MW00927831

FIRE AND
Glass

BY LINDA SEED

The Main Street Merchants

Moonstone Beach
Cambria Sky
Nearly Wild
Fire and Glass

The Delaneys of Cambria

A Long, Cool Rain
The Promise of Lightning
Loving the Storm
Searching for Sunshine

The Russo Sisters

Saving Sofia
First Crush

LINDA SEED

FIRE AND

Glass

ISBN-13: 978-1539567707
ISBN-10: 1539567702

First Trade Paperback Printing: October 2016

Cover design by Kari March.

For Evan, my best book buddy. With love and appreciation.

Chapter One

"Lacy, will you marry me?"

Lacy Jordan stood frozen, looking down at her boyfriend, Brandon, who was kneeling in front of her on one knee. She was having an odd, out-of-body sensation, and she suspected that some of her essential physical processes had stopped working. For instance, she knew she couldn't have been hearing him right.

"What? What did you say?"

He was looking up at her with the brilliant, confident smile of an insurance salesman, or a guy in a toothpaste ad. She could see the comb tracks in the flawless, dark gloss of his hair.

He laughed, apparently mistaking her shock for happy surprise. "Lacy, I asked if you would be my wife. You'd make me the happiest man in the world. Come on, say yes."

Was this some sort of reality TV setup? Was it some kind of elaborate joke? Lacy wondered if perhaps this was one of those dreams you had when you'd eaten too much pizza before bed.

"Brandon, I—"

"Say yes," he said again. He fidgeted a little, and she could see that he was becoming annoyed at finding himself on his knee on a hardwood floor longer than he'd anticipated. Also, holding that ring out to her had to have been taxing, considering that the rock was almost as big as a bowling ball. "Lacy?"

Instead of answering, Lacy imagined how happy her mother would be if she could see this scene. Nancy Jordan had set Lacy up with Brandon, a chiropractor, several months before, after Nancy had seen him for a bout of sciatica. Nancy, concerned about her daughter's single status, had immediately looked for a wedding ring on the young doctor's left hand, and had found it blessedly absent.

A chiropractor with a solid practice checked all of Lacy's mother's boxes. He was tall and attractive, and he was gainfully employed, with a 401K and a good health plan. Lacy's own boxes—the ones labeled *passion, adventure,* and *romance*—remained unchecked, but she'd given things a chance anyway because she was lonely. Because she was past thirty and single. Because she wanted a family, wanted children, and her prime childbearing years were upon her. And because—she could admit it—all of her three best friends were paired up, and she was jealous as hell.

They all had happy relationships, and Rose was expecting a baby. And what the hell did Lacy have? A job at a coffeehouse and a trailer in her parents' backyard.

"Lacy," he said again, and she realized that she still hadn't answered him.

"Brandon, this is … sudden." It wasn't an answer, but it was, nonetheless, true.

"Don't you like the ring?" he said.

How could she not like the ring? It was a stunner, a two-carat emerald-cut diamond with tiny round stones lining the band. She stared at it. "It … it's gorgeous."

He seemed to take that for her answer, in the absence of any other. He took her left hand and slipped the ring onto the fourth finger. It fit as though it had been made for her, and it occurred to her that it probably had been.

She held out her hand and gaped at it, her mouth slack. Maybe she was hypnotized by the sparkle; maybe she was influenced by his obvious confidence; maybe she was thinking of the kids that would come with the package. Whatever it was that was clouding her judgment, she didn't object when he stood and enfolded her in his arms.

"Lacy, sweetheart, you won't be sorry," he murmured into her hair.

Had she missed something? Had she missed, specifically, the part where she had said yes?

"We're going to be so happy," he told her. "You're going to be such a beautiful bride."

She stiffened slightly, and he held her away from him so he could look into her face. "Sweetie? What's wrong?"

"Nothing." She forced herself to smile. "I was just thinking about what my mother is going to say. I'd better call her and tell her the news."

But as she pulled out of his arms and grabbed her cell phone from the kitchen counter in Brandon's apartment, she couldn't have said for sure whether she really wanted to call her mom, or if she'd said it as an excuse to have a moment of blessed solitude.

"Oh, honey, that's wonderful!"

Lacy was standing on the back deck of Brandon's place with the sliding glass door closed to keep him from hearing the conversation. Brandon's Morro Bay apartment was four blocks from the beach, and she had a thin strip of an ocean view in front of her as she squinted against the September sun.

"Is it? I didn't even say yes. He just assumed." Lacy could hear the bitterness in her own voice as she held out her left hand and peered at the diamond, which was sparkling in the sunlight.

"But why wouldn't you say yes? He's everything you want."

"Maybe not *everything* …"

"He's got a good career. He can provide for you. He's smart, and he's so handsome, Lacy. He could give you a family. Isn't that what you've always wanted?"

It was. But she'd also wanted the kind of passion she read

about in the romance novels she'd loved since she was a teenager. Brandon wasn't the type to give a woman passion. He was more the type to give her a sweater at Christmas, and twice-a-year vacations at a time-share in Florida.

"He said … He told me I'd be a beautiful bride."

"And, honey, you will be."

What Lacy's mother didn't understand—what nobody seemed to understand—was that for Lacy, beauty was as much a curse as it was a gift. Her porcelain skin, golden blond hair and pale blue eyes, the tall, willowy figure that had drawn the looks of boys and men since she'd hit puberty, had undoubtedly made life easy for her in more ways than even she knew. But it also made every man who approached her suspect. How many of the boys she'd dated in high school had been drawn to her by her looks alone? How many had pursued her for the bragging rights of dating Lacy Jordan? How many men, in her adult life, had even bothered to get to know the person behind the body, the face?

If Lacy was more than a little concerned that Brandon wanted her for how she'd look in the wedding photos, well, she came by that worry honestly, after years of hard-earned experience.

Nancy was saying something, and Lacy tried to focus.

"… the engagement party. You won't have to worry about a thing, your sisters and I will handle everything. Oh! I wonder if we can rent the veterans' hall!"

"Mom, I don't need—"

"Now, don't be silly, Lacy. Of course you're going to have an engagement party. I'll call Brandon and we'll set a date."

"Um … okay." It just seemed so much easier to agree than it was to make her mother understand the reservations that roiled within Lacy, threatening to overwhelm her.

"Wonderful, sweetie. And, Lacy?"

"Yeah, Mom?"

"Honey … I just love you so much." Lacy could hear the emotion in her mother's voice, and it made her own eyes hot with suppressed tears.

"I love you too, Mom."

Nancy and Brandon both seemed so happy. Was it completely out of the question that this marriage might make Lacy happy, too? She looked at the ring again and imagined her future in its bright, shining light.

Daniel Reed held his hands on his narrow hips as he surveyed the glassblowing studio toward the back of the lot where his little house stood. Too small; the place was just too damned small. If he wanted to work on more of the larger projects like the one he was doing for Eden, a hotel that had just gone up a few blocks off the Vegas Strip, then he was going to have to hire assistants. Assistants took space, and so did the glass itself. The Eden job had taken up just about every square inch he had. He could either stick to smaller jobs, or he could expand the studio.

Screw the small jobs. Ever since the Vegas thing, which was going to be unveiled next month, he was starting to think big.

Big meant moving to a better space. Or, it meant renovations.

Daniel was leaning toward the renovations. For one thing, he liked the lot where his house and studio were located. Just south of Cambria, on the Central Coast of California, the lot sat amid rolling hills and tall grass that was emerald green in the winter, golden in the summer. Oak trees studded the property, bringing him welcome shade.

If he moved, he'd have to customize whatever property he chose anyway. It was hard to find a house with a ready-made glassblowing studio, even in Cambria.

The Vegas job meant his bank account was more flush than it had been in some time. If he was going to add on, now was the time.

He left the studio, walked the dirt path to his house, went inside, and gave it a good look. Little more than a cottage, the house had two tiny bedrooms, a sitting room, and a kitchen that had last been updated in the 1970s. Why not add on to the house while he was expanding the studio? He could use an office to manage the bookkeeping, the supply ordering, and the other day-to-day paperwork of his business. The kitchen had good bones, but visitors had a way of cringing at the sight of the ancient, harvest gold appliances and the ceramic tile countertops with their dark brown grout.

He had to admit, it was ugly as hell.

What would it hurt to put down some granite counters, buy some new, stainless steel appliances? Maybe redo the cabinets while he was at it. He had the money, but money had a way of getting spent. If he didn't get the work done now, there was no telling when it might happen.

Daniel wasn't an architect, but he did know a thing or two about making a decent sketch. He got out a pad of paper and a pencil, and went to work on some ideas. He sketched the outline of the cottage as it stood, then added a room to the east side of the house, with generous windows to catch the sunrise. And how about a loft? He peered up toward the cottage's generously high ceilings. That could work.

After he'd played with it a while, and thought about it some, he fished his cell phone out of his jeans pocket and called Ryan Delaney, a good friend who'd just had a house built on his ranch property north of town.

"Ry?" he said when his friend answered. "Who'd you use

for the architect on your house?"

"What are you planning?" It was midday, and Daniel could hear from the background noise that Ryan was in the barn. The new one, the state-of-the-art one that, from the sound of it, was currently occupied by a number of irritated cattle.

"Thought I might add on to my house," Daniel said. "Expand the studio."

Ryan let out a bitter laugh. "You make that sound like a good thing."

"You mean it's not?"

"It can be," Ryan told him. "But if I had the choice of building a custom house again or having my appendix taken out through my nose, I'd have to carefully consider my options."

And Ryan hadn't been living in the house while it was being built. Daniel supposed he wouldn't be able to live in his, either. He'd have to find somewhere else to stay while the work was being done. Still, that was doable.

"Maybe the less you tell me about that, the better," Daniel suggested.

"Maybe," Ryan agreed.

"So, anyway. The architect?"

"Right, right. We used Vince Jordan."

It seemed to Daniel that he knew the name. Then, it came to him. "Lacy's father?"

"That's the one. He did good work. You've seen the house." Somewhere near Ryan, a cow moaned. "I won't say it went smoothly, because these things never do. But I can't argue with the end result."

Lacy Jordan's father. Daniel considered it. He didn't know Vince Jordan, but he did know Lacy. The woman looked like a Victoria's Secret model crossed with a Botticelli painting. And she made a damned good cup of coffee.

He asked Ryan for Vince Jordan's number, and wrote it down on the pad of paper next to his sketch.

The idea of running into Lacy during the course of the project gave the whole idea the edge over having his appendix removed through his nose.

Chapter Two

Lacy pulled a shot of espresso, then steamed some lowfat milk in a small, stainless steel pitcher. She piled a cloud-like layer of foam atop the coffee in a thick ceramic cup, and then finished the drink by adding a sprinkling of cinnamon on the top.

She passed the cup across the counter to Kate Bennet, one of Lacy's best friends and the owner of Swept Away, a bookstore a few doors down on Main Street. Lacy had passed the cup to Kate with her left hand, and as she began to pull the hand back, Kate reached out and grabbed, pulling it to her so she could examine the engagement ring that sparkled like starlight in the coffeehouse's overhead lights.

"Good God, that stone is huge," Kate exclaimed. "Whatever else he may be lacking, Brandon has excellent taste in jewelry." As an afterthought, she added, "And when your back starts to hurt from lugging that thing around, he can give you an adjustment. So that's handy."

Jitters, the coffeehouse where Lacy worked as a barista, had a light crowd—about average for nine a.m. on a Tuesday in September. She was alone behind the counter. Connor, her coworker, was in the back room, organizing the stock and taking out the trash.

"What do you mean, 'whatever else he may be lacking'?" Lacy asked defensively. "What is he lacking?" Lacy was well aware of what Brandon was lacking—ranging from his fashion sense to his taste in movies—but with the ring on her finger and the plans for the engagement party underway, she felt the need to defend him.

"Nothing," Kate said. "I didn't mean anything. It's just … he does have that thing he does with his throat." Kate raised her eyebrows and regarded Lacy.

Lacy wanted to protest that she didn't know what Kate meant about Brandon's throat. Unfortunately, she did know. Brandon had a tendency to clear his throat when making what he thought was a particularly salient point. When discussing politics or personal finance, he sounded like he was suffering from smoke inhalation.

"So he has one annoying habit," Lacy said. "We all have annoying habits. I leave wet towels on the bathroom floor!"

"She does." Genevieve Porter, owner of Main Street's Porter Gallery, had just come in the front door to grab a coffee to go. She was dressed in her usual gallerywear: a form-fitting black dress and high-heeled black pumps. Her hair, a glorious mass of unruly red curls, was pinned up in a loose bun. She'd heard the tail end of their conversation, apparently, and chimed in to support Lacy regarding the towels. "I shared a hotel room with her that time we spent the weekend in San Francisco. She's a slob."

"Hey!" Lacy said.

"I'm sorry, honey, but you are."

Lacy knew without asking that Gen wanted a large black coffee, no sugar. She poured it into a to-go cup, added a lid and a cardboard sleeve, and moved to the register to ring her up.

"Somehow, I can't see Brandon being okay with the towels-on-the-floor thing," Gen observed as she dug into her purse for her wallet.

"Is Ryan okay with the way you make that whistling noise in your sleep?" Lacy asked.

"I don't do that."

"You do. The trip to San Francisco, remember? You sound like my mother's tea kettle." Lacy took three dollars from Gen, put it into the cash register, and handed her some change.

Gen protested. "Well, that's just—"

"We'll work it out," Lacy said, interrupting her. "People work things out."

"I guess." Gen sulked, looking put out about the whistling remark.

"What are we working out?" Rose Watkins had just come in the front door, and she wanted to get caught up.

It wasn't an accident that all of Lacy's three best friends had come into Jitters at about the same time. Their routine on workdays was to pop in for coffee sometime between nine and nine thirty just to check in with each other. But now, Lacy was starting to wish they'd all made their coffee at home.

"We're working out the fact that Brandon clears his throat when he talks, and that Lacy leaves wet towels on the floor," Gen informed her, her brows still gathered in an irritated pout.

"And that Gen whistles in her sleep," Kate added helpfully.

"Ah. I guess that brings me up to speed," Rose said.

Rose, who was more than five months pregnant and who was, therefore, watching her caffeine intake, had taken to ordering half-caff lattes in a compromise she'd reached with the baby's father, a biology professor who'd moved in with her the same day that news of the baby had come out. One thing Rose had been unwilling to compromise on, though, was hair dye. Her hair was fire engine red this month, and her facial piercings—a delicate silver ring in one nostril and a silver barbell in her left eyebrow—appeared faintly pink in its reflection.

Lacy went to the espresso machine to pull the coffee for Rose's drink.

"Honestly, Lacy, are you sure you even want to?" Rose asked. "Work things out with Brandon, I mean? It's better to break it off now than to make a run for it at the church on your wedding day. Although, if you do that, I've totally got your back."

The other two nodded in agreement.

"That's just … Why the hell would I want to make a run for it?" Lacy was wiping the counter with a white towel, and she threw the towel down irritably. Ever since Lacy's friends had learned about her engagement, they'd been dropping hints that Lacy might not want to go through with the wedding. At first, she'd just been puzzled, but now it was annoying the hell out of her. Marriage to Brandon meant a home, children, stability—all the things she wanted. Or, most of them, anyway. Why shouldn't she have those things? Why shouldn't she want them?

"It's just … the two of you don't seem all that … compatible." Gen was looking at Lacy earnestly, standing at the counter with her coffee cup in her hand.

"We're compatible!" Lacy threw her hands into the air in frustration. "We are! We're compatible! He's handsome, and smart, and he's nice to me, and … and it's easy for all of you to criticize, when you have what you want! You've all got these … these *perfect* men! What do you want from me? Do you want me to be alone? Is that it?"

Lacy hadn't planned the outburst, but now that it had happened, she could see that it had been brewing for some time.

"Oh, sweetie." Kate's eyes were brimming with sympathy. "Can you take a little break and come sit down with us?"

She was on the verge of saying no—of kicking all of them out, in fact—but she was due for a ten-minute break, and she didn't feel that she could leave things like this. If she'd had doubts about Brandon—which she told herself she *didn't,* regardless of what they thought—then she could live with that. But when things weren't right between her and her friends, well, that was something that just couldn't stand.

❖

"We don't want you to be alone." Kate was rubbing Lacy's forearm as they all sat at a café table in a corner of the coffeehouse, with Connor peering over at them curiously from where he was manning the counter.

"Well … it seems that way sometimes," Lacy said, her voice sullen.

"We just think … we're not sure that Brandon is the guy who's going to make you happy," Rose said.

"You don't want me to *be* happy!" Lacy tossed her hands skyward again. "You don't want me to have what you have! Why not? Why shouldn't I have what you have?"

"You should," Gen said. "You should have exactly what we have. That's why Brandon isn't the right guy for you. Because he's not going to give it to you. He'll try, but he can't. Lacy, he can't." Gen was looking at Lacy with the intense, serious gaze of someone staging an intervention. Which, now that Lacy thought about it, she was.

It was easy for Kate, Gen, and Rose to judge Lacy's relationship. After all, each one of them had found what appeared to be true love. Kate was living with Jackson, one of the top chefs in Cambria. Gen had married Ryan, a hot, ridiculously rich rancher. And Rose was having a baby with Will, a truly sweet guy who, Lacy had no doubt, would walk through fire if Rose asked him to.

So what if Lacy's relationship with Brandon lacked that kind of passion? It didn't make Brandon any less of a good man. It didn't make Lacy any less worthy of love.

"Does this mean none of you are coming to my engagement party?" Lacy sat with her arms folded over her middle, her gaze firmly on the tabletop. "I wouldn't, if I felt that way."

"Of course we're coming. Don't be stupid," Kate said.

"Honey." Rose put a hand on Lacy's arm. "We're your best friends. If you killed somebody, we'd tell you that murder is wrong. But we'd still help you hide the body."

The Vegas job hadn't been installed and unveiled yet, but after months of intense work, the glass was done. That meant Daniel had to get back to work on the bowls and vases, the plates and candleholders that usually made up so much of his income.

Bowls and vases might not be as artistically satisfying as a big installation, but they were popular with the tourists who streamed through Cambria year-round. He regularly had pieces in a half dozen shops around town. He placed the lower-priced items—the kinds of things a middle-class shopper might buy on impulse during a weekend in town—in boutiques on Burton Drive and Main Street. The higher-ticket items—the larger pieces that would appeal to collectors—usually were shown at the Porter Gallery.

The Vegas deal had already gotten him some press, and Gen Porter said some of her clients were inquiring about buying his pieces—even clients who'd never shown an interest in him before. The flip side of that was that he'd been so busy he had nothing new to show them.

If he wanted to capitalize on the publicity from the Eden job, he had to get back to work, and he had to do it now.

That was fine with him. The business of art—the schmoozing, the accounting, chasing publicity—was a necessary part of his work, and he knew that. But in his heart, he didn't give a rat's ass about that end of things. He wanted to work. He wanted to create things. He wanted to put his soul into the glass and see what that looked like.

The rest of it only mattered because he had bills to pay.

At the moment, he was working on a vase. A vase wasn't flashy, it wasn't high-profile. A vase wouldn't get him a mention in *Art in America*. But there was a certain satisfaction in the shape, in the graceful lines. He started by gathering molten glass on the end of a blowpipe. Then he rolled the glass back and forth on the marver—a flat steel slab—to get a rough cylindrical shape. Into the furnace, then back to the marver for shaping. Back into the furnace, and then he rolled the hot glass over dark red powder and put that into the furnace again to melt it onto the piece. Now more shaping, this time with an inches-thick slab of wet newspaper that was rounded and blackened with use. The color streaked across the piece in fiery waves.

He had to keep the glass hot—somewhere in the neighborhood of a thousand degrees Fahrenheit—and he had to keep it in constant motion to preserve the shape. One hand on the blowpipe, turning and turning, one hand on his tools, shaping the glass, forming it into the vision he had for his piece.

Sometimes the vision changed in the middle of the work; the feel of the thing suggested to him what it wanted to be. Daniel believed in rolling with the intuition, in being as flexible and malleable as the molten glass itself. You had to listen to the glass. You had to hear the story it had to tell.

Somewhere in the middle of the meditative process of heating and shaping, heating and shaping, Lacy Jordan popped into his mind. If he worked with Vince Jordan on the house thing, then maybe Daniel would get to spend some time with Lacy. He'd been around her a lot, mostly as part of the big group that included his friends and their significant others. He'd been intrigued by Lacy, and yeah, he could admit that at first, it was about how she looked. But there was more to it than that. He wanted to know how she *thought*. Images of Lacy worked their way through his mind as he carried the blowpipe back to the furnace and heated the glass until it glowed.

What he did—it was all about the fire.

The heat was everything.

Daniel repeated the cycle of blowing and shaping and heating. He was starting to get somewhere with the piece. He'd been doing this long enough that he didn't have to think about it much anymore—he *felt* it. The process relaxed him, soothed him, as he thought about everything from books he'd read to movies he'd seen to problems with family, with women.

He looked at the glass form on the end of his pipe and admired the streaks of color. He wondered if Lacy would like it.

Lacy. There she was again, in his thoughts, unbidden.

Jesus, it was hot in here.

Chapter Three

Daniel probably would not have been invited to the engagement party if it hadn't been for Vince. Daniel considered Lacy a friend by virtue of the friends they had in common, but he wasn't someone Lacy's mother and sisters would have thought about when writing up the guest list.

That oversight was corrected when Daniel called Vince to set up an initial appointment to talk about the renovations. After the usual chitchat about what Daniel was looking for and the basics of how Vince did business, the older man had asked whether Daniel could be expected at the party the following weekend.

Not only hadn't Daniel known about the party, but until that moment, he hadn't even known that Lacy was engaged. Fortunately, Vince took the dumbstruck surprise in Daniel's voice for affront over the fact that he hadn't been invited, instead of what it was: dismay over the idea that the lovely and delightful Lacy Jordan, subject of many a happy daydream over the years, was going to marry that stiff she'd been seeing.

Vince, in his misunderstanding of the situation, rushed to correct the faux pas he thought he had made.

"Oh, jeez. I'm sure Nancy and the girls meant to invite you. I feel like an ass."

"No, no, don't." Daniel was pacing in his kitchen, his cell phone pressed to his ear. He didn't correct Vince's assumption, but he also didn't want him feeling bad over something that wasn't even a problem. The problem—the real one—was that Lacy was engaged in the first place. And if Vince wanted to feel bad about that, then he could sure as hell have at it.

"If I'd known—" Vince began.

"Nah, nah, it's fine," Daniel answered. "It's just … are you sure she's doing the right thing?" Daniel wasn't sure whether to broach the subject with Vince, but the opportunity had presented itself, so what the hell?

"Why?" Vince's voice turned wary. "Do you know something I don't?"

"Not really. It's just … I've met this Brandon guy a few times, and … are we sure he's good enough?"

The sound in Vince's voice changed from suspicion to knowing amusement, and he chuckled. "You got someone in mind who'd be better?"

"What?" Daniel's eyebrows rose in innocence. "No. But a woman like Lacy is … she's special. And that Brandon guy strikes me as … well … not."

Vince chuckled again, a low, throaty sound that made a man want to have a beer with him. "You go ahead and come to that party," he said. "And if you've got a mind to make some sort of move, you'd better get on it, son."

"What, me?" Daniel was genuinely surprised at the suggestion. "I'm not gonna make a move. I'm just concerned."

Daniel didn't want to pursue Lacy. At least, he'd never seriously considered it. And the woman was engaged. But if a guy was concerned about a sort-of friend's life choices, well, that was just … friendly.

"Listen, when's that party going to be?" he asked Vince.

The thing about living in an Airstream trailer was that there wasn't space for anything. The fact that the trailer where Lacy lived—its tube of a body perched like some oversized metallic pill bug in her parents' backyard—had just one miniscule closet meant that Lacy had very few clothes. And most of those clothes were the jeans and T-shirts appropriate to her job at Jitters.

She did have one dress, but when she'd suggested that it would do well enough for the engagement party, her sisters had openly scoffed at her. That was how she ended up crammed into a Ford Fiesta on a Wednesday morning with her three sisters, traveling south on Highway 1 toward the Nordstrom in Santa Barbara.

"For God's sake, Lacy," said Jessica, Lacy's oldest sister, who was manning the wheel. "It's your engagement party! How did you let it go this long without buying a dress?" Jessica, who was almost seven years older than Lacy, had the soft, comfortable look of a woman who'd long since settled into motherhood. She had the same glossy blond hair as Lacy, the same pale blue eyes, but the fifteen extra pounds and the smile lines around her eyes made women want to confide in her and children want to settle in for a long hug.

"But I have a dress," Lacy protested.

"*Pfft.* That old thing?" Whitney, one of Lacy's younger sisters, scoffed. "You wear it to every wedding, every funeral, every—"

"It's a nice dress," Lacy insisted.

"It's okay, I guess, if you're a hotel concierge," quipped Cassie, the youngest of the Jordan siblings. "But you want to look sexy at your engagement party. You don't want to look like you're ready to book somebody's tickets for *Hamilton.*"

Cassie had a point, Lacy supposed, but Lacy shuddered at the thought of what her baby sister would choose for her. Cassie, with her messy pixie haircut, her bright red lipstick, and her dramatic, cat's-eye eyeliner, tended more toward Timberland boots with cutoff shorts and band T-shirts than toward Lacy's no-fuss style.

Lacy would have to lean on Whitney in choosing a dress.

While Jess was too conservative and Cassie was too grunge, Whitney hit a nice middle ground of sexy but not too sexy, classic but not fussy. Whitney, who ran a day spa in town, always looked appropriately polished without appearing to be trying too hard. Whatever extra gene Whitney had received at conception that told her what to wear, how to do her hair, and what accessories to choose for any given situation had obviously not been gifted to Lacy. Whitney bemoaned that fact from time to time, complaining that Lacy's statuesque figure and elegant facial features were wasted on someone who didn't give a crap about fashion, and who made even Levi's and a plain white T-shirt look good.

The drive to Santa Barbara was just over two hours, which was a long time when you were five foot ten and you were wedged into the back of a subcompact car that barely provided enough knee room for a five-year-old. Lacy was stuck with the back, though, because Jessica, as the oldest, had insisted on driving, and it was Cassie's car. That left Lacy and Whitney with their knees shoved sideways in an effort to maintain circulation to their lower extremities.

"I don't know why it has to be Nordstrom," Lacy complained. "I could have found something at one of the boutiques in town."

"It's an engagement party. It has to be Nordstrom," Whitney said, as though this fact were so obvious that no further explanation was necessary.

"Anyway, it'll be fun," Jess said as they cruised through San Luis Obispo on their way toward Highway 101. "When was the last time we all went shopping together?"

Cassie put a forefinger on her lips and gazed upward in thought. "Hmm. I think it was sometime around last ... never."

"Never?" Lacy said. "That can't be right."

"Well, I guess you could count the times Mom dragged us down to Santa Maria to buy school clothes," Cassie said. "But I don't think Jess was there for that, so ... "

Lacy thought about whether it was true, and she decided it probably was. Jess hadn't gone on those school shopping trips because she was so much older than the rest of them that by then, she'd preferred to do her shopping with her friends. And as adults, they all had such different fashion sense that it simply hadn't occurred to any of them to hit the shops together.

Until now.

"We've really never done this," Lacy said in wonder. "Not even once."

"Well, it's about time, then," Whitney asserted. "It's my chance to smack some fashion sense into you people."

"I've got fashion sense," Cassie said.

Whitney rolled her eyes extravagantly.

"What's wrong with my clothes?" Jess demanded. Her mom jeans and poly-blend tops weren't exactly frumpy, but they did broadcast her maternal status like a neon sign, especially when they were adorned with juice box drippings and a dusting of Goldfish cracker crumbs.

"Nothing," Whitney said, in an effort to keep peace with her older sister. "Nothing. I just think your style could use a little extra ... *oomph*."

"Lacy's idea of dressing up is to put on a clean apron at Jitters," Cassie said, smirking.

"My style is simple," Lacy said, a little bit stung. "I like simple."

"It's simple, all right," Whitney said. "But an engagement party doesn't call for simple. It calls for *sexy*."

"I gotta tell you, honey. She's right," Jess agreed.

❖

Lacy had to admit, she could get used to having Whitney choose her clothes.

She was standing in a fitting room at Nordstrom, gazing at herself in a three-sided mirror with a surprising amount of satisfaction. The dress she was wearing was midnight blue, in a satiny fabric with ruching down the front that made the dress hug her hips and cling to every inch of her curves. The wrap-style neckline made a deep V that displayed a creamy expanse of Lacy's cleavage. The three-quarter-length sleeves were midnight blue lace, offering a peek at the pale, smooth skin beneath.

"Come on out. I want to see," Whitney called over the top of the fitting room door.

"Just a minute. I'm adjusting," Lacy said. She tugged at the shoulders and hemline of the dress, but the truth was, it fit perfectly. Which was good, since she'd waited so long it would be impossible to have it altered before the party.

"Stop stalling," Cassie called. "Get out here and twirl!"

Lacy took a deep breath, steeled herself for the comments she was certain to receive, and opened the fitting room door. All three of them were waiting on the other side, their faces displaying various states of impatience.

When the door opened, those expressions fled and they all just stared.

"What?" Lacy prompted them. "What's wrong? Is the neckline too deep-cut? I knew it. God. I'll just go back in and—"

"No!" Whitney said, recovering herself. "It's gorgeous. You look gorgeous."

"You do." Jess's face looked stern, as it so often did, but she was nodding firmly. "Whit's right. Give us a little spin." She twirled a finger to demonstrate.

Lacy did a full, slow turn.

"God, your ass looks fabulous," Cassie said, shaking her

head in mock disgust. "It's so not fair that you were the one to inherit Mom's ass."

Jess closed her eyes and waved her hands in front of her face in a warding-off gesture. "Do *not* make me think about our mother's ass." She dropped her hands in defeat. "Too late."

"Mom really does have a nice one," Whitney acknowledged. "Even still, at her age. And Lacy got it, all right."

"It's like that dress was made for maximum ass advantage," Cassie observed.

Lacy took a couple of steps back into the fitting room and turned her rear toward the three-sided mirror, peering over her shoulder to see what all the fuss was about. The satiny fabric was clinging to her butt, following its contours and highlighting the curves with its sheen.

"Wow," Lacy said.

"Right?" Cassie agreed. "That's it. That's your dress."

Lacy hadn't looked at the price, but since this was the dress, she figured she'd better take a peek. She fingered the tag that hung from the sleeve and focused on the number printed across the bottom. When she saw it, her knees nearly buckled.

"Oh, God," she said.

"Honey, it's your engagement party," Jess said. "You only get one of those."

"Hopefully," Whitney added.

"I think we should try Kohl's." Lacy felt light-headed.

"Bullshit," Cassie said. "This is the dress."

Since it was rare for all three of her sisters to agree on any-thing—let alone something related to fashion—Lacy figured they must be right: This must be the dress.

She mentally calculated her bank balance and winced. But if she looked as good as her sisters said she did, it might actually be worth it.

Chapter Four

From Daniel's perspective, the money Lacy had paid for the dress was worth every penny, and then some. When he walked into the Cambria veterans' hall that Saturday and saw her, he nearly lost the power of coherent thought. Lacy in jeans, a T-shirt, and an apron behind the counter at Jitters was a lovely and alluring sight. But Lacy all done up in a dress that fit her like it was painted on was enough to strike a man speechless. He just stood there for a minute, because he couldn't feel his feet.

"Daniel!" Lacy saw him from across the room and smiled, and her smile was like the sun coming out after the biblical flood. He half expected to see pairs of animals exiting an ark. "I'm so glad you could come," she said, approaching him and taking his arm to draw him into the room and into the crowd.

"I … uh …" He tried to answer her, but he was still stupid from the sheer impact of her beauty. "Congratulations," he said finally. That was always a safe bet.

"Thank you. Come and say hello to Brandon."

She drew him deeper into the room, which was decorated with votive candles, fairy lights, and blue and white banners proclaiming, WE'RE ENGAGED. The center of the room was dotted with round tables covered in white linen, and at the edges of the room, food tables were groaning with casseroles, salads, and dessert trays brought by the assembled guests.

Brandon, a guy Daniel knew only a little, was all done up in a suit and tie, his hair combed with too much product, looking smug as hell. Why wouldn't he look smug? He was engaged to Lacy Jordan. If Daniel had been in that position, he'd have been pretty damned pleased with himself. He'd have been so smug he'd have wanted to kick his own ass.

"Brandon," Daniel said in greeting, extending his hand.

"Daniel." The smug smile stayed in place as Brandon shook Daniel's hand with exaggerated firmness. "What do you think of our girl here?" Brandon released Daniel's hand and put an arm possessively around Lacy's shoulder.

Daniel wasn't sure he liked the *our girl* thing—as though Lacy were the possession of the collective men in the room. Now wasn't the time to deconstruct it, though. "I think you're a very lucky man," he said instead.

Brandon laughed a little too exuberantly, especially considering that Daniel hadn't been joking.

"Isn't that the truth!" Brandon declared.

Brandon had missed a spot while shaving, and a tiny patch of whiskers on his jawline, just below his chin, bobbed as he talked.

"I hear you're planning to fix up your place," Brandon said.

"Well, I—"

"That's great, that's great," Brandon responded, without waiting for Daniel's answer. "You know, I've been in the market for a house in Cambria for the two of us. In my price range, we were thinking ..."

Brandon continued, citing the exact price range he was considering, the housing options available, the current interest rates on home mortgages, his average income over the previous five years, and his performance investing in stocks and mutual funds. Daniel was astonished both by the amount of financial information Brandon was furnishing, and by the sheer number of words that were coming out of his mouth. Daniel looked around the room frantically for some hope of rescue, and then he felt Lacy's hand on his arm.

"Daniel," she said, interrupting Brandon's economics lesson, "I think I saw Jackson and Ryan over by the bar. Why don't you go get yourself something to drink and say hello?"

Daniel tried to express his gratitude with his eyes as he said brightly, "I think I'll do that! Brandon, I'll let you mingle with your other guests. Nice to see you. Congrats again! We'll talk later." And with that, he hauled ass to the bar before he could hear about Brandon's tax bracket.

Jackson and Ryan were indeed at the bar, as was Will Bachman, a biology professor who was one of Daniel's close friends.

"Did he tell you about his gross adjusted income?" asked Jackson, a tall, auburn-haired man in jeans and a leather jacket. He had his elbows propped on the bar and was drinking a craft beer from the bottle.

"What's with that guy?" Daniel wanted to know. "I thought he was going to show me his pay stubs."

"He's marking his territory," Will said, adjusting his glasses. "It's a common behavior in courting and mating rituals." Will was an evolutionary biologist, which inevitably colored his take on any situation.

"I guess you're lucky he didn't pee on you," Ryan added, his dark eyes warm with amusement.

Daniel ordered a beer from the rent-a-bartender, a guy he knew a little bit from the gym where he and Will sometimes worked out. When it came, he took a deep drink and leaned against the bar.

"Lacy looks good," he said, in what could only be described as understatement.

"You think?" Ryan said.

"I've never seen her all ... *done up* like this," Jackson added. "It works."

"It does," Daniel agreed, following Lacy with his gaze as

she greeted guests, talked with friends, and checked on the food tables.

"I can't help but wonder …" Will began.

"What?" Jackson prompted him.

"Well … it's just … Brandon."

"I think what Will is contemplating," Ryan broke in with an easy grin, "is what Lacy's doing with an assclown like that."

"Well … yeah," Will admitted. "I wouldn't have used that word, but, basically."

"She could do better," Daniel grumbled. He took another swig from his beer.

"Gen thinks it's the biological clock thing," Ryan said, referring to Gen Porter, his wife. "She wants kids, and she's past thirty …"

"Aw, jeez," Jackson said. "That kind of talk makes me think of them … *together*. And I really don't want to think about that."

Daniel didn't either. He squirmed a little in discomfort.

Further discussion of what Lacy and Brandon might or might not do with their reproductive systems was cut short as Vince Jordan stepped to the head of the room and started talking into a wireless microphone.

Vince was a big, gruff-looking guy with a ruddy face and hair that had been buzz-cut to minimize the effect of his receding hairline. His pink scalp showed through the quarter-inch-long bristles of hair that had once been blond, but were now gray. He looked intensely uncomfortable in a suit that had probably hung in the back of his closet, untouched, for years. The soft folds of his neck spilled over the collar of his dress shirt.

"Could I just have everybody's attention for a minute?" Vince said into the microphone, squirming a little under the growing attention of the crowd.

Vince started off by thanking everyone for coming, and he

called out a few family friends in particular who had traveled to attend the event. Then he began talking about Lacy, about what kind of child she'd been, happy and loving, with a sweet demeanor and a goofy sense of humor. He started to tear up a little as he moved on to Lacy as an adult, her kindness, her devotion to her family, her compassion and empathy for those around her.

He finished the speech, wet-eyed, by looking at Lacy and saying, "Your mom and I wish you nothing but happiness, baby. Always." He swiped at his eyes, shoved the microphone into the hands of one of Lacy's sisters, and hurried off to gather himself.

Daniel looked at his friends in surprise. "Is it me, or … ?"

"He didn't mention Brandon," Jackson said, picking up on Daniel's train of thought. "Not once."

"Jeez," Will said.

"From that speech, she could be marrying herself," Ryan agreed.

"That would probably be better," Daniel said. It gave him comfort that Lacy's father apparently had some of the same reservations that he did. On the other hand, young women weren't known for embracing their father's choices in men.

"Huh," Daniel said.

He looked across the room to where Lacy was surrounded by a group of well-wishers, including Kate and Rose, who both looked pretty, all dolled up in their fall dresses. A young blond man Daniel recognized as Lacy's brother, Nick, was just releasing Lacy from a bear hug.

Daniel was thinking about Vince's speech, and about Lacy, when Gen came up to the bar and slipped her arm around Ryan's waist. Gen was wearing some kind of tight-fitting black dress, and her curly red hair spilled down over her shoulders.

"I thought I'd better check on you guys," Gen said, looking

up at Ryan with undisguised love.

Newlyweds, Daniel thought.

"We're fine," Ryan said. He planted a kiss gingerly on the tip of Gen's nose. "We've got beer, and we've got guys to talk to. It's all good."

Just then, Daniel spotted Brandon standing at one side of the room talking to a pinched, elderly woman who, from the resemblance, could only be his mother. Brandon looked up and caught Daniel's eye, said something to the woman, and then headed toward the bar.

"Oh, shit," Jackson said. "He's coming over."

"Ryan? Could you help me check on the … the thing?" Gen said, pulling at Ryan's arm.

"Absolutely," Ryan said, following her away from the bar and toward safety. "Can't neglect the thing."

"Will," Jackson said, an urgent tone in his voice. "Let's get some food."

Will looked a little bit confused. "But I'm really not—"

"Food," Jackson said, glaring at him. "*Now.*"

The two of them fled, leaving Daniel alone at the bar in Brandon's laserlike sights.

"Daniel!" Brandon said, all bluster and hearty greetings. "How are you enjoying the party?"

"Well, I—"

"I was thinking about that lot of yours," Brandon went on. "How much has that baby appreciated since you bought it?"

"Oh, God." Kate was looking across the room with sympathy to where Brandon had cornered Daniel at the bar. "Do you see the look on Daniel's face? He looks like he wants to find a high window to jump out of."

"Unfortunately, we're on the ground floor," Rose observed.

"Come on, you guys," Lacy said, irritated. "Brandon isn't that bad."

"Compared to what?" Kate said. "A televangelist?"

"You act like someone having to talk to him is … is torture," Lacy said. "He's going to be my *husband*."

"About that …" Rose began.

"Do not start." Lacy pointed one finger at Rose.

"Sorry," Rose said glumly.

"Oh, honey." Lacy's mother rushed up to them, her face glowing with maternal pride. "Isn't the party wonderful? Didn't your sisters do a beautiful job with the decorations?"

"They really did," Lacy agreed, looking around in admiration.

"I can't wait to start planning the wedding," Nancy went on. "Oh, it's going to be so gorgeous. I was thinking Ragged Point, but there's still time to talk about that. Do you think we have enough salads?"

The abrupt change in topic was jarring. "Well, I'm sure we—"

"I'm going to go check," Nancy said. "Oh, honey, you look just stunning. I'm so proud of you." Nancy squeezed Lacy in an embrace that almost took the wind out of her before rushing off toward the food tables.

"Wow. That's a happy mother," Kate said, watching her go.

Somehow, her mother's ebullience had the opposite of its intended effect. Instead of making Lacy feel warm with joy, it made her insides hum with an anxiety she couldn't quite place.

Music began playing over the speaker system, and people started calling for Lacy and Brandon to dance. She put a smile on her face and went to the center of the room to meet her fiancé.

Chapter Five

Vince had suggested that Daniel should make his move if he was going to. But the thing was, he wasn't going to. Why would he? He and Lacy had never been more than friends, and that sure as hell wasn't going to change now, with that rock on her finger.

Okay, yeah, maybe he should have asked her out at some point. Maybe he should have given that a chance, to see if it would go anywhere. But it was too late for that now. The woman was spoken for. And if the guy who'd spoken for her was kind of an asshole, well, that wasn't his problem.

Daniel thought about all of that on the Monday after the party as he waited for Vince Jordan to show up at his house to start planning the renovations. The day was clear and warm, with the faintest bite of fall in the air. In a setting as beautiful as this, outside was usually better than inside, so he sat on his tiny deck in a patio chair and drank from a steaming mug of coffee while he waited. Maybe expand the deck, too, he thought as he sipped. Hell, might as well, while he was doing it. He could have barbecues out here, invite his friends.

Maybe invite Lacy. Except that Lacy now came as a package deal with that Brandon guy, and *that* was a prospect too exhausting to think about.

Vince Jordan came rolling up the dirt road that led to Daniel's place a few minutes before ten a.m.—right on time. Vince's truck, a Ford F-150 that looked like it had seen better days, came to a stop in what passed for the driveway, and Daniel waved at him.

"Nice piece of land out here," Vince said as he climbed out

of the truck. He looked around at the tall golden grass on the rolling hills that surrounded the little house.

"I like it," Daniel replied amiably.

"I'll bet you do." Vince squinted at the property. "Probably a fire hazard out here in the dry season, though, considering your line of work."

Daniel stood and carried his coffee mug out to where Vince stood by his truck. "What are you thinking?"

"Once we do the expansion, we gotta get some fire-safe landscaping in a zone around the house." Vince gestured with his arms to indicate the area surrounding the cottage and the studio. "Gotta be drought-tolerant, obviously. Maybe some hardscape combined with some fire-resistant native plants."

"I can see that." Daniel nodded. "Come on up to the house. I'll get you some coffee and we'll talk about it."

Vince chuckled. "I wouldn't say no to coffee."

Daniel had thought they would get right down to business, but once Vince had his coffee—cream, no sugar—in front of him at the kitchen table, the discussion drifted toward Lacy and the engagement party.

"Well, I suppose it went all right," Vince said, rubbing at the back of his neck with one paddle-sized hand. "Sure made my wife happy. That woman lives for this kind of stuff. Five kids and she's only managed to marry off one of them." He shook his head mournfully. "I worry that she's rushing Lacy into something she's not ready for."

Daniel considered how to proceed. Part of him didn't think that things like women's engagement parties were a proper topic for discussion for manly men such as themselves. But another part of him wanted to know what was going on in Vince's head. That part won.

"What makes you think that?" he asked.

Vince winced at him. "You met the guy."

"Well, yeah." No elaboration was needed—they both knew what that meant. "He seems decent enough. I mean, it seems like he treats Lacy okay, he's got a good job, he's got plans …"

"Now you sound like my wife," Vince remarked. "Seems to me, a young woman like Lacy should be able to do better than a guy who has a solid job and treats her okay."

Daniel opened his mouth to make some kind of argument—for some reason, he felt like he should be defending Lacy's decisions—but in the end, he couldn't think of a valid position to take.

"Yeah," he said, finally.

"But I don't suppose Prince Charming's going to come riding in on some damned white horse," Vince concluded, looking glumly into his coffee.

"You never know," Daniel said.

"Hmm. I guess you don't." Vince was looking at Daniel pointedly. Why the hell was he looking at him like that?

"Maybe … ah … maybe we should take a look at the house," Daniel suggested.

Lacy's book collection was getting to be a problem.

It wouldn't have been an issue if she'd lived in a regular house or even a small apartment, but the Airstream had precious little storage space for the essentials, let alone for things like the romance novels that constituted Lacy's one true indulgence.

She looked at the box crammed with books that she'd pulled from the storage nook beneath her bed, and tried to think about which ones to donate to the Friends of the Library.

She couldn't get rid of the Jennifer Crusies or the Susan Mallerys, obviously. She'd had to say goodbye to some of her

Nora Roberts novels, despite her love for them, because there were just so damned many. The Robyn Carrs could go either way.

On the other hand, maybe she should keep everything. After all, she wasn't going to live in the Airstream forever. She'd either be moving into Brandon's apartment or into a house in Cambria, once he found one he liked enough to make an offer.

The idea of a house gave Lacy mixed feelings. On one hand, moving into a home—an actual house that wasn't on wheels—would bring her one step closer to her dream of having a big, noisy family like the one she'd had growing up. On the other hand, a house came with so many *things*: furniture, kitchenware, clothes, appliances—maybe even knickknacks. Lacy had grown attached to her minimalist lifestyle in the years she'd been living in the stripped-down, streamlined confines of the trailer.

Well, things were going to change, she thought. A *lot* of things were going to change.

Lacy considered the box of books, crammed a couple more into it, and then put the box back in the cabinet beneath the bed. No sense in doing away with her excess belongings now—not when she was about to increase those belongings exponentially.

With that done, Lacy thought about all the things she should do before her shift at Jitters started that afternoon. She needed to take her laundry to the house and wash it. She needed to stop by the Cookie Crock for a few basic grocery items. And she needed to get started thinking about the wedding.

She and Brandon hadn't set a date yet. He'd wanted to, but Lacy had argued that the date would be influenced by the venue they chose. What if the place they really wanted wasn't available for the date they'd selected? What if the venue—wherever it turned out to be—was more beautiful during one season than another? What if the cost of renting the place was dramatically different one time of the year versus another?

Brandon couldn't argue with the logic of Lacy's argument, and neither could her mother. But now they were both pushing her to choose a venue, showing her websites, magazine spreads, and brochures for hotels, churches, restaurants, and wineries.

Lacy's mother was growing increasingly exasperated with Lacy's indecision. But it had to be right, didn't it? You only got married once—at least, you *should* only get married once. Where was the sense in rushing it?

She walked to her tiny kitchen table, where she'd left the information her mother kept giving her. By now, she'd amassed a sizable stack of pages Nancy had printed from the Internet, each page adorned with Nancy's barely readable scrawl: *Your cousin Brian's best friend got married here—it was lovely.* Or, *Book early, they fill up months ahead.* Or, in one case, *Your father and I can send a deposit today!!!*

Lacy picked up the stack of papers, flipped through a few of them, and then plunked them back onto the table with a sigh. She went to her bed, picked up the paperback romance that sat open on the shelf over the mattress, and flopped down onto the bed with the book.

Maybe the story would inspire her to start planning the wedding. And if it didn't, well, there was always tomorrow.

The upshot of Vince Jordan's visit was that Daniel had given him a deposit, and Vince had taken photos and measurements and had promised to start on some plans. Daniel had told him what he wanted, but said he was open to ideas, as long as it fit into his budget for the project.

Now, with Vince gone, Daniel was starting to get excited. Expanding the studio was one thing. He needed that if he was going to attract more clients like Eden. But the house? That was something else. That was pure luxury.

Daniel had been living in the little house south of Cambria for about six years, and he liked it, maybe even loved it. But there was no denying it was small, old, and outdated. When he was younger, that kind of thing hadn't seemed to matter much. How much luxury did a guy like him really need? But as he grew older, now into his midthirties, he began to want more. More comfort, more convenience. More room. More style—one that didn't include harvest gold appliances and dark brown grout.

Another factor was his financial situation. Because of the Eden job, he had more money now—with additional set to come in when the installation was done—than he'd had in a long time, maybe ever. And money had a way of getting spent if you didn't do something with it. It seemed to Daniel that renovating the house would be a good investment if he ever decided to sell the place. He'd likely get all of his money back, and then some. And in the meantime, he could enjoy it in the form of a bigger, more aesthetically pleasing house.

His personal life was another area that needed some work—it had been a long time since he'd been in a relationship that was anything more than brief and casual. But he could worry about that later. Right now, he could work on the house. And he could work on getting the Vegas thing off the ground— literally.

The job he'd been commissioned to do for Eden, a tropical-themed hotel and casino, was a ceiling fixture inspired by the Dale Chihuly installation at the Bellagio. Of course, Eden wasn't paying the forty million that had reportedly been put out for *Fiori di Como*. They weren't paying one million—not even close. That was why they'd hired Daniel Reed instead of Dale Chihuly, and that was also why the Eden installation would be a fraction of the size of the one at the Bellagio.

Still, it was the biggest commission Daniel had ever done, and it represented months of work, months of stress over the fact that the thing would make or break his reputation.

The glass was done, packed, and cluttering up his studio—a vivid illustration of why he needed more space. The pieces were ocean-inspired, in keeping with Eden's tropical island theme. But not ocean-inspired like some of Chihuly's work, with its shapes mimicking sea kelp and coral. Daniel's pieces were inspired by the water itself, the white-capped waves of wind-whipped seas and the gentle undulations of a body of water at rest. Done in shades of blue, green, and white, when it was lit from above it would make the viewer feel that he was standing beneath the ocean's surface, looking up into sunlight filtering through water.

At least, that was the hope.

He'd let Eden know that the pieces were done and ready for transport, and they were sending some guys out from Vegas with a moving truck to pick them up and drive them to the hotel. He hoped to God they knew what they were doing, because one broken piece could delay the unveiling, which was scheduled to happen in just a few weeks.

Daniel would have to go out there early to supervise the installation, because positioning the pieces together would be like assembling a jigsaw puzzle—one of those really confusing ones, where everything was close to the same color. He'd written up detailed instructions, complete with diagrams, but he couldn't trust strangers to do the job right. He had to be there.

The thing about the comped rooms came up the day of Vince's visit, while Daniel was on the phone with the reservations desk at Eden, arranging for his accommodations.

"Of course, Mr. Reed. We have your room reserved, at no charge, for the dates you requested, covering the period of the installation and the unveiling." The guy recited the dates. "And, of course, we can give you complimentary rooms for any guests you'd like to invite to the event."

Daniel raised his eyebrows in surprise. "You can?"

"Certainly. We're not at capacity for that weekend, so you're welcome to invite friends or family as our guests. How many rooms will you require?"

Daniel did some quick mental calculations. "Five? I'll have to ask who can make it, though."

"I'll put you down for five, from the Friday before the unveiling through Sunday. You can confirm the number when we get closer to the date." The guy on the phone was crisp, efficient, and professional. And right now, Daniel wanted to kiss him.

A Vegas getaway with his friends seemed like just the thing to relieve the stress of finishing this job.

He just hoped he wouldn't blow all of his earnings at the blackjack tables.

Chapter Six

"**V**egas, baby!" Rose said, raising a fork in triumph. "In your case, literally," Gen said, pointing her soup spoon at Rose's baby bump. They were all gathered at Kate's dining table around platters, bowls, and crocks full of Jackson's rejects.

Jackson had been testing new crab recipes for the menu at Neptune, and he'd declared that the crab puffs, crab pasta, crab soup, and crab cakes that sat in front of them were not fit for the restaurant's diners. He'd also been experimenting with wine pairings, which had resulted in five open bottles of various varietals, each of which had only a few ounces missing.

After Jackson had left for work, Kate had looked at the abundance of food and wine in their refrigerator and had decided that the only thing to do was to invite the girls over for a crab-themed feast. The occasion presented a perfect opportunity to celebrate the news about the Vegas trip.

"God. I can't wait to sit by the pool and drink a mai tai," Kate said, between nibbles on a crab puff. "I've never even had a mai tai. It just sounds like something someone should drink by a pool."

"I want a mai tai," Rose said, scowling at the glass of iced tea she had in front of her instead of wine. "Once this baby's born, I'm having a mai tai."

When Daniel had called everyone to tell them about the comped rooms, a flurry of excitement had rippled among the group. A Vegas getaway, on its own, was enticing enough. But doing it with a crowd of friends had even more appeal. Lacy was probably the most excited, because she'd never been to Vegas.

Lacy couldn't say exactly why that was true. Las Vegas was only six hours from Cambria by car, so it was a natural choice for a three-day weekend. But for whatever reason, she'd never been there. Probably because she'd rarely been anywhere.

Born and raised in Cambria, Lacy had often longed to see the greater world. When she was growing up, it had been impossible for her family to travel very far with the expense of six children. Family vacations then had usually meant camping, or a road trip to Disneyland. But Lacy craved more. She craved New York City, Boston, New Orleans. She craved Europe. Cambria was great—she loved it in the deep, immutable way she loved her family—but at times, she felt that love was a little bit smothering, much like her own mother's affections.

"Last time I went, I stayed at the Bellagio," Kate said, sipping a smoky chardonnay from her wineglass. "This was before Jackson. I got a hot rock massage. Bliss." She closed her eyes in memory.

"I want to see the fountains at the Bellagio," Lacy put in. "They sound amazing."

"That's right. You've never been, have you?" Rose asked. "How is that even possible?"

Lacy shrugged. "I don't know. I just … never have."

"Well, you're going to love it," Rose said. "I'm going to need you to get drunk for me. I mean, you have to get drunk for yourself first, obviously. But then, after that, get drunk once for me." She rubbed her belly affectionately with one hand.

Lacy sighed theatrically. "The things a girl has to do for friendship."

Kate's house had one of the best ocean views in Cambria. Situated on a hill in the Marine Terrace neighborhood, the house had one wall of windows that offered a nearly one hundred and eighty degree vista of crashing waves, blue horizon, and dazzling sunsets. The sun had already set in a blaze of oranges and reds, and now the dusky shades of twilight were darkening the sky.

The sky was never fully dark in Las Vegas, Lacy supposed.

She considered herself lucky to have been invited on the trip. Daniel was a friend, yes, but in the twice-removed way of people who had to accept each other because of their mutual relationships. If he'd left her out of the Vegas gathering, it would have been completely understandable. And yet, he'd invited her. Or, more accurately, Kate had invited her at Daniel's prompting.

Lacy had been finishing up her shift at Jitters that day when Kate had called her cell.

"Do you want to go to Vegas in a few weeks?" Kate had asked.

Lacy, a little uncertain what the hell Kate was talking about, had replied, "Sure, but I can't afford it." Her paycheck from the coffeehouse was woefully meager, and tips were rare.

Then Kate had explained that the trip would be for the unveiling of Daniel's installation, and that the rooms would be comped.

"And he invited me?" Lacy asked, confused.

"Well … yes. In a circular sort of way."

The way Kate told it, Daniel had offered a free room to Kate and Jackson, and then had said he had an extra in case she knew anyone who might want to go. *Like maybe … I don't know … Lacy.* That's how he'd said it. As though he hadn't had her in mind at all, but was scrambling to think of someone, anyone, who could fill that extra room.

It was kind of cute, when Lacy thought about it.

She had looked the way she looked since puberty, so she had the experience to know when a man was interested in her but was trying to pretend he wasn't.

This—this invitation that wasn't exactly an invitation—was

Exhibit A.

It was clear to Lacy that he was attracted, but that he was trying to avoid the appearance of impropriety because of her engagement to Brandon. Lacy found it endearing, and if it meant a free trip to Las Vegas, so much the better.

"I wonder if Brandon will be able to clear his schedule," Lacy said.

The other three looked at her.

"What?" she said. "He has weekend office hours."

The others didn't say anything, and instead focused on their various crab dishes. Kate poked her crab bisque with her spoon.

"Okay." Lacy put down her fork and raised her voice slightly. "What's the issue here?"

Gen was the one to venture an answer. "It's just ... Brandon doesn't seem much like a fun-loving, Vegas party guy." She shrugged and offered a weak smile.

"That's true," Rose said. "He doesn't."

"Well ..." Lacy picked up her napkin, fiddled with it a little, and then threw it back down onto the table. "That doesn't mean he can't enjoy himself! It doesn't mean he can't ... I don't know ... see the sights! See a show! Enjoy a nice restaurant!"

"Of course it doesn't," Kate reassured her in a soothing voice. "You're right."

"Now, Jackson," Rose said, raising her pierced eyebrow skyward. "I'll bet *that* guy knows how to party in Vegas." Jackson had a reputation with women—earned before he'd started seeing Kate—that suggested a certain level of hedonism that would mesh well with the *what happens in Vegas stays in Vegas* ethos.

At that moment, as if on cue, Jackson came in the front door of the house, looking exhausted after a day of work at Neptune. He looked up, saw them sitting around the table full of crab, and scowled.

"You weren't supposed to eat that," he said.

"Oh. God. Did you need it for something?" Gen asked.

"No, no." He ran a hand through his thick auburn hair. "It's just … It's crap. That's the stuff that wasn't good enough to serve at the restaurant. I was gonna throw it away when I got home."

"The hell you say." Rose moved to block the crab dishes with her pregnant body. "You're going to have to get through the both of us to take it."

"Aw, it's fine." He waved away her objection. "It's just … I can do better. You should taste the stuff I was working on today. The puffs have just a hint of horseradish—"

"Jackson," Rose began, testing her theory. "What are you looking forward to most about the Vegas trip?"

He gave her a Jackson look, the one that said you were a fool if you didn't already know the answer to the question you'd just asked. "Hookers, obviously."

"You didn't really just say that." Kate picked up a potholder she'd used to bring hot dishes to the table and hurled it at Jackson.

"What?" Jackson raised an arm to deflect the potholder. "I meant for Daniel. The guy hasn't gotten laid in months. Or so he tells me."

"Still. Ew," Rose said.

"Yeah, yeah. I've gotta take a shower. Excuse me, ladies." He disappeared into the little house's lone bedroom with its attached bath.

"See what I mean?" Rose asked when he was gone. "Brandon would never think of hookers."

"And that's a bad thing?" Lacy quipped.

"Lacy has a point," Kate allowed.

"Ryan would never think of hookers either," Gen said.

"Unless he was worried about them."

"Aww. He's such a sweet guy," Rose said.

"He is," Gen said fondly. "I'm lucky. And married life is … well. It's great."

They all looked at Lacy.

Somehow, she didn't think it was because they expected her to be equally happy after her own wedding to Brandon.

Lacy and her friends spent the next couple of weeks thinking about the Vegas trip, planning which shows they wanted to see, which casinos they wanted to visit, which restaurants they wanted to try, and where they wanted to shop. They'd made a group trip down to San Luis Obispo to buy new bathing suits—all except for Rose, who said she wouldn't be caught dead in one in her current condition.

Kate and Gen experienced a certain amount of angst about what they would pack, uncertain whether to lean toward comfort, fashion, or a balance of both. Rose was more fixated on the unfairness of the fact that the trip would be happening during her nine-month sobriety. How was she supposed to have Vegas-level fun and protect her unborn child at the same time? Obviously, the baby came first. But she moaned that the trip would have been so much more satisfying had it happened several months earlier.

Lacy wanted to properly enjoy the dilemma of clothing choices and the planning of activities, but she couldn't. She was too busy fighting with her fiancé.

"God, Brandon. It's a free trip to Las Vegas. Why wouldn't you want to go?"

"I do want to go. I just don't like the fact that *he* invited you."

They'd had this fight—or some version of it—at least three

times since they'd gotten news of the trip. Lacy was giddy with excitement, but Brandon couldn't get over the fact that the room was being provided to Lacy by another man.

"He's a *friend,* Brandon. He congratulated you at our engagement party!" The two of them were at Brandon's apartment in Morro Bay—where they always went. He refused to spend time in her Airstream, saying it made him feel like a canned sardine. Lacy was pacing amid the clean, sterile furniture, growing increasingly frustrated with him, waving her arms as she talked, as though the motion might distract him from his argument.

"Yeah, well, I've seen how he looks at you. He's not just a friend. Not from his perspective, anyway." Brandon stood with his arms crossed over his pale blue polo shirt. His hair was immaculately combed, and Lacy had the irrational desire to throw something at it.

"I have known Daniel Reed for years. He has never made a pass, never said anything inappropriate …"

"That doesn't mean it isn't on his mind," Brandon insisted.

In the heat of the argument, Lacy somehow forgot that she herself had noticed that Daniel was attracted to her. And anyway, why did it matter, when there was nothing going on between them?

"I can't control what he's thinking!" Lacy insisted.

"No, but you can control whether you encourage him." Brandon's voice was annoyingly calm, as though he were explaining a difficult concept to a toddler.

This made Lacy sputter with barely suppressed rage. "I … You … I never … *How am I encouraging him*?!"

"Maybe you're not right now," Brandon said, his face arranged into an unattractive pout. "But if you accept that room, you will be."

"Brandon. Jesus Christ!" She threw her hands into the air in frustration. "He invited Kate! He invited Gen! He invited Rose! Do you think he's making a play for *all* of us?"

"He didn't invite them."

Now thoroughly flustered, Lacy rubbed at her eyes with the heels of her hands. "*What?*"

"He invited the men. Jackson, Ryan, and Will are his friends. That's who he invited. They're just bringing their significant others. But I'm not his friend. He invited you. Specifically."

"He … no. No." Lacy waved her arms in front of her to clear away the haze of his argument. "He didn't invite me. He asked Kate if she knew anyone who wanted to come, and *she* invited me."

"Oh, that was just a ruse, and you know it."

Lacy didn't have an immediate response to that, because he was right. It *was* a ruse, and she *did* know it.

"So, what?" she said finally, recovering herself. "What do you want to do, then? Are we supposed to stay home?"

"Yes."

"No!" Lacy was back in her state of sputtering outrage again. "You … I …" And then she regained her footing and advanced on him, driving him back into a corner of the condo as she pointed one finger at the middle of his chest. "I never go anywhere, Brandon. Not anywhere! I was born here. I was raised here. I've been here since I was one goddamned day old, and I will *not* miss an opportunity to get out of this town and see some other part of the world, even if it *is* only a six goddamned hour drive away. I'm going on that trip, and I'm taking that free room, and if you want to go with me, fine. But if you don't, Brandon, I swear to God I'll go without you, and when I do, I vow to you—yes, I make a solemn vow—that I will get drunk and lose money and wear a bikini by the pool and maybe even *flirt with other men,* and I will goddamned well *enjoy it!*"

She ended her rant with her face two inches from his, her skin flushed with anger, the finger she'd been pointing at him buried in the fabric of his polo shirt.

The look on his face was one of shock. He'd never seen this side of Lacy before, though others had; she'd had to bring the thunder to Jason Nix after he'd spread sexual rumors about her in the eleventh grade. It was no less satisfying this time.

"Well." He recovered himself and straightened out his shirt where she'd wrinkled it. "That's fine, Lacy. I didn't know you felt that strongly about it. We'll go. Of course we'll go."

"We will?" She looked at him with wide eyes, surprised at having won.

"Sure. But we're not taking that room."

"Brandon—"

"We'll get our own room. One that doesn't come from Daniel Reed."

"But he's not even paying for it! The rooms are comped!"

"That's not the point." Brandon's mouth was in a firm line, his lips having vanished into the chasm of his indignation.

Lacy thought about continuing to fight, but decided there was no point. She'd gotten a concession from him: They were going. Why did the details matter?

"I'll call Eden and make the reservation," Brandon went on, looking smug. "I'll let you know the rate, and then you can reimburse me for your half."

"My ..."

"I'm glad we've got this worked out, sweetie," Brandon said, planting a quick, chaste kiss on Lacy's lips. "Now, where should we go for dinner?"

"Let me get this straight. He's insisting on paying for the

room, and he's charging you for half?"

Lacy handed Rose's half-caff latte to her at Jitters.

"That about sums it up."

"What an asshole."

Lacy wanted to argue with Rose—she wanted to protest that the man she planned to marry was both wise and emotionally mature—but in this case, she couldn't. Brandon really was being an asshole. The best she could come up with in his defense was, "He doesn't usually act this way."

Rose side-eyed her. "If you say so."

"I do."

"Okay. But … Lacy, please tell me you're thinking about this. Tell me you're thinking about how it's going to be to live with him day after day, year after year …"

"Rose."

"All right." Rose raised the hand that wasn't holding the latte in a show of innocence and surrender.

Lacy wouldn't have said it out loud, but she couldn't muster up much outrage over what Rose had said. In fact, she *had* been thinking, extensively, about what it would be like to live with Brandon forever, especially after the fight over the hotel room. Was she really up to a life of jealousy, chiropractic advice, polo shirts, and hair gel? And if she wasn't, what was she supposed to do, now that she'd agreed to marry him?

"The important thing is that I'm going to Vegas," Lacy said, putting the bigger issues aside for the moment. "Is Will excited about the trip? Oh, and didn't you have an appointment with your OB this morning? How's that baby?"

"She's doing great," Rose said, rubbing her baby bump lovingly. "But I'm losing the Baby Name Derby." Rose had learned a couple of weeks before that her baby would be a girl, and since then, she and Will had been competing in a contest for naming rights. The rules were complicated, but they had something to do with a sophisticated points system based on housework completed, sexual favors granted, and letters of endorsement from friends and family.

"How can you be losing?" Lacy fretted. "Don't you get points for sex? You love sex!"

"Yes, but so does he," Rose reminded her. "Every time I earn points, he earns them right along with me." Rose considered. "Not that I want him to stop earning points."

"Well, of course not," Lacy agreed. Then a thought struck her. "You should get extra points for use of your uterus."

Rose's shoulders fell. "I did. I got twenty bonus points. I'm still losing."

Lacy wiped drops of coffee and foam off of the counter with a white bar rag. "So, what name are you going with if you win?"

Rose's face lit with enthusiasm. "Poppy."

"Oh, my God, that's adorable," Lacy said.

"Isn't it?"

"Rose and Poppy. I love the flower theme."

"Me too." Rose took a sip of her latte and grimaced at the lack of full-powered caffeine. "I've gotta find a way to earn more points."

"So what name does Will want?"

"Harper."

"Oh, jeez. That's cute, too."

"Yeah. I guess I'll be okay either way," Rose admitted. "But it's not just about the name. I hate losing. On the other hand, one of the reasons I'm losing is that he's been doing all of the laundry. So there's that."

Lacy grinned, feeling the vicarious warmth of Rose and Will's relationship. The two of them really were unbearably sweet together. They weren't married, and in fact had moved in together only after learning about Rose's pregnancy. Still, the sense of love, friendship, and fun that surrounded them made Lacy happy for both of them, and also a little sad for herself. She had no doubt that Brandon did care for her, but she couldn't pretend that they had what Rose and Will had. She worried that if she held out for that kind of connection, she would be waiting forever.

Chapter Seven

A week before the big unveiling at Eden, Daniel packed his things, locked up his house, got into his SUV, and made the drive out to Vegas. He wished he weren't going alone. Sure, his friends would be meeting him before the actual event, but that left almost a full week with him on his own in Sin City.

Of course, he'd be working a lot of that time. The reason he was going early was that he had to supervise the installation of his piece. The ceiling fixture had a lot of parts that had to be joined together in a very specific way. He didn't trust anyone else to do it right. He had to be there.

Daniel usually didn't feel lonely. He was an independent guy who enjoyed his solitude, enjoyed being able to hear his own thoughts. But being at home or at work alone was one thing. Being alone in Las Vegas, capital of hedonism and impromptu marriage, was entirely another.

Of course, it was always possible that he could hook up with someone during the trip, someone he might meet at the bar or the pool. But that sort of thing had lost its allure as Daniel had grown older. While he used to see impulsive hookup sex as harmless fun, these days it just seemed kind of sad. He didn't really want anonymous sex. He wanted someone he could talk to. He wanted the kind of connection that came with mutual affection and respect.

Might as well start shopping for a walker, Reed, he told himself as he maneuvered his SUV through the light traffic of Interstate 5 as it passed through Kern County. *You're getting old.*

But even as he thought that, he realized it was bullshit. He wasn't getting old. He was growing up.

The day was hot and bright, even though it was late October. That was one thing he missed about Colorado, where he'd grown up: the seasons. In this part of California, it was just as likely to be seventy degrees in February as it was in June. It just didn't make sense. It defied the natural order of things. He'd moved to the state years ago, and yet he'd still never really adjusted.

He drove, blasting Vampire Weekend and Givers on the sound system as he tried not to think about Lacy Jordan.

Lacy.

She was coming to Vegas for the unveiling, and that was good. But that asshole fiancé of hers had refused the room he'd offered, and that was stupid. Daniel asked himself, not for the first time, why she was marrying that guy.

His interest wasn't personal. Of course not. It was more … curiosity. Why would a lovely, kind, smart, funny woman like her decide to spend a lifetime with an uptight, boring, fashion-challenged prick like Brandon Lewis? It didn't make sense, and Daniel liked for things to make sense.

Still, he figured it was her business, not his. And maybe Brandon had some fine qualities Daniel didn't know about. Maybe he was kind to animals. Maybe he was better socially one-on-one, with Lacy, than he was in group situations. Maybe he wrote sensitive poetry. Women liked sensitive poetry.

Whatever it was, Daniel envied the hell out of it, because it had gotten him Lacy. *A woman* like *Lacy,* he amended. Because this wasn't about Lacy specifically. Of course it wasn't.

Daniel made the rest of the drive, stopping once in Barstow for a Big Mac and fries. When he got to Eden, a couple of blocks off the Vegas Strip, he gave the valet his car, got checked into his room, and dropped his bag on one of the two queen-size beds.

He peeked into the bathroom and saw that he had a Jacuzzi tub in there. He sighed.

A queen-size bed and a Jacuzzi tub weren't nearly as much fun alone.

Lacy and Brandon fought again on the way to Vegas. The fight wasn't just about the hotel room, though that was part of it.

It started when Lacy told Brandon that Kate and Jackson had invited them to see a Cirque du Soleil show the following night, but from there, it spread in many directions, like a particularly virulent virus.

"I don't want to see Cirque du Soleil," Brandon said. "Or, actually, I do. But I don't want to see that particular production. I want to see the aquatic one. You know, the one at the Bellagio."

"Oh. But everyone's going to the one at the Mirage. We were all going to go together, and—"

"Nah." Brandon wrinkled his nose as though he were smelling something unpleasant, like dirty sweat socks or French cheese. "Let's skip it and do our own thing."

Lacy began to feel uneasy, because one of the most attractive things about this trip was the fact that she would be doing it with her best friends, sharing the experience, doing a little girl bonding at the same time as she was enjoying a weekend with Brandon. But now, his nose wrinkles were calling the entire plan into question.

"Well ... I guess we don't have to see that particular show," Lacy allowed. "But ... I do want to spend some time with Kate and Gen and Rose."

Brandon let out a weary sigh, the same weary sigh he used whenever he wanted to belittle something Lacy was saying.

"I would think you spend enough time with them at home. More than enough."

"What's that supposed to mean?" Lacy said. "They're my *friends.*"

"Oh, I know." Brandon chuckled bitterly. "Believe me, I know."

Lacy shifted in her seat so she could face him more directly as he drove the I-15 toward the Nevada state line. "Brandon? Do you have a problem with my friends?"

He didn't say anything at first, but she saw his knuckles whiten as his grip on the steering wheel tightened.

"Brandon?" she prompted him.

"It's just ... do you have to see them every day? Every day, Lacy? You don't even see *me* every day."

Lacy threw her hands into the air in frustration. "Of course I see them more often than I see you! They live in Cambria! They all work on Main Street! They come into Jitters every day, and I serve them their coffee! You're all the way down in Morro Bay with your ... your office and your chiropractic patients and your ... your golf!"

He threw her a weary look before returning his gaze to the road. "Now you have a problem with me playing golf?"

"No! It's none of my *business* if you play golf, just like it's none of yours if I like to spend time with my friends!"

He was silent for a few moments, but now his jaw was flexing along with his clenched knuckles.

"You know I'm looking for a place in Cambria," he said, his voice tight.

"I know. That's not—"

"And I would think that it will *all* be my business once you're my wife."

Lacy recoiled as though she'd been slapped. Not because

what he'd said was so shocking or horrible, but because he was simply telling the truth about how he saw the world—a truth she hadn't understood until now.

He *did* think it would all be his business once they were married. He really did believe he should have a significant say in how she would spend her time. And he didn't approve of her spending time with her friends.

What would that mean once they were married? What would her life look like? She would have the house in Cambria and the kids, sure. But would she be expected to retreat into a world centered on Brandon? Did he expect to become the sun around which she, a minor planet, would orbit?

"Lacy?" he said when she hadn't spoken for more than five minutes.

"Yeah?" Her voice sounded vague, distracted.

"All I'm saying is that—"

"I know what you're saying."

"And?" he prompted her.

If he wanted to get into it, well, then, they would get into it.

"My friends are a big part of my life, Brandon. That's not going to change once we're married. I'll be seeing them every day, just like I do now, so you need to get used to that. They're my family. And you wouldn't expect me to just ... cut off my family."

"Now that you mention it ..." A wry smile tugged at his lips.

Lacy glared at him. "Now that I mention it, what?"

"Well. You do spend a lot of time with your mother. And your sisters. I really think they're a bad influence."

"A bad *influence*?"

"You wouldn't still be working at a coffeehouse if your parents had insisted that you go to college. You wouldn't be living in a … a *tin can* in the backyard." His voice picked up force as he warmed to his topic. "You know, Lacy, you need someone like me to guide you. To help you get your priorities in order."

"My priorities? My *priorities?*"

"Yes! Yes! Your priorities!"

"I think friendship and family and … and *honest work* are good priorities, Brandon!"

"And wasting your time reading those idiot novels you love so much?" He was taunting her now, playing with her, coming in for the kill.

Lacy waved her hands in front of her face as if to clear away the noxious fumes that were his words.

"Now you have a problem with the *books* I read?"

"Yes. Yes. Now that you're bringing it up, I do."

"You brought it up, Brandon! Not me!"

"Well, now that it's out there, I think it's time we talked about it."

Brandon's car shot down the I-15 at 70 miles per hour amid sparse traffic, the great expanse of barren desert stretching out around them. A flock of birds flew overhead, and a wiry brown rabbit took cover under a scrubby bush.

"What the hell is wrong with my books?" Lacy demanded.

"Like this one?" Brandon snatched up a paperback that had been sitting on the center console between them. A historical romance, it featured a shirtless man embracing a woman whose breasts were perilously close to spilling out of her dress. "This is garbage, Lacy. It's … it's the worst kind of trash. You need to be reading quality books. The classics."

"The classics? This is my *life*, Brandon. This isn't senior English."

"No, although when you *were* in high school, you probably cut class every day, or you might have a real job."

Lacy felt stunned and sickened. Was this how he felt about her? Was this how he'd felt all along?

"Give me the book," she said, her voice low and even.

"No."

"Give me the book, Brandon."

"No!"

She reached for it, and he yanked his arm away. He hit the button for the automatic window, and when the glass had rolled down, he dodged her reaching hand and hurled the book out the window, where if flapped and fluttered to the roadside like a dying bird.

There wasn't much to say after that. Lacy turned away from him to look out her window at the passing desert landscape. She crossed her legs and folded her arms over her chest. If she could just make herself very small, maybe she could pretend that she wasn't here, beside this man.

Chapter Eight

On day eight of his trip to Vegas, Daniel had just finished his final inspection of the ceiling installation and was crossing the casino on his way to the hotel's burger joint for lunch when he saw Lacy Jordan sitting at the bar. He headed toward her, buoyed by the sight of a friendly face, but then stopped short when he realized she had been crying.

"Lacy?"

She turned toward the sound of his voice, her eyes red and puffy. "Oh. Daniel." She had in front of her the remains of what looked like a Long Island iced tea. Those things were lethal. He could recall more than one hangover caused by that particular cocktail, and shook his head to clear the memory.

"Hey, Lacy. Are you okay?" He slid onto the barstool next to hers.

"No." She shook her head. "Really, no. I'm apparently stupid and childish, and I don't have a real job. Plus, my friends and family are a bad influence."

"Jesus. Who told you that?"

"Brandon. My fiancé. My future husband."

Of course it was Brandon. That asshole.

"Where is he now?" Daniel was asking because he thought it might be refreshing to find the guy and punch him in the face.

Lacy shrugged, a big, theatrical gesture that involved the entirety of her arms. "The room, I guess. The one he wouldn't let you pay for."

"I didn't pay for any of them," Daniel reminded her.

"Whatever. I left while he was in the shower. Shithead. I hope he drowned."

Well. It seemed to Daniel that people usually were well into a marriage—say, ten or twelve years—before reaching that level of hostility. Of course, that probably varied.

Daniel looked at Lacy and assessed the situation. From the sound of her voice and the slightly unfocused look of her eyes, he deduced that the drink wasn't her first. She wasn't fully drunk, but she was at least buzzed, and the sadness in her face cut right through him. He wanted to help her somehow, but felt woefully unprepared. "Should I … Do you want me to see if Kate's here yet? Or Gen?"

"No, no." Lacy waved a hand and let it flop heavily onto the bar. "They already hate him. They'd just say 'I told you so.' "

"No, they wouldn't."

"Okay. Maybe they wouldn't. But they'd be thinking it."

Daniel couldn't argue with that, as much as he wanted to. Lacy's friends *had* told her so, on more than one occasion. He knew that because guys talked, sometimes about whatever their girlfriends were currently obsessing over. So, yeah. They'd told her, and so far, she had ignored them. But, hell. You couldn't control what other people thought, and there wasn't much payoff in trying.

"It doesn't matter what they think," Daniel said, going with the theme. "What matters is that they care about you. They want you to be okay."

She gave him a long, tearful, meaningful look that said she knew he was right. But then she turned back to her drink and pounded what was left in the glass. Which wasn't an insignificant amount.

"You know what I want?" she said after a while.

"No. What?"

"I want to have fun. I want to see Vegas. And I don't want to think about Brandon."

"Okay." He could work with this. "Okay. Why don't you give Kate or Gen or Rose a call, see if they've checked in yet. When you hook up with them, you can—"

"I can't talk to them. Not right now." She stood up decisively. Lacy tried to pull the strap of her purse over her shoulder, but she got her hand tangled in it. She looked at the hand and the strap as though she were puzzled by what she was seeing. She tugged at the strap and flapped her hand around, trying to free it.

It occurred to Daniel that she was more drunk than he'd thought.

"Here. Let me help with that." Daniel gently unwound the strap from around Lacy's hand, and laid it gently and carefully onto her shoulder.

"There!" Lacy said, as though she'd been the one to fix it. Then she walked away from the bar and headed toward the exit of the casino. Daniel hurried to catch up with her.

"Lacy? Where are you going?"

"Vegas!" she said, waving her arms in an extravagant gesture that encompassed the casino, the hotel, and the city beyond.

She walked away from him, and he weighed his options. Unless he restrained her by force—which he sure as hell wasn't going to do—it seemed to him that he had no choice.

Drunk and upset, she wouldn't be safe out there amid the anonymous crowds on the Strip.

He sighed and let out a curse under his breath, and then followed her out the door, into the afternoon sun, and into a waiting cab.

❖

"So. Where to?" the cabdriver asked.

Lacy made her voice bright. "To a place where my asshole fiancé can't tell me what to do, and who to see, and … and what to read!" she announced.

The cabdriver looked at her over the back of his seat. "I don't know that place. You're gonna have to be more specific."

"Just take us to the Strip," Daniel told him. "Caesar's Palace."

The driver turned on the meter, and they headed into the desert toward the sparkling skyline in front of them.

When they arrived at Caesar's, Daniel paid the fare plus tip, and they went inside. Within ten minutes, Lacy had bought a strawberry daiquiri in a plastic cup that was as tall as a toddler. Daniel wasn't sure more alcohol was a good idea, but he was her friend, not her father. And it seemed to him she'd had more than enough of being told what to do. So he watched her sip the drink through a straw as they wandered through the designer shops under a ceiling made to resemble blue skies dotted with fluffy clouds.

"God, this is good," Lacy said as they paused outside the Louis Vuitton store. "You should try it." She held the ridiculously tall cup out to Daniel.

"I'd better. If you drink the whole thing, I'll have to carry you back to the hotel." He took a sip from the straw and tried to hand the cup back to her.

"Have a little more," she said. "You look tense."

Lacy herself didn't seem tense in the slightest. Her anger at Brandon seemed to be burning off, and the alcohol she had consumed had combined with her excitement at being in Vegas to make her seem loose and happy.

Daniel scowled at her. "What do you mean I look tense? I'm not tense."

"Not even with the unveiling tomorrow?" Lacy said.

"Okay," he admitted. "I might be a little tense."

He took another, longer, drink from Lacy's cup, and then

they caught the Fall of Atlantis animatronic show in the Forum Shops. Lacy noticed a Cheesecake Factory right behind the fountain where the show was, so they bought a slice of lemon meringue cheesecake and shared it on a bench while the crowds in their jeans and slogan T-shirts flowed around them like water.

Daniel pointed out that he wasn't getting much of the cheesecake—Lacy was devouring it like a swarm of locusts attacking a wheat field.

"How can you eat like that?" he asked her. "There are about a thousand calories in that. What are you, a size four?"

"Six," Lacy corrected him. "And I'm blessed with a fast metabolism. I don't gain weight."

Daniel guffawed. "That must make you a hit with your girlfriends."

When they were done with the cheesecake, Lacy hefted what was left of her daiquiri and they headed out onto the Strip and walked north toward the Venetian.

Lacy wanted to go on a gondola ride. Daniel couldn't see the point of riding a fake gondola on a fake canal through a fake Venice, but Lacy announced that she was doing it with or without him, so he grumbled a little and then climbed into the boat.

Daniel had regarded the gondola ride as a silly waste of money. But once they were underway, with the gondolier in his striped shirt guiding them along the waterways of the massive hotel, he had to admit it was worth it if it made Lacy this happy. She was looking everywhere—at the building, the shops, the other tourists, the gently rippling water—but Daniel found himself looking only at her.

The look of childlike bliss on her face was enchanting. And that wasn't a word he would use lightly—or, usually, at all. But there it was.

He wanted to see more of that bliss, so he went along with whatever she wanted to do. So what if he didn't like designer purses or fake European cities? She did, and that was enough.

"Ooh, St. Mark's Square!" Lacy squealed when they got off the gondola. He could barely keep up with her as she took it all in, wandering through the shops, watching the street performers, and craning her neck to look at the architecture mimicking that of the real Venice.

"You ever been?" Daniel asked.

"Where?"

"To Venice. The real one."

Lacy scoffed at him. "No. I've never been anywhere."

Being in Vegas made Lacy feel like a five-year-old on her first trip to Disneyland. Except, Disneyland didn't serve alcohol, so this was better.

She'd never been to Vegas before—hard to believe, considering that it was reasonably close and she was in her early thirties—but it was true. So the spectacle laid out before her—the lights, the sounds, the sheer audacity of everything that passed into her line of sight—was awe-inspiring.

She felt such giddy pleasure that Daniel's question, which reminded her of one of the main flaws in her otherwise happy life, jarred her.

"What do you mean you've never been anywhere?" he asked.

They were standing on a bridge over the mock Grand Canal, Lacy with her elbows propped atop the railing.

"Well, I mean that I haven't seen Venice. I haven't seen anywhere in Europe. I've barely seen anything in America. I hadn't even been to Vegas until today."

Daniel looked dumbstruck. It would have been comical, if

his reaction hadn't been prompted by such a sad truth.

"How is that possible?" he said.

She turned to face him and leaned her back against the bridge railing. She swayed a little, but the walking and the sights and the activity seemed to have settled her head, and she felt less drunk than she had when they'd started this adventure, despite the yard-high daiquiri.

Throngs of tourists streamed past them, but she was focused only on him.

"When I was a kid, my parents weren't all that interested in traveling. They said we lived in one of the most beautiful places on the planet, so why go somewhere else? I think that was partly true, but I also think that was easier than admitting they couldn't afford it."

"I know what your dad does. But your mom's what? A teacher?"

"Yeah. Fifth grade. They did okay, moneywise. There was enough. But having enough to support your family isn't the same as having enough for a vacation. Especially when you've got five kids."

He shook his head in wonder. "Yeah, I get that. I can't imagine taking five kids on a road trip to Walmart, let alone on vacation."

"Right. And once I was old enough to travel on my own, I was too broke. I'm a barista. I can barely afford a trip to Paso Robles." She looked into the water and grinned as a gondola full of elderly women, cameras in their hands, floated by.

"Huh. Well, I'm glad you came on this trip, then."

"How about you?" she asked, still looking at the water and at the people milling around on the other side of the canal.

"Which part? The family, or the traveling?"

"Both. But start with the family."

"I'm an only child."

"Oh, God," Lacy said, sighing. "That sounds so peaceful. Nobody to fight with. Nobody to borrow your clothes without asking, or to make you take the blame for stuff they did."

"Also nobody to play with when you're a kid," Daniel pointed out. "And nobody to commiserate when your parents ground you or take away your TV privileges."

Lacy tried to imagine the loneliness of life as an only child, and couldn't. Her memories of childhood were too full of noise, and chaos, and people.

"Now the travel part," she prompted him. The alcohol had made the world soft around the edges. Listening to his voice amid the noises that surrounded them lulled her into a feeling of contentment.

"Well …" He rubbed at his chin. "I grew up in Colorado. Talk about your natural beauty. My parents were on this quest to visit all of the fifty states, so we did that. A lot."

"That sounds like fun," she said.

"It was, some of the time. The rest of the time it was hours and hours in the back seat of my dad's station wagon, listening to him and my mom argue about whether to take Route 40 or Route 36 to get to whatever place was next on the list." His mouth curved into a wistful grin as he lost himself in the memories.

"So, did they make it?"

"Make what?"

"All fifty states," she reminded him. "Did they do it?"

"All except Delaware."

"Why Delaware?"

He shrugged. "My mom got cancer, and that sort of put a stop to the whole thing."

"Oh, Daniel." Lacy put a hand on his arm. "I'm sorry."

"She's okay," he reassured her. "She got through it, went into remission. It's just, I think that after a year and a half of cancer treatment, not knowing whether she was going to live or die, Delaware kind of lost its importance."

"I can imagine," she said.

She was swaying a little, gently, feeling the movement of the people around her, listening to the cacophonous sounds of the giant hall where the faux St. Mark's stood.

"So, where would you go?" he prompted her. "If you had a chance?"

She looked around them, then grinned at him. "Italy."

"Really?"

"Absolutely."

"Huh. Well, let's keep walking around here, then. It's not the real thing, but at the moment, it's what we've got.

Chapter Nine

When they finished wandering through the Venetian, Lacy and Daniel went back out onto the Strip and headed south toward the Bellagio. Daniel wanted to get one more look at the Dale Chihuly art glass ceiling installation that had prompted the commission for the job at Eden. Of course, since this was Lacy's first trip to Vegas, she had to see the fountains.

They decided to walk instead of taking a cab or a shuttle. The evening was unseasonably warm for October, and the street was packed with cars and pedestrians. Some of the pedestrians were drunk; some were locals hawking shows, helicopter tours, or photo opportunities with showgirls or comic book characters; and some were families with backpacks and strollers.

As they made their way down the sidewalk, a guy held out a flyer and Lacy took it. She peered down at an image of a scantily clad woman along with the promise of fulfilled fantasies.

"Is this a prostitute? Did this guy just give me an ad for a whore?" Lacy inquired.

"Ah, jeez. Yes. Let me just …" Daniel, embarrassed, reached out to take the paper from her.

"No, I'm keeping it," Lacy said, folding up the paper and putting it into her back pocket.

"Why?" He quirked an eyebrow at her. "Are you interested in her services?"

She smacked him on the arm. "Of course not, you idiot. It's a souvenir."

"Okay. But personally, I'd rather have a mug or a T-shirt."

They walked amid the lights and the glimmering billboards,

across bridges that spanned the busy street, past water features and moving sidewalks beckoning visitors into the casinos, where fortunes would be won and lost—but mostly lost.

When they got to the Bellagio, Daniel checked the time on his cell phone and saw that they had twenty minutes until the next fountain show. With a little time on their hands, they followed a walkway around the artificial lake and into the hotel, where they made their way to the lobby.

Daniel had seen *Fiori di Como*—Dale Chihuly's two thousand-piece glass installation that adorned the ceiling of the hotel lobby—many times before. He'd studied it, pondered it, even dreamed about it in the time since he'd been commissioned to do something similar, but much smaller in scale, for Eden. But for Lacy, it was all new. As they emerged into the lobby with its gleaming floors, its graceful arches, its front counter that seemed to be a mile long, Daniel watched Lacy's face as she tipped her head back, gazed upward, and saw *Fiori di Como* for the first time.

"Oh. My. God." Her mouth dropped open and her neck craned back. "I've seen pictures, but …"

Daniel watched her as her eyes took in the shapes, the colors, the textures, the light streaming through the field of glass flowers.

"What do you think?" he asked after she'd had a chance to process it.

"It's …" She seemed to be struggling for a word. "It's amazing. But you're the expert. What do *you* think?"

Her gaze broke from the ceiling and she looked at him. She seemed to really want to hear his answer, and he didn't want to disappoint her, so he thought carefully before he responded.

Instead of answering directly, he gestured toward a group of five middle-aged men who were standing nearby, gazing up at the ceiling. The guys, in their typical tourist attire of shorts, T-shirts, and ball caps, were transfixed, their jaws slack, their eyes wide, as they looked upward toward that magical field of flowers forged of fire and sand.

"Look at those guys," Daniel told Lacy.

"What—"

"Just take a moment, and look at them."

She did, and then she looked back at him in question.

"Right now, they're not thinking about how much they lost in the casino, or the fights they had with their wives, or the electric bill. They're not thinking about their crappy jobs or their car that needs to be serviced. They're not thinking about one damned thing … except that." He pointed toward the ceiling. "They're transported." His voice had taken on an emotion that he hadn't planned, hadn't expected. But there it was. "Now, I could talk to you about what it takes to complete a project like that, the supplies you'd need, the techniques for getting the color, the texture. I could talk about the challenge of installing it, with the weight, the square footage, the number of pieces involved. But none of that matters. What matters is those guys, and what they're feeling right now." He nodded, and looked skyward. "That … Well. It's magic. It's just … magic."

"And now you've done something similar," Lacy pointed out.

"Similar to this?" Daniel waved a hand to dismiss the idea. "My deal's nothing like this. I mean, yeah, they said they wanted something inspired by the Chihuly. But mine … it's smaller, it's simpler. It's a whole hell of a lot cheaper." He rubbed at the back of his neck with one hand.

Lacy cocked her head to one side and regarded him. "Do you always do that?" she asked.

"Do what?"

"Minimize your accomplishments."

He looked at her in surprise, started to say something, and then stopped. Was that what he was doing?

"I … Kind of. Yeah. I guess I do." He hadn't realized it until she'd pointed it out.

"Come on," she said, nudging him with an elbow. "It's almost time for the fountains."

By the time they got outside, a crowd had gathered along the concrete railing lining the water outside the Bellagio. They moved through the throngs of people until they found a spot on the railing where they could get a good view. An announcement over the loudspeaker told them the show was about to begin, and Lacy squirmed in excitement. She wiggled up and down on her toes as she waited for the display to start.

"Have you seen this before?" she asked Daniel, peering over her shoulder to where he was standing behind her.

"I have, yeah."

"Is it great? Because I really want it to be great."

He grinned at her in amusement. "Wait and see."

Under the late afternoon sun, bathed in the glow of neon lights and surrounded by festive crowds of people, Lacy watched the still water, waiting for some sign of something on a surface dancing with reflected light.

A voice over the loudspeaker announced the Fountains of Bellagio, and Lacy leaned in to watch.

The soundtrack was a mix of contemporary and vintage, from Mariah Carey to Frank Sinatra, and Lacy stood there spellbound as the water alternately swayed, pulsed upward in a tap-dance staccato rhythm, arced in graceful patterns, and exploded skyward with the swell of the music's crescendo.

She didn't know what she had expected. Fountains, water, music, sure. Maybe some colored lights. But this—this spectacle of excess, this miracle of engineering, this masterpiece of complexity—was pure magic. As the show ended and the fountains retreated, she felt something hot and insistent rise in her chest, and tears filled her eyes. She noticed Daniel watching her, and blinked hard, swiping at her wet cheeks.

"You okay?" He grinned at her.

"Yeah, yeah. Yes. Gah!" Embarrassed, she waved him off. "It's a thing. I cry when I'm happy."

"That's cute," he said.

"*Humiliating.* I think the word you're looking for is *humiliating.*"

"What? Nah." He shrugged. "There's nothing embarrassing about being happy. About feeling joy. I mean, Jesus. How many of us even know what that's like anymore?"

She cocked her head at him under the glow of the streetlights as dusk began to fall. "Don't you?"

"Don't I what?"

"Don't you know what it's like? Joy?"

He scowled and took her arm. "Come on. I think it's time for us to head back."

They caught the shuttle back to Eden, and as they rode, Daniel thought about Lacy's question. To say that he didn't know what it was to feel joy would be a mistake. He felt it when he worked in his studio, using heat of up to 2,400 degrees to bend glass to his will. He felt it when he was held in the grip of an idea, a concept, a vision for a work of art he would create. And he'd felt it when he'd watched Lacy crying over the fountains.

And *that,* he had to admit, was playing with fire every bit as much as what he did in his studio.

Lacy was engaged. And he and Lacy were friends, part of a

larger network of friends who cared about and supported each other. What the hell was he thinking, feeling joy with her? He should have been feeling joy with some other woman, while Lacy was feeling joy with Brandon.

Though he got the feeling that *joy* wasn't the dominant emotion in that particular relationship.

He couldn't help watching her as she looked out the window of the cab, pointing out things of interest, exclaiming over the world of manufactured pleasures that was passing outside.

Had he ever felt that much simple happiness? Not without a blowpipe in his hand.

Her joyful spirit—that was one thing. And then there was the way she looked.

Lacy and all of her friends were attractive, no question. Each of them had a quality, an allure, all her own. But Lacy had the kind of beauty that could strike a man breathless, or mute, or both. Long, golden blond hair, pale blue eyes, a face like a Renaissance painting. And her body. Holy shit. Best not to think too much about that.

He was feeling things he shouldn't feel, and thinking things he shouldn't think, and the best thing to do was to excuse himself when they got back to the hotel so he could hide in his room before he did anything stupid.

But somehow, that wasn't what he did. Because when they arrived at Eden, she charged over to the bar as though she was ready to pick up exactly where she'd left off when he'd first found her there. And he couldn't just leave her there, drinking alone, so he followed her as she sat down on a barstool and ordered another cocktail.

Chapter Ten

Lacy's cell phone had rung at least ten times since she'd left Eden with Daniel. One of those calls had been Kate, and one had been Rose. The rest had been Brandon. She had ignored them all, because she didn't want to talk to him, and she wasn't ready to admit to her friends that they had been right.

She would deal with all of that later. For now, it was so much simpler just to turn off her ringer and pretend no one was looking for her—that no one wanted to fight with her or belittle her, or even comfort her. It was so much simpler to pretend that she and Daniel were the only ones here, the only ones who mattered.

Lacy had always been the responsible one, the one who did the right thing, the one who looked out for everyone else. For once, she didn't want to do the right thing, the responsible thing. What she wanted was to ignore her cell phone and sit here at this bar, drinking with Daniel.

The main bar at Eden was a big, gleaming, circular affair with an enormous light fixture cascading down from the ceiling; towers of bottles in various colors backlit against a mirror; music pulsing through the sound system; and people—in couples, singular, and in groups—drinking, laughing, and playing the video gaming machines that were always close at hand.

They ordered their drinks—a mojito for her, a gin and tonic for him—and took in the sights and sounds around them.

"I should go," Lacy told him when she was about halfway through her drink. "You were sweet to babysit me, but I'm okay."

He waved a hand like he was shooing away a bee. "Ah, hell.

It wasn't babysitting. I'll admit it started out that way, but I had a good time." He took a deep drink of his gin.

"Still."

As they talked, Lacy was aware of a presence on her other side. She looked up when she felt a nudge against her shoulder. A guy, probably in his late thirties, had climbed onto the barstool next to her. He had slicked-back hair and was wearing a Hawaiian shirt. He'd clearly been drinking for a while, and Lacy had to lean back to escape the foul fog of his breath.

"Buy you a drink?" the guy said, leering.

"I have one, thanks." Lacy turned back toward Daniel. "So, what should—"

"I'll buy you another, then. Bartender! Get the lady a … " The guy gestured toward Lacy's mojito. "A whatever. That thing. Whatever that is."

"No thank you," Lacy said to the bartender. "I'm good."

The bartender, a crisply uniformed woman with her hair in a tidy ponytail, nodded and went back down the bar to attend to another patron.

Lacy kept her back to the drunk guy, facing Daniel, hoping that her body language would dissuade Hawaiian Shirt Man from persisting. But maybe he was too drunk to read body language. Or maybe he was just that socially inept.

"Hey!" the guy said. "I'm Trevor. What's your name?"

Now Daniel faced Hawaiian Shirt Man and said, "Hey, Trevor? The lady doesn't want a drink. And she doesn't want to flirt. She's here with me, okay?"

"I don't believe I was talking to you," Trevor said, his words slightly slurred. "I was talking to … What's your name? Miss? Are you too stuck up to even tell me your name?"

And here we go, Lacy thought. Looking like she did, she was familiar with the situation. A guy makes a move. She shuts him down. Guy gets more aggressive. Then guy turns insulting, and things get ugly. Usually, it ended with Lacy picking up her purse and leaving. But this time, Daniel was added into the mix. Most of the time, Daniel was a fairly mild-mannered guy. But who knew what might happen when he was defending a woman from an aggressive drunk?

"Let's move to a booth," Daniel told Lacy, gesturing to a faux leather-lined booth at the edge of the bar area. "Come on. Bring your drink."

Lacy grabbed her stuff and they started to move away from the bar.

Trevor wasn't going to give up that easily.

"You really going with him, honey?" Trevor called after them. "Come upstairs with me and I'll show you a real man."

Lacy looked at Daniel and put her hand on his bicep. "Daniel. Don't. It's okay."

There was a set to his jaw, a fire in his eyes. "No. It's not okay."

Daniel put himself between Trevor and Lacy, and the two of them started doing that puffed-chest thing men did when they were sizing up which one was going to be the alpha.

"Step away, asshole," Daniel said.

"What did you call me? What did you call me?" Trevor's face was turning red.

"Daniel. Trevor. Just … stop. Both of you. Stop."

Lacy thought Trevor was going to take a swing at Daniel. Instead, he reached around Daniel, grabbed Lacy's arm, and pulled her toward him.

"Come on, honey. Let's go. You don't need him." He hauled Lacy in his direction, almost pulling her off her feet.

Daniel's hand clamped down on Trevor's wrist where he was holding Lacy. "You're gonna want to take that hand off of her," he said.

"Or what are you gonna fuckin' do, you pussy?" Trevor's words were belligerent enough, but he was starting to look scared.

Out of the corner of her eye, Lacy saw a security guard approaching.

It's about time, she thought. She just hoped the guard got here before the first blow landed.

Too late.

Daniel set his feet, and without taking his left hand off of Trevor's arm, he sent his right fist crashing into Trevor's face hard enough to drop him and his Hawaiian shirt to the floor.

Her arm now free of Trevor's grip, Lacy jumped back from the heap of drunk guy at her feet. The security guard, now in a hurry, got to them and grabbed Daniel's forearm.

"Whoa, whoa, take it easy," the guard said, hauling Daniel a few feet back from Trevor, who was moaning and holding a hand over his eye.

"That's the guy you want, Neil," the bartender said to the security guard, pointing to the man on the ground. "He grabbed the lady."

Neil gave Daniel a skeptical look, let go of his arm, and grabbed Trevor under the arms and helped him to his feet.

"Are you injured, sir?" Neil asked Trevor.

"Hell, yes! I'm fucking injured!"

Neil rolled his eyes. "Would you like me to get the police here so you can press charges?" Trevor started to answer, and Neil interrupted him. "Because I'm sure, while they're here, they'd like to hear this lady's story about how you assaulted her."

Trevor opened his mouth, then closed it, then opened it and closed it again. Then he gingerly fingered his eye. "That's … I … Just fucking forget it."

"Good choice, sir." Neil smacked Trevor on the back a little too hard to be friendly. "Now I'm going to have to ask you to leave the premises."

Neil led Trevor out of the bar area, and Lacy turned to Daniel. Her eyes were wide, and she was trembling.

"Oh, my God, Daniel. He … You … Holy shit. Are you okay? How's your hand? Are you …"

"You're shaking," he said.

"He scared me."

"You're okay," he told her, rubbing her shoulders with his warm hands. "You're all right."

She was still shaking, so he pulled her to his chest, and she let him fold her up in the warmth of his arms.

It felt so good, being here, being held by him, that she began to calm down, began to feel safe and protected. She was still standing there with his arms around her when they heard Brandon's voice.

"So, what's going on here, exactly?"

They both looked up to see Brandon standing three feet away, his lips pursed, his arms folded over his chest, his face turning blotchy and red with anger.

"Oh, God. Brandon. This isn't—"

Lacy had backed away from Daniel like he was on fire, and she was now trying to explain to Brandon that there was nothing going on—that it wasn't how it looked. Bar patrons were looking on with amusement, and the part of Lacy's brain that wasn't in crisis mode heard a guy chuckle and mutter, "Girl is in deep *shit!*"

"It isn't what, Lacy?" Brandon demanded. With his crossed arms, his tightly compressed lips, and his neatly combed hair, he resembled an unliked office supervisor about to fire someone for stealing a stapler. "I told you in the car on the way here that he had ulterior motives." He gestured at Daniel with his chin. "And now I come down here and see the two of you—"

"He was comforting me!" Lacy insisted. "This guy grabbed me, and I was scared, and—"

But before she could finish, Brandon had turned crisply away and was walking purposefully toward the elevators.

"Oh, shit," Lacy said to no one in particular. And then, to Daniel: "I'd better go after him."

"Do you want me to come with you? I can tell him what happened."

"No." She shook her head. "Just … no. I'd better go alone."

Still shaking with adrenaline from the confrontation with the drunk at the bar, Lacy went to the elevators to catch up with Brandon. He was already gone, so she punched the up button and waited, her arms wrapped around her torso, bouncing a little on her feet with excess nervous energy.

Lacy didn't feel drunk anymore—that was one benefit, she supposed, of sudden personal upheaval. It tended to cut through the fog. As she waited for the elevator, and then as she got in and rode toward the twelfth floor, she wasn't sure exactly what she wanted the outcome of all of this to be. She knew what she was supposed to do. She was supposed to convince Brandon that nothing was going on between her and Daniel, so they could reconcile and proceed with their plans together. On the other hand, considering everything he'd said in the car, this could be her opportunity to avert what would likely be a disaster of a marriage.

She surprised herself with the thought. How long, exactly, had she felt this way? How long had she known that she didn't want to marry Brandon? How long had she been looking for a way out?

None of that mattered, she supposed. What mattered was that she knew now. And that she needed to make it official.

The elevator doors opened on the twelfth floor, and Lacy walked down what seemed like an endless hallway toward her room. When she got there, she found her bag, which she hadn't taken the time to unpack, sitting outside the door.

She slid her key card into the lock and tried to open the door, but he had locked it from the inside with the security latch, so she could only get it open a couple of inches.

"Brandon?" she called into the space.

"Go away, Lacy! I don't want to talk to you!"

Brandon's voice sounded muffled. Was he *crying*?

"Just … come on. Let me in, and we'll talk, and—"

"What is there to say? You were hugging him!" She heard movement from inside the room, and then Brandon's face appeared in the two-inch space between the door and the jamb. "Do you mean to tell me you're not having a fling with him?"

Lacy paused, considering what to say. This was the moment. She could convince him that she was innocent, or let the entire relationship go to hell.

She had a choice.

"Well?" he demanded.

"I … You're right. It's been going on a few weeks. I'm sorry, Brandon. I didn't want you to find out like this."

If it was possible for him to compress his lips even more tightly, he did it, so that the lips themselves disappeared and all that was left was the skin around them, white with pressure.

"Give me back the ring," he said.

"Oh." Lacy pulled it off of her finger and poked it through the door, and he snatched it out of her hand.

"And your key card."

"What?"

He didn't answer; he just held out his hand for the card.

Not knowing what else to do, she held the key card through the door, and he grabbed that, as well.

"Where am I supposed to sleep?" she said.

"I don't know! Ask your boyfriend!" The door slammed so fast that Lacy had to yank her fingers out of the way to avoid getting them smashed.

She stood in the empty hallway, looked at her bag, and looked back at the door.

"Brandon!" She knocked again.

The door opened two inches, the slide bar still in place.

"What?"

"I … I'm pretty sure I left my jacket in there."

A couple of seconds later, her jacket emerged through the crack in the door, the fabric poking through inch by inch until she had the garment in her hand. Then, the door slammed again.

Lacy picked up her suitcase, pulled out the handle, and began wheeling it down the hallway and back toward the elevators.

She was free.

But she was also abandoned more than four hundred miles from home without a room and without transportation.

Ah, well. If your friends couldn't help you when your ex-fiancé left you stranded in Las Vegas, then what the hell were they for?

Chapter Eleven

Lacy, her friends, and their significant others held an emergency meeting via phone and text, since some had arrived in town and some had not, to figure out an action plan. First, Daniel tried to get another comped room, but that didn't work out; the hotel had unexpectedly filled up when a plumbing problem at the place next door had caused the guests there to seek refuge at Eden.

When that didn't pan out, Jackson, Ryan, and Will agreed to do rock, paper, scissors via text—a procedure they'd worked out long ago in response to a disagreement over where to eat lunch—to decide who would give up his hotel room for Lacy.

The idea was that one of the guys would bunk with Daniel—the only one of the men who wasn't there with a partner—so that Lacy could take his place in his original room. That would result in Lacy sharing a room with one of her friends, which the women all agreed was the optimal situation given her fragile emotional state. Nobody thought that a woman who'd just broken her engagement should be alone overnight with a minibar.

Jackson lost the game, due to an untimely selection of "scissors" during a sudden death round against Will. So Lacy moved in with Kate, who'd checked in an hour earlier, while Jackson, grumbling about the lack of opportunity for Vegas sex, took up temporary residence with Daniel.

The second part of the plan addressed how Lacy would get home. She could have caught a ride with anyone, since they all had space in the backseats of their cars. But all of the couples planned to stay the entire weekend. Daniel, who'd already been in Vegas for more than a week and was, frankly, getting sick of it, would be heading out the next day after the unveiling of his ceiling fixture. Since Lacy had neither the budget nor the heart to continue with the trip after all that had happened, they decided that she would catch a ride home with Daniel.

With all of that worked out, the next item on the agenda was to tend to Lacy's emotional state. Once everyone had arrived and checked in, the women gathered in Kate's room and sent the men off to do whatever men did in Vegas. There was a little grumbling from the guys, but it was mostly for show; they could see the need for Lacy to be with her friends at a time like this, and besides, who wouldn't enjoy a guys' night on the Strip?

"Okay, so he saw you hugging Daniel. There was nothing going on. Surely Brandon can understand that, right? You'll talk to him. This can be fixed." Kate was sitting on the bed next to Lacy, looking concerned and earnest.

"She's right," Rose said. She was also on the bed, sitting propped up against the headboard with her feet on a stack of pillows to relieve her swollen ankles. "I mean, the guy's a stiff, but he's not stupid. He's not going to let you go over a simple misunderstanding."

"He always struck me as a little bit stupid," Gen put in. Kate and Rose glared at her, and she put her hands up in surrender. "Sorry, sorry."

"I might have … It's possible that I told him I was sleeping with Daniel." Lacy avoided eye contact, focusing instead on the white linen comforter.

"What?" Kate and Gen said in unison. Rose simply stared at her, too stunned to speak.

Lacy shrugged miserably. "Well, he accused me of it. And it just seemed easier than arguing. And … and it was easier than telling him that I couldn't marry him."

The three women stared at Lacy in silence, until Gen finally recovered herself and said, "Go on."

Lacy gestured wildly with her hands as she spoke. "We had a fight on the way here. In the car. He doesn't even *like* me! He belittled my job, and my trailer, and the books I read. And ... he said I spend too much time with you guys and my family. He wants me to change *everything*! He wants me to be this ... this person I wouldn't even recognize! By the time we got to the state line, I wanted to punch his stupid face in."

Kate, who had been listening raptly, slumped in relief. "Oh, thank God." Gen and Rose high-fived each other.

"What? Wait, you're high-fiving? My life is falling apart, and you're high-fiving?" Lacy's voice rose in indignation.

"It seems to me your life isn't falling apart at all," Gen said, unable to conceal a grin. "It seems to me that it's in pretty good shape for the first time since you started seeing him."

If Lacy were being honest with herself, she had to admit that she didn't feel as bad as she would have expected. In fact, what she felt was ... light. As though a burden she'd been carrying had at last been lifted.

"You guys really couldn't stand him, could you?" she asked sheepishly.

"We tried. For you," Rose said.

Lacy could see that was true. They'd warned her, and they had made their concerns known. But they had been willing to go through with it all—the engagement party, the wedding, including him in their lives—to make Lacy happy. She'd never felt more love for her friends than she did at this moment. How could she ever distance herself from them for a man? How could anyone think for a moment that she would?

Tears filled Lacy's eyes, not in grief over Brandon, but in

gratitude for the women in her life.

"I love you guys," she said. Kate and Gen enveloped her in a hug, while Rose, who had trouble moving these days, reached out and rubbed her upper arm.

When they finally pulled apart, misty-eyed and choked up, Kate said, "Are you sure you don't want to stay for the whole weekend? I'll be a lot of fun."

"No." She shook her head. "I can't afford it without a comped room, and I can't put Jackson out for more than one night. Plus, you guys all need your Vegas couple time. And anyway, I'm just not up for it. All I want to do is go home and hide under the covers for a while."

"Then that's what you should do," Gen said in a soothing voice. "Let your mom spoil you a little."

Lacy straightened in alarm. "Oh, God. My mom."

She didn't have to elaborate; they all knew what she was thinking. Nancy Jordan had been more excited about Lacy's wedding than Lacy herself had ever been. To her, it meant safety and security for Lacy. It meant stability and happiness. It meant a beautiful wedding, and it meant the promise of grandchildren. Now, all of that was lost.

"How am I going to tell her?" Lacy said helplessly.

"Text message," Rose said decisively. "Today. Right now. That way you don't have to see her face or hear her teary voice when she hears the news, and by the time you get home, she'll be mostly over it."

"You know, she's right," Kate said.

On one hand, it seemed a little cowardly and insensitive to break that kind of news over a text message. But on the other hand, Lacy could see the benefits. And anyway, if this was some kind of tragedy—and Lacy had to think it really wasn't—then it was Lacy's tragedy, not her mother's. She couldn't make her life decisions based on what made her mother happy.

"Somebody give me my phone," Lacy said.

After the text was sent, the girls decided that if Lacy was only going to have one night in Vegas, it was going to be a good one. So they ordered room service, then grabbed a cab to the nightclub at the Hard Rock Hotel for dancing.

They didn't mention Brandon again.

While all of that was going on, the men gathered in the lobby at Eden to plan their next move.

"I just know Jackson's going to suggest strippers," Daniel said with a wry grin.

"God, no." Jackson shook his head sadly. "Kate would kill me. Not metaphorically, either. With actual blood and mangled body parts. Then there'd be the question of where to hide the corpse."

"Okay, then," Will said. "Blackjack? Play some slots?"

They went to the casino and settled in for some video poker. Within a half hour, Daniel hit a straight flush for a five hundred dollar payout. Most people would have put the money right back into the machine, but Daniel wasn't an idiot like most people. Instead, he cashed out and consulted with the others.

"It's found money," he told them. "I think we should spend it. What do you guys want to do?"

"We could see a show," Ryan suggested.

They considered that, then rejected it, reasoning that the women would be disappointed if they were left out.

"I've got an idea," Jackson said.

Daniel should have known that Jackson's idea would involve food. His plan was to blow the whole five hundred—and then some—on a five-course meal at a Michelin-starred restaurant where Jackson knew the chef. Daniel had never spent that kind of money on a meal, even when you divided it four ways, but since he didn't have a better idea, he agreed.

The restaurant in question was a French place inside the MGM Grand. The dining room was huge, with purple velvet curtains cascading from the ceiling to the floor; purple velvet upholstery on the tufted banquettes; and a crystal chandelier so big it reminded Daniel of the one from *Phantom of the Opera*.

With their destination in mind, they'd all gone back to their rooms before leaving Eden to put on jackets and ties, and now Daniel tugged uncomfortably at his as they were escorted to their table and took their seats.

"Frog leg fritters?" Will said, peering uncertainly at the menu. "I'm glad someone else is paying for this." He adjusted his glasses and squinted at the small print.

"Sea urchin," Daniel said, zeroing in on another menu item. "I'd be glad someone else was paying for this, too."

"Listen," Jackson said. "It's your jackpot. If you don't want to do this …"

"Nah, nah." Daniel waved him off. "I'm game. I'm just kind of … out of my element."

"Me too," Ryan agreed. "I can't even pronounce this one." While Ryan could certainly afford a restaurant of this stature—the Delaneys were flush with Central Coast land wealth—his family tended more toward casseroles and chili cookouts.

"*La soupe folichonne,*" Jackson said, leaning over to look at where Ryan was pointing on his menu. "It's herbs in an aromatic broth." At Ryan's blank look, he said, "It's soup, basically."

They all decided that the best course of action was to let Jackson order for them. When the waiter came, Jackson placed one order for himself, Daniel, and Will, and another for Ryan, who was the only vegetarian cattle rancher any of them knew.

Jackson ordered a bottle of wine for the table, and when their full glasses were in front of them, they started to deconstruct the events of the day.

"So, this thing with Lacy," Ryan said, kicking off the conversation. "You mind telling us how, exactly, Brandon caught you two in a clinch over in the bar at Eden?" Ryan's dark eyes were mischievous, and a half smile quirked his lips.

"Ah, jeez." Daniel rubbed at his eyes with one hand. "That was just … She was upset. She was shaking. I was comforting her. What the hell else was I supposed to do?"

"She was upset because of the bar fight. The one where you punched someone in the face," Will provided.

"Yeah, well …" Daniel said.

"Generally speaking, if I find out that one of my friends punched somebody in the face, I'm going to think it's Jackson," Ryan observed mildly.

"Well, Jackson wasn't there, and the guy had his hands on Lacy," Daniel told them, squirming a little under their scrutiny.

"Here's to punching assholes in the face," Jackson said. He raised his glass in a toast.

"I'll drink to that," Ryan said.

Daniel grinned sheepishly and raised his glass. "I'll tell you, though, I kinda wish the asshole I punched was Brandon."

"Maybe next time," Will suggested.

They drank their wine and pondered that.

"Seems to me it all worked out," Jackson said after a while. "I mean, Lacy's not going to marry that guy, and that's got to be a good thing."

"Yeah, but …" Daniel shrugged. "She's sad. And that kind of sucks, even if it is for the best."

Ryan grinned and leaned back in his chair. "What are the chances that hug in the bar was more than just you trying to comfort her?"

"Well, jeez. I don't know." Daniel's first instinct was to flatly deny it, but that would have been disingenuous. The truth was, he couldn't begin to understand everything that had been in that embrace. He'd been trying to comfort her, yes. But his need to do so came from something more than kindness, something more than basic sympathy. Her distress over the guy in the bar had made Daniel ache with the need to protect her. And then, when she'd stepped into his arms …

"You ought to think about it," Ryan said. "You two would be good together. I could really see it."

"Yeah?" Daniel said.

Jackson made a grumbling noise and shifted uncomfortably in his seat.

"What?" Will asked him.

Jackson glared at Daniel. "She's practically my sister-in-law. If you make a move, and you hurt her, I'm gonna have to kick your ass. And you're my friend, so that's gonna be awkward as hell."

It seemed to Daniel that if he made a move and he hurt her, he would deserve a good ass-kicking. Jackson would be welcome to it.

Chapter Twelve

The unveiling of Daniel's ceiling fixture was scheduled for two p.m. the next day, a Saturday. Daniel wore a suit; he had very little need for a suit in his daily life, so he felt uncomfortable as he fiddled with the shirt collar in the hotel lobby before the event.

"Stop fidgeting, for God's sake. It makes you look like a kid dressed up for church," Jackson told him when they'd all arrived for the event.

"Do I look okay?" He combed through his hair with his fingers as he peered into a mirror mounted on the wall behind a huge flower arrangement.

"You look fine."

He found his gaze drifting across the room to where Lacy was chatting with Kate. She was more dressed up than usual, in a pair of black pants and some kind of turquoise top that draped down at the neckline to show a tantalizing amount of cleavage.

He pushed thoughts of Lacy aside, because this wasn't the time to go there. He wondered whether it would ever be wise to go there; his heart would be safer if that was a journey he never made.

The unveiling was a lot like any other art opening. White wine and hors d'oeuvres for the invited guests. A speech by the hotel manager praising Daniel and his art work, and then talking about the owner (a celebrity billionaire who wasn't present) and his magical vision for the hotel. After the first thirty seconds, it sounded to Daniel like the adults in a Charlie Brown cartoon: *wah, wah-wah, wah wah.*

He smiled politely, nodded modestly at the right moments, and grabbed a glass of wine at the first opportunity.

He looked at all of his assembled friends: Jackson and Kate; Ryan and Gen; Will and Rose. And, of course, Lacy. He felt humbled that they'd done this. They'd come all this way. They'd made an effort. For him. Who the hell was he, for them to go out of their way like this?

Daniel was asked to say a few words, and of course, he'd prepared for that. He took the podium that had been positioned under the tarp that covered his work, and cleared his throat to speak. He looked at Lacy first. He tried not to, but his eyes seemed to be drawn to her by some irresistible force.

He took a deep breath and said the words he'd planned for the occasion. Words like *honored,* and *privileged,* and *inspired.* And then they released the tarp, which fluttered to the lobby floor like fall leaves.

There was a collective gasp, followed by applause.

Daniel was so nervous, so pumped full of adrenaline, that he could barely hear what the people around him were saying to him. But he felt the pats on the back, felt the hearty handshakes. He saw the smiles of satisfaction.

It could all be bullshit, of course. But there was always a chance that it wasn't.

There was always the chance that he had actually done okay.

When the tarp came down, Lacy wasn't sure what to expect. She'd seen the Chihuly installation and had been moved by it. What if Daniel's work suffered in comparison? What if it looked like a cheap copy? She was prepared to smile and congratulate him. She was prepared to say that it was brilliant, whether it was or not. She was ready to tell one of the kind white lies that one tells at such times.

As it happened, the lie wasn't necessary.

She saw Daniel's installation, drew in a breath, and her eyes filled with tears.

It didn't suffer in comparison to the Chihuly, because it wasn't like the Chihuly at all. It might have been conceived as a cheaper alternative to the Bellagio ceiling, but this was pure Daniel Reed.

The Bellagio piece and Daniel's were both glass, and they both were attached to a ceiling. But that was where the similarity ended.

While the Bellagio installation was a field of colorful flowers, Daniel's was all undulating blues and whites with light streaming through from above, creating the illusion that the viewer was on the ocean floor looking up through the water toward a sky filled with sunlight.

The feel of the work was so harmonious with the tropical theme of the hotel that it felt as though it had always been there, as though the hotel had been built for the artwork, and not the other way around.

Lacy wiped her eyes and saw Daniel watching her. She beamed at him across the crowd and mouthed, *It's beautiful.* He lowered his eyes from hers and grinned, and she thought he might even be blushing.

Daniel and Lacy got on the road soon after the unveiling was over. They each went to their rooms, changed into comfortable clothes, and packed up, and then Daniel checked out. They were in Daniel's SUV on the I-15 South while the sun was still high in the sky, shining brightly on the desert landscape.

An awkward tension filled the air between them, like cigarette smoke in a Glitter Gulch casino. Lacy didn't break the heavy silence until the towering city was well behind them.

"Thank you for doing this." She glanced at him out of the corner of her eye before returning her gaze to the road. "After … you know … the bar, Brandon checked out and left without even asking me how I was going to get home."

Daniel grunted. "The guy's an asshole." He saw her stiffen. "I'm sorry, but he is. If you didn't see that before, it should be pretty damned clear now. Who leaves his fiancée stranded in Las Vegas? An asshole. That's who."

Lacy crossed her arms over her chest. Her eyebrows nearly met, causing the space between them to furrow. "Well, I *was* there with seven other people. It's not like I was going to have to hitchhike."

Daniel grunted again. Okay, so Lacy was a little bit pissed. But at whom? At him? The fact that she was defending Brandon when she should have been trashing him suggested that her anger was a little bit displaced. She needed a target—someone other than Brandon—and Daniel was handy. He got that. And he knew he should just keep quiet to stay out of the firing line. But he couldn't seem to manage it.

"Did he even give you a chance to explain about the Neanderthal in the bar, or did he just jump to conclusions?"

Her silence gave him his answer.

"Why was his immediate reaction not to trust you? Can you tell me that?" He was warming to his subject, so he just rolled with it as they passed the state line. "That kind of suspicion, that kind of … of emotional manipulation"—he shook his head in disgust—"that's not what you deserve, Lacy. You deserve better. If he can't even give you the benefit of the doubt—"

"I let him think we were sleeping together, okay?" Lacy threw her hands up in surrender. "I had the chance to tell him what happened, but instead, I told him you and I were a thing."

Daniel, stunned, could only open his mouth and close it

again like a ventriloquist's dummy robbed of its partner.

"But … why?" he finally managed to ask.

"Because I wanted out." She slumped down in her seat and blew out a puff of air. "I wanted out, and I made you the bad guy. Basically, I suck."

Daniel took a few minutes to process what she'd told him. When he spoke again, his voice was tentative.

"But … if you wanted out, then why do you look like you want to rip off my right arm and hit me with it?"

"Because!" Now she was yelling at him. "My life is in upheaval! I'm single, yet again, and my eggs are aging as we speak! I'm not going to have a dream wedding, and I'm not going to have kids, and … and my mother is going to kill me! And … and I can't be mad at Brandon, because I was the idiot who chose him! And I can't very well rip off my own right arm, now can I?!"

"Yeah, okay." Daniel nodded. "That's a lot to deal with."

"Thank you!"

They drove a little more, and he said, "I think I know what might help." He pulled off the highway and parked at a gas station with a mini-mart.

"What are we doing?" she demanded, her voice still steely with anger.

"Just … wait here." He got out of the car and went into the mini-mart. A few minutes later he came out with the biggest red ICEE she'd ever seen, and a paper bag that was so full it was bulging. He got back into the car, handed her the drink cup, and plopped the bag into her lap.

"What's all this?" She looked into the bag, which was packed with Oreos, potato chips, mini donuts, Cheetos, and Funyuns. She looked at him and arched one eyebrow. "Funyuns?"

He shrugged. "I wasn't sure what you like to eat when you're upset. I wanted to cover all the bases."

She grinned at him and pulled the pack of mini donuts out of the bag as he drove the SUV back onto the highway.

"If you're not going to eat those Funyuns, pass them over," he said.

The junk food really did make Lacy feel better. What was it about sugar, salt, and fat that elevated a person's mood? And her mood really did need elevating. Last night, when Kate, Gen, and Rose had made Lacy their project, taking her out on the town, she'd been able to forget her problems—at least, mostly. But once she and Daniel had gotten on the road, there'd been nothing to distract her from the state of her life. She hadn't been angry at Daniel, not exactly. But he was wrapped up in all of this because of the hug, because of the lie she'd told Brandon to free herself from the bear trap of her engagement. Yelling at him had seemed like the natural thing to do. Therapeutic, even.

But the donuts and the ICEE were proving to be even more therapeutic. The only problem was that the large drink was making her want to pee.

"I need a gas station," she told him. She held up the drink cup, which was now almost empty. "You should have bought a smaller drink."

He pulled off the highway at a station just south of Baker. Lacy got out of the SUV, retrieved the bathroom key from a pimply teenage clerk who seemed half asleep, and peed. When she was done and had returned the key to the front counter, she came outside to find a scruffy, oversized rat sniffing at her feet.

Or, maybe it wasn't a rat. It was possible that it was a dog.

The thing barked once, a light, happy yap, and that settled it: The thing was definitely a dog.

"Hey there," Lacy said to the creature, who was studiously sniffing her ankles. "Where's your person?"

She bent down intending to look for a collar, but the dog, either alarmed at her overture or under the mistaken impression that she was playing a game, dashed about thirty feet away and then stood there looking at her, wagging its little stump of a tail.

Daniel had seen the exchange between woman and dog, and got out of the SUV to join her.

"What the hell is that thing?" he asked, his hands on his hips.

"It's possible that it's a dog," Lacy answered. The animal was about the size of an opossum, with triangular ears that stood up at attention from its head. It was covered in white, wiry hair that stuck up from its body at a variety of angles, but the hair was so sparse that it left a clear view of the gray, wrinkled skin beneath. All in all, the thing put Lacy in mind of the creatures from the movie *Gremlins*—post-midnight-feeding, but with a better disposition.

The dog barked at them optimistically.

"I wonder where his owners are," Lacy said, looking around to see if anyone was looking for the little dog.

"Huh," Daniel said thoughtfully.

In a repeat of its earlier game, the dog approached and sniffed Daniel's ankles, then darted away when he bent down toward it. Once it was more than arm's length away, it crouched down on its forepaws, its butt in the air, and wagged its tail, its tongue lolling out of the side of its mouth.

"Friendly little guy," Daniel observed.

After a couple more failed attempts to check for a collar, Daniel went to the SUV and retrieved the leftover Funyuns. He crouched down and held out a Funyun for the dog's inspection.

"Hey. Those are my Funyuns," Lacy protested.

"I'll get you more," Daniel said.

The dog inched closer, sniffed the oniony treat, and then finally took the crispy ring gingerly into its mouth. As it ate, Daniel scooped the dog up into his arms.

"No collar," he observed. Daniel looked around, as Lacy had, to see if the dog had any prospective human parents. There was no one around; Daniel and Lacy were the only customers at the moment, and the gas station's employees were all inside.

Lacy caught a whiff of the dog's smell—a combination of intestinal gas and whatever he'd been rolling in—and wrinkled her nose. "What are we supposed to do with him? Should we call Animal Control?"

"What? Nah." Daniel shook his head. "He'd end up in a shelter, and they'd probably put him down."

"I can't imagine there'd be a lot of people clamoring to adopt something that looks like … well, like this," Lacy agreed.

The dog had finished its Funyun and stretched its head up to lick at the underside of Daniel's chin.

"We can't leave him here," Lacy said after a while. "It's the desert. He'll die of dehydration or get eaten by a coyote or a hawk or something."

Daniel scratched at a spot behind the dog's ears, and the dog whined happily in response.

Lacy went into the mini-mart to ask the pimply clerk if he knew anything about the dog. The clerk, barely roused from his state of tired indifference, shrugged. "He's been out here the last couple of days."

She thought for a moment, then filled a drink cup with water from the soda fountain and bought a small plastic container of dog food that she found on a dusty bottom shelf near the windshield wipers and the car air fresheners. She carried her purchase outside and knelt down near the dog.

"Here you go," she said, offering him the cup of water. The dog lunged at the water, lapping it up as though he hadn't had a decent drink in days. Which he probably hadn't.

She peeled open the top of the dog food and set the container on the ground next to the water. The dog whined in delight and gobbled up the food. When it was gone, the dog held the container in place between his paws and licked the plastic until all remains of the food and its juices were obliterated.

Daniel sighed and nodded. "All right then." He picked up the dog, held it in his arms, and started walking back to the SUV.

"What are you doing?" Lacy demanded.

"We're bringing him with us."

"What?!" Lacy didn't know what they were supposed to do with a strange-looking, foul-smelling dog on the long ride back to Cambria.

"You said it yourself, nobody's going to adopt him. And if we leave him out here, he doesn't have a chance." He shrugged. "We'll bring him. We can find him a good home in Cambria."

Lacy squinted at the dog skeptically. "You think?"

"He'll have a better shot there than he will here. Come on." With no further discussion, he got into the SUV with the dog.

Lacy sighed heavily and followed him.

"Zzyzx? You're naming the dog Zzyzx?" Lacy said. The dog, which had been squirming, wiggling, and thrashing about on her lap for the last ten minutes, was finally starting to settle down. She stroked his back to calm him.

"Why not?" Daniel gave a half grin. "That's where we found him."

It was true that the gas station where they'd discovered him was not far from Zzyzx Road, an exit off of the I-15 just south of Baker. But it never would have occurred to Lacy to name a living creature that.

"Seems like he's got enough challenges in his life without being saddled with a name like that," Lacy said sympathetically.

"He looks like a Zzyzx," Daniel said.

Lacy wanted to argue with that, but she couldn't. If ever there were a dog that looked like a Zzyzx, it was this one.

"I'm going to call him Z for short," she said. "It's easier to spell, for one thing. And anyway, it's only temporary. I'm sure whoever ends up adopting him will name him something else."

If Zzyzx had an opinion on his name, he didn't share it with her. Instead, he curled up on her lap and whined softly as they continued down Interstate 15 toward Barstow.

They were just on the outskirts of town when Zzyzx rose up in her lap and began convulsing slightly, making the horrendous retching noise that every dog owner dreaded.

"Oh, God," Lacy said. "He's going to throw up. Pull over, pull over!"

"I can't pull over." Daniel had a big rig in the lane to his right and a pickup truck in front of him that prevented him from speeding up to pass.

"Oh, shit. Oh, shit," Lacy said. She picked the dog up off of her lap and put him on the floor, thinking she could at least spare her clothing if the worst-case scenario happened.

It did.

Zzyzx made another grand, wrenching noise from the bowels of his stomach, and the entire contents of the dog food container, plus one chewed-up Funyun, emerged, steaming, onto the floor mat of Daniel's SUV.

"Jesus …" Daniel said.

Zzyzx, much relieved, stepped through the mess, jumped onto Lacy's lap, and then darted between the two front seats to dash around the back of the SUV.

Lacy looked at the puddle of vomit at her feet, and at the pukey paw marks that dotted her clothes.

She turned to Daniel wryly. "Think you can pull over now?"

They spent the next half hour at a gas station, cleaning Zzyzx off with a water hose, then doing what they could to remedy the situation inside the car. Daniel pulled the passenger side floor mat out of the SUV gingerly, to avoid spillage, and peered at it with distaste.

He considered the option of hosing it off and then giving it a good cleaning when he got home, then calculated the price of a new floor mat. Taking all things into consideration, including effort, the grossness factor, and the likely aroma inside the car, he made his decision. He walked the mat to a nearby Dumpster and threw it in.

That done, he and Lacy, using paper towels and water, worked together to clean the areas where Zzyzx's feet had left little vomity paw prints on the upholstery.

Finally, Lacy dug some clean clothes out of her bag and went into the restroom to change. She came out carrying the dog-puke clothes in a plastic bag she'd gotten from the gas station clerk.

"Do you suppose he has a problem with carsickness?" Lacy peered skeptically at Zzyzx, who was nestled happily in Daniel's arms. "Or did the food just disagree with him?"

Daniel shrugged, worried about the same question. If the dog had an issue with motion sickness, this would likely happen again—maybe more than once—before they reached Cambria. "I guess we'll find out."

"Maybe I should drive while you hold him," Lacy suggested.

"Like hell," Daniel said, and then grinned slightly. "I don't want to be in the firing line any more than you do. And it's my car."

"But you're the one who wanted to bring him along," Lacy pointed out. "If it were me, we'd have called the Animal Control people."

"Who would have gassed him!" Daniel waved his free arm in indignation. "Or given him a lethal injection, or … or whatever they do!"

Lacy didn't argue the point, but she didn't give up her ground, either.

"Fine. We'll flip a coin," Daniel said.

Lacy dug around in her purse, pulled out a quarter, and got ready to flip it. "Call it."

"Heads. No, tails. Tails seems appropriate, given the circumstances."

Lacy flipped the coin into the air, and caught it in her open hand. She smacked it onto the back of her other hand, and they both leaned in to read the results.

"Heads," Lacy said. There might have been a hint of smugness in her voice.

"Well, shit," Daniel said. But in truth, he wasn't too upset about his assignment to dogsit for the next leg of the drive. Lacy did nearly get puked on, after all. And it really had been his idea to bring the little guy along.

They took Zzyzx around the back of the gas station to give him a chance to pee, or to throw up again if he needed to. Once he was done—pee, but no puke—they got back into the car with Lacy in the driver's seat.

She pulled the car back onto the I-15, and it became apparent within just a few miles that their cleaning efforts had been substandard.

"Oh my God," Lacy said, holding her nose against not only

the smell of the residue of dog puke, but also against the smell of Zzyzx himself. If the dog had ever had a bath, it was now so far in the past as to be only a fond and vague memory.

"Holy hell," Daniel said, grimacing against the stench. "That's just … I think I'm gonna have to burn this car."

In Daniel's lap, Zzyzx whined hopefully.

It seemed like the thing to do was to open the window. No sooner had Daniel done it than Zzyzx shoved his face into the rush of air, sticking his head out the window and squinting his eyes happily against the gush of the wind.

Daniel, afraid the dog was going to fall out of the car, got a grip around the animal's furry middle.

"That helps a little, I guess," Lacy said, referring to the air, which was a little more breathable with the window open.

"I guess," Daniel agreed.

It was ridiculous—utterly ridiculous—but sitting here with an ugly, smelly dog in his lap, the smell of vomit in his car, and Lacy driving his SUV beside him, Daniel felt unaccountably happy.

What the hell was that about?

The only sense that he could make of it was that he usually spent so much time alone that the sensation of someone needing him—Lacy for the ride home, Z for his very survival—made Daniel feel hopeful in a way he usually didn't.

He sat back with the wind from the window blowing the crap out of his hair and began to enjoy the ride.

Chapter Thirteen

After Daniel dropped Lacy off outside her parents' house, she gathered her stuff from the back of the SUV, gave Z a fond pat on the head, and thanked Daniel for the ride. Then, grateful to have the entire Vegas misadventure behind her, she walked quietly around the house and into the backyard, hoping to get to her Airstream undetected.

She was just unlocking the door when her mother came out the back door of the house, a pissed-off look on her face to match the sound of her voice.

"Lacy Ann Jordan," Nancy said, her hands on her hips. "You get your butt into my kitchen right this minute." Nancy disappeared back into the house, the screen door closing with a snap.

So much for making a quiet entrance.

"It's not so much that you broke up with him. Though I simply don't understand that at all. It's that you told me over a *text message*." Nancy was using a look that Lacy was very familiar with from her childhood. The look said, *You might think you're getting away with something, but you have another think coming, missy.*

"I was afraid to tell you." Lacy sat at the kitchen table and looked down at her hands in her lap. "I knew you'd be upset."

"Upset!" Nancy said in exasperation. "Upset! Of course I'm upset! Brandon is a perfectly nice man, he's a doctor … He could have provided for you! He could have given you a house, a family!"

"I've got a family! I've got a really big family, and lots of friends, and … and I can provide for myself!" Lacy had been cowed when she'd come into the house, but she was starting to feel the indignation of the misunderstood. "And I didn't love him, Mom. Not really. Is that what you want for me? Marriage to a man I don't love, just because he's a doctor?"

"Well, I ..." Nancy sputtered in surprise and frustration. "Why did you agree to marry him if you didn't love him?"

"Because it just seemed easier!" Lacy stood and started pacing the kitchen. "Easier than telling him no and going through a breakup. Easier than figuring out what I really want to do with my life. Easier than telling you that it wasn't going to happen." She came to rest in front of the refrigerator, facing Nancy, her arms folded over her chest, her lips tight.

Nancy let out a deep sigh. "Well, honey, of course I don't want you to marry someone you don't love. I just want you to have all of the things you deserve. I don't want to see you living in a trailer the rest of your life."

Lacy gestured widely with her arms. "What is it with everybody and the trailer? Brandon and I fought over the damned trailer! It's one of the things that led to all of this! I like the trailer! Of course I don't want to live in it forever. But for now, it's my home, Mom."

"I understand that, honey. I do. Oh, Lacy, come here." Nancy stood up and opened her arms, and Lacy stepped into them. Lacy felt herself getting teary-eyed, not because of her breakup with Brandon, but because it felt so good to have her mother's love.

"I just want you to be happy, honey," Nancy said.

"I know, Mom. Brandon wasn't going to make me happy."

Nancy sighed and patted her daughter's back. "To each her own, I guess. But a hundred and twenty thousand dollars a year and a 401K? That would have been a lot to be happy about."

❖

Knowing that her mother was so worried about her financial prospects made Lacy consider the state of her career.

Or lack thereof.

She liked being a barista. She liked the aroma of the coffee, the background music that played over the sound system at Jitters, the chatter of the customers, the sound of the coffee grinders. She liked the satisfaction of making a perfect latte. And most of all, she liked chatting with the people who came into the coffeehouse day after day. Not just her friends, but the tourists, the locals, the people who were such integral threads in the fabric of her life.

She liked the idea that by providing superior coffee, she could make a customer's day just a little bit better.

But her mother was right—she would never be able to pay for a real house on a barista's wages. Part of her had always felt that she was just biding her time, anyway. In her ideal future, she would be a stay-at-home mom to a gaggle of kids. Five, maybe more. She had nothing but respect for the women in her life who sought success in their careers—Gen, Kate. Even Rose was planning to start college part time once her baby was born. But Lacy imagined a different life for herself. She imagined nurturing her husband and family, making nutritious and comforting dinners, making a home. She wanted her house to be the one the neighborhood kids flocked to for the warm, welcoming environment it provided. She wanted her children to come home from school to feel the safe cocoon of her maternal love.

Basically, she wanted to give her kids what she'd had growing up.

She couldn't fault her mother for wanting to see her with Brandon. After all, Lacy was in her thirties now. If she wanted kids—not one or two, but a gaggle—she'd have to get on it sooner rather than later. And Brandon had seemed like a likely prospect to father that gaggle.

As Lacy unpacked her things in the trailer, recovering from the disastrous Vegas trip, she shuddered slightly at the thought of Brandon as her husband and the father of her kids. Her house wouldn't be that place of warmth and love as long as he was in it. Not that he was a terrible person; he just wasn't the person for her.

Putting her clothes and other belongings away, she realized she'd forgotten a sweatshirt in the back of Daniel's car. Also, more troubling, she couldn't find her topaz earrings. The earrings had belonged to her grandmother, and had been a gift to Lacy on her eighteenth birthday. She refused to consider the idea that they were lost. She must simply have misplaced them somewhere in the trailer. She would have to scour the place for them later.

With the unpacking finished, Lacy flopped back onto her bed. Lying there, looking at the ceiling of the trailer, her thoughts drifted to Daniel. There was no sense denying that her attraction to him was growing. Seeing him cradling that ugly little dog in his arms had made her melt a little. A man who could be kind to a helpless, unsightly animal—even after that animal had thrown up in his car—was a man with some real father potential. Not to mention the way she'd felt in the bar when he'd held her in his arms …

But Lacy was smart enough to know that it was unwise to jump into a relationship just after ending one. That was a recipe for sorrow and regret.

Still. God. When he'd held her, she'd felt safe. She'd felt whole. She'd felt things that she had never felt with Brandon.

Even if Brandon did have a goddamned 401K.

Daniel looked down at Zzyzx with a scowl.

"Well, what are you waiting for?"

He had given Z a bath, and with that done, he'd set a blanket on the floor of his laundry room, thinking the dog could sleep there until Daniel could make other arrangements for him. But Z just looked up at him expectantly, leaving the blanket untouched on the floor.

"Just try it," Daniel coaxed him. "It'll be a hell of a lot more comfortable than sleeping out in the desert, and you didn't seem to mind that."

Z's tail thumped on the floor as he wagged it lazily.

"Okay, let's try this." Daniel took a dog treat out of his pocket and placed it on the blanket. His theory was that if he could get Z to step onto the blanket, he'd see that it was an inviting place to lie down. Z did step onto the blanket, but only long enough to snap up the treat. Then he dashed back off of the blanket and crunched the treat in his little jaws, looking up at Daniel happily.

"Hey, look," Daniel said, irritated. "I haven't had time to get a proper dog bed. I don't know what you expect."

Finally, he decided to leave Z in the laundry room with the blanket for a while. If the dog could get used to the room and the blanket, then maybe he'd decide it was acceptable accommodations. "You stay," he told the dog, pointing one finger at him.

Daniel opened the door that led from the laundry room into the kitchen. As soon as the door had opened the few inches Z needed to make his way through, the dog hit the door at a run, darting through and into the house before Daniel could stop him.

"Hey, hey … wait a minute!" Daniel called after him.

With a sigh, Daniel found Z curled up on the sofa, looking up at him hopefully, tail rhythmically thumping against the cushion.

Daniel reached down to pick up Z and put him back in the laundry room where he belonged, but as soon as his hand was in range, Z gave it a lick, with a happy little whine.

"Well, hell," Daniel said. He looked at the dog with exasperation, his hands on his hips.

He guessed it wouldn't hurt anything if Z had a little nap on the sofa.

At least he was clean, though that didn't seem to help with the rotten-egg smell that was wafting up toward him from Z's body.

"Ah, jeez," Daniel said, grimacing. "We're going to have to find you a dog food that doesn't give you gas."

Z laid his head on his paws and closed his eyes, apparently not nearly as troubled by his gas as Daniel was.

Daniel knew he was going to have to get busy finding a home for Zzyzx, before the dog got attached to him. Wasn't going to be easy, given the fact that Z looked something like a miniature, fuzzy warthog, but without the tusks. Most people expected cuteness from a dog, or, if you wanted it for protection, fierceness. Z wasn't about to provide either of those things.

Daniel figured that was fine. It wasn't like Z owed anybody anything. He was who he was. They would just have to find him a home with someone who got that.

But that would be a job for tomorrow. Right now, tired from the drive home from Vegas, Daniel got a beer out of his refrigerator and plopped down onto his sofa next to Zzyzx to drink it.

As he sat there, he couldn't help thinking about Lacy.

He had so many mixed feelings.

Under the negative column, he was sorry that she'd gone through what she had with Brandon. Breakups were a bitch, even when the person wasn't right for you. He could attest to that. And he felt a little bit guilty that he'd had a part in causing that breakup. The embrace in the bar—well, he'd told himself it was about comforting her, and to some extent, it had been. But he'd be a liar if he said it wasn't more than that.

And he wasn't a liar.

And that brought him over to the plus column.

The way she'd felt when he held her, the way she'd sighed as she kind of melted into him—that was a hell of a big plus. He couldn't quite get the impression of it out of his mind. Not that he wanted to. He'd been happily replaying it in his memory ever since it happened. Also a plus, it was a good thing that Lacy wasn't with that stiff anymore. That she wasn't going to marry him. Sure, the guy was a doctor, and he supposed that counted for something. But he didn't deserve Lacy. Daniel wasn't sure who exactly would. He, himself, sure as hell didn't. Lacy was special. He supposed it was that—his conviction that she was both rare and extraordinary—that had prevented him from making any kind of move with her.

Didn't stop him from thinking about her, though, about the joy in her face when they'd ridden in the gondola, the tears in her eyes when she'd seen his artwork. The way she'd sighed and relaxed into his embrace.

He was still thinking about her as he drifted off to sleep with Z snoring softly on the sofa beside him.

Daniel woke to the sound of Z whining. He figured he was only asleep about an hour; it was still before midnight.

His neck was a little bit sore from the way he'd been positioned on the sofa, and he stretched it and rubbed at it.

He looked around for the dog, figuring Z probably had to go outside to pee. He didn't find him by the door, though—

either the front or back. Instead, he found him in the bedroom, on his hind legs, front paws reaching up the side of the dresser toward Lacy's forgotten sweatshirt, which was on top. Daniel had been planning to return it to her the next day at Jitters.

"Come on," Daniel told him. He scooped up the dog and held him in his arms, scratching him behind his ears. "You can't have that. It isn't yours."

He took Z outside, let him pee one more time just for insurance, and brought him back into the laundry room, where Daniel had originally planned for the dog to sleep.

Daniel put him on the blanket, crouched down, and said in a stern voice, "This is your spot. Just settle in and get used to it." He patted the dog on its back. "Goodnight, Z."

Daniel left the laundry room, closed the door behind him, and turned out the kitchen light, planning to go to bed.

He didn't even make it all the way to the bedroom before he heard Zzyzx scratching at the laundry room door, whining.

"Aw, for Christ's sake …" Daniel went to the laundry room door and opened it. At the first opportunity, Z darted through the door, past the kitchen, and into the bedroom.

Daniel found him up on his back legs again, reaching for the sweatshirt.

"What if I give you this and it's her favorite sweatshirt or something?" Daniel asked, as though Z had some kind of answers. "You're gonna get it all … doggy. She'll be mad at us."

Z whined, scrabbling at the dresser with his paws.

"Ah, hell," Daniel said. He picked up the sweatshirt and put it on the floor, mentally promising to buy Lacy a new one.

Z stepped onto the sweatshirt, turned around two or three times, and then plopped down and curled up on the shirt. He let out a contented sigh and promptly went to sleep.

"I get it," Daniel said in resignation. "I miss her, too."

Chapter Fourteen

Lacy was waiting for Daniel to come into Jitters. At first, she didn't realize she was waiting. She just knew that she felt unsettled, as though she'd forgotten to do something important, or was missing something that mattered.

Then, someone who looked vaguely like Daniel—a tourist with the same build, the same way of carrying himself—walked into the coffeehouse, and Lacy felt a surge of excitement, followed by bitter disappointment when she realized it wasn't him.

That was when she realized she'd been waiting for him—and that she was a hopeless idiot.

An idiot, because what was she doing longing for one man barely five minutes after breaking up with another one? Who did that? A hopeless idiot, that was who.

Because, yes, she was longing for him. She'd been pretending that she wasn't, but that was before the pseudo-Daniel had walked through the door and sent her spirits soaring and then plunging.

If that didn't clarify things, what would?

She tried to tell herself that she was just looking forward to seeing a friend, one who'd helped her out when she'd been in a crisis. That was all. Who didn't enjoy seeing a friend?

But usually, she didn't fantasize about seeing her friends with their clothes off. So, there was that.

And where the hell was he, anyway? Daniel came into Jitters almost every day, except when he was out of town visiting his family or doing business related to his glass. He wouldn't be out of town today, just two days after coming home from Vegas, would he?

Was he making his coffee at home? And if so, was he trying to avoid her?

All of this Daniel-related thinking and waiting was making it hard for her to concentrate on her job. As a result, she'd used the wrong kind of milk in Mrs. Watkins's latte, had given decaf to someone who had ordered regular, and had burned herself on the milk steamer.

So it was a mercy when Daniel finally did come into the shop just after lunchtime, as Lacy was getting ready to finish a shift that had started before dawn.

When he walked in the door, she felt the same surge in her spirits that she'd felt with the tourist. But this time, the feeling stuck, because it really was him. The thing about her being an idiot popped back into her mind. Damn her stupid girly feelings.

"Hey," he said, waving to her a little before shoving his hands deep into his jeans pockets.

"Hey," she said back. They needed to work on their sexy banter. She reminded herself that she was at work and that she needed to be professional. "What can I get you?"

"Low-fat latte with cinnamon."

It was his usual. She rang him up, and then got to work on the drink.

He stood just across the counter from her as she pulled the espresso and steamed the milk.

"Z misses you," he said.

For a moment, she wasn't sure what she'd heard. He missed her? But then, it hit her. He was talking about the dog.

"Zzyzx?" she said, just to make sure.

"Yeah." Daniel didn't meet her eyes. "He sleeps on your sweatshirt. If I take it away, he whines." He looked sheepish. "It's probably ruined. I owe you a new one."

"Oh." She slid a cardboard sleeve onto his drink and passed

the cup over the counter to him. "I thought you were going to find him a home."

"Yeah, well." Daniel looked embarrassed. "I was going to, but … I can't imagine there'd be people lining up to take him. He's got a face even a mother would have a hell of a hard time with."

Lacy guffawed. It was true. Zzyzx hadn't been blessed with beauty. Still, there was something to be said for that. At least when people liked him, it would be for the right reasons.

"I was wondering …" Daniel shifted from foot to foot uncomfortably. "I thought maybe you could come by and visit him."

"Visit him," Lacy said, as though to confirm she'd heard him correctly. "Visit Zzyzx."

"Yeah. He … well. I thought, the thing with the sweatshirt … He spent a lot of time with you on the drive, and I think he's sad without you."

She gave him a wry half smile. "I wouldn't want Zzyzx to be sad."

"Of course not," he agreed. "So … you'll come over? To my place?"

Lacy thought about it, trying to figure the angles. Was Zzyzx actually suffering over her absence, or was Daniel using a roundabout, adorably awkward way of asking her on a date?

If it was the former, then she figured she could help out a little, spend some time with the dog to reassure him. If it was the latter, well … then it was likely she was in trouble. Because another relationship so soon after the last one would be an epically bad idea. And yet, she found herself irresistibly drawn to say yes to him. Yes to his place, yes to a date. Yes to so very much more.

"Yes," she said. "Yes. I'll come over."

❖

Lacy had wondered if Daniel was telling the truth about the dog missing her, or if it was just a ruse to get her to his house. All of her doubts vanished, though, when she walked in his front door and Zzyzx lost his damned mind.

He stood there on the hardwood floor looking curiously at her for a moment, and then surprise registered on his face when he realized who she was. What followed was complete canine pandemonium. He ran to her and jumped as high as he could, crashing into her body before falling to the floor. Then he sprinted around her in circles a few times before jumping again, getting twisted in midair, and landing on the floor on his back. He circled her five or six more times before rolling onto his back with his quivering legs in the air, whining for a tummy rub.

"Wow. He really did miss me," Lacy said. She got down on her knees and obliged with the tummy rub as the dog made happy noises from deep in his throat.

Daniel stood over them and scowled. "I mean, you're great and everything, but I'm the one who feeds him. I'm the one who's giving him a place to stay. Where's the enthusiasm for me?"

"Aww." Lacy cooed in sympathy. "I'm sure he loves you. He just has a different way of showing it."

"Yeah, yeah," Daniel said.

After a long and thorough belly rub, Lacy picked up Zzyzx and stood up with him in her arms. His little tail wagged rapidly, thumping against her side.

"You bought him a collar," Lacy observed. The collar was blue, with a little gold bone-shaped tag hanging from it. "And a tag," she added.

Daniel tucked his hands under his arms and looked at the floor, embarrassed. "Yeah, well."

"I'm just gonna take a quick guess," Lacy said, a wry grin curving her lips. "You're not trying to find him another home."

He shrugged. "Well, what am I supposed to do? Somebody pukes in your car, it's like a bonding thing. You can't just abandon them."

Lacy laughed. "That's the most ridiculous—"

"Look at him," Daniel said. "He likes us. He's happy here."

Lacy looked at the dog, whose homely face was aglow with love and joy.

"Well, I guess that settles it, then," she said. "Looks like you've got a new friend." She sniffed the dog. "He smells a lot better. You gave him a bath."

"Yeah."

"Tell me he doesn't sleep in your bed."

"No. I do have some boundaries." Daniel shrugged. "And anyway, he'll only sleep on your sweatshirt."

"Huh. I really liked that sweatshirt," Lacy said with some regret.

After a brief discussion, they decided to take Zzyzx to the dog park on Main Street. Z was too small to play with a tennis ball—it was too big for his mouth—so Daniel had picked up a miniature version the day before when he'd bought the collar, some kibble, and a leash at Maddie Mae's Pet Pantry.

Now, he gathered the leash, the ball, and the dog himself and they got settled in the SUV for the short ride into town.

Zzyzx sat on Lacy's lap for the drive, gazing at her adoringly as they headed down the dirt road on Daniel's property toward Highway 1.

"I'm a little nervous after last time," Lacy admitted.

"Ah, you'll be okay," Daniel reassured her. "I don't think he gets carsick. I think it was just the gas station food. Maybe it had been sitting there too long or something. I've had him in the car a few times since then, and he hasn't blown any chunks."

"Well, that's good to know," Lacy said. She stroked Zzyzx's fur—what there was of it—as they got onto the highway and headed north toward the Main Street turnoff.

The weather was the kind that drew people from all over the world to California. Clear blue sky, light breeze, temperatures in the mid-70s. The rolling hills to either side of the highway were carpeted in long, emerald green grass, which was being chewed by the occasional cow.

For Daniel, it felt good, but frightening, to be alone with Lacy. Last time, he'd been doing her a favor, so it didn't count. The outing in Vegas didn't count, either, because she'd been drunk and he'd been making sure she stayed safe. Besides, she'd been engaged. This time, they were on what could, arguably, be called a date. Even if it wasn't a date—he'd gotten her here on the pretense of comforting the dog, after all—it was still social. Here they were, the two of them, being social alone together, and it scared the crap out of him. It felt stupid to admit that, even to himself. But there it was.

The thing about Lacy was that she had some sort of … aura. There was a kind of light or energy field or some damn thing around her, as though all of the beauty and joy in the room had her right at its center. He couldn't explain it, even to himself. He just knew that he wanted to be near that light, that energy.

Zzyzx felt it too, obviously. Right now, he was blinking slowly in utter contentment, his head on her thigh, as she stroked his head.

"Did you have any pets growing up?" Lacy asked.

The question pulled him out of his reverie. "Uh … yeah. I did. I had a beagle named Winston. Got him when I was about sixteen. He just died a couple years ago. My mom was heartbroken. I guess I was, too."

"Winston," Lacy said, amusement in her eyes.

"Yeah, he was a great dog." He glanced at her. "Your parents' house seems like a place that would have a lot of pets."

"Oh, God." Lacy rolled her eyes. "Cats, dogs, rabbits. Even a chicken."

He shot a look at her, surprised. "You had a pet chicken?"

"Yeah." Lacy laughed. "My brother, Nick, was raising chickens for 4H when he was about twelve. They were supposed to be sold for meat once they were grown. But Cassie bonded with one of the chicks, and she had an epic meltdown over the idea of somebody eating it for their Sunday dinner. So, all of the others were sold, and we kept Roger as a pet."

"Roger? It was a rooster?"

"No. It was a hen."

Daniel glanced at Lacy, puzzled. "Okay, but *Roger*?"

"Cassie was always a weird kid," Lacy said fondly, as though no other explanation was needed.

When they got to the dog park, a fenced-off area where the local dogs could commune with one another off-leash, only two other dogs were there—a Maltese with a blue bow in its hair, and a basset hound who looked like he wasn't amused by the outing. They pulled up into a parking space, and a thought suddenly occurred to Lacy.

"Oh! Is it really safe for Z to be here? I mean, we don't know what shots he's had...."

"I got him the full deal yesterday," Daniel said. "Rabies, Bordetella, parvo, and whatever else it is that dogs get. I don't remember all of them."

Lacy turned in her seat to face him more fully, a wry smile on her face. "You took him to the vet."

"Well, yeah."

"Yesterday."

"Yeah, yesterday afternoon."

"And you bathed him and bought him a collar and a ball."

Daniel was starting to feel uncomfortable. "Yeah, and?"

"And, you started doing all of that less than twenty-four hours after coming home from Vegas." Her voice softened. "You were never going to find him another home. You were always going to keep him."

Daniel squirmed a little in his seat. "Well, I did call around to some of the animal shelters out there to see if anyone was missing him. But … yeah. It gets lonely out there at the house. Is it a crime to want some company?"

Still holding Zzyzx in her arms, Lacy grinned and leaned over to give Daniel a gentle kiss on the cheek. "No," she said. "It's not a crime at all. In fact, I think it's really sweet."

She got out of the car with Z and put him on the ground, and the two of them walked toward the gate of the dog park together.

Daniel sat in the car and watched her go. God, she was a vision with those long legs and that hair and the … Well. Best to stop there.

It occurred to him that he'd be happy to adopt three or four more dogs if that was what it took to get her to kiss him.

Maybe even a chicken, too.

Chapter Fifteen

By the time they took Z back to Daniel's place, the dog was exhausted and panting from a playtime that had included chasing the mini tennis ball, barking at a squirrel, peeing on every available surface, and sniffing the butts of the other dogs at the park. He fell asleep in Lacy's lap before Daniel had even pulled the SUV out onto Main Street for the ride back home.

Lacy felt that she'd had almost as much fun as Zzyzx.

Someone in the dog's past had taught him to fetch, and he'd brought the little ball back countless times, breathlessly plopping it at Lacy's feet and waiting with trembling anticipation for her to throw it again. The dog's joy was infectious, and Lacy had found herself aglow with contentment as she and Daniel had played with Z, talked, and shared easy companionship.

Now, as they headed back toward Daniel's place, she didn't want the day to end. It had to, though. Being with Daniel was making her head fuzzy—full of visions of what it would be like to kiss him and how he would look with his shirt off—and none of that was doing her any good. She knew the proper thing to do was to retreat into the safe burrow of her trailer and lick her wounds post-Brandon.

But right now, she really wanted to lick other things.

She gently stroked the dog in her lap and stole a glance at Daniel as he drove. God, he was beautiful. He had a pure masculinity about him, with his rugged features, his broad shoulders, and his day's worth of stubble, that made her want to curl up on his lap the way Z had curled up on hers.

It was ridiculous, though. Who broke up with her fiancé

only to curl up in another man's lap two days later? Well, lots of people, probably, now that she thought about it. That didn't mean it would be smart.

They pulled up in front of Daniel's house, and he parked next to Lacy's car. She told herself that she was going to get out of his car, hand over the dog, and then leave. So she was proud of herself when he invited her in, and she said she had to get going. She was still mentally patting herself on the back when he let Zzyzx into the house and then returned to walk her the twenty feet to her car.

"I really had a good time today," he said, rubbing at the back of his neck in a way that made her wonder if he was nervous. About what? About her?

"Me too," she said. "I think Z's going to need a long nap now."

"Yeah." He grinned. "He really wore himself out." The sun was just above the western horizon, and a light breeze ruffled his hair.

Daniel tucked his hands under his arms and said, "Hey, listen. It's getting to be close to dinnertime. Did you want to …"

Be strong, Lacy, she told herself. *Be strong, be strong, be strong.*

"I would, but I really need to get back," she said, scrambling for some kind of excuse. "I … uh … I told my mom I'd be home for dinner. My sisters are coming over, so …" She had no idea if it was true. It might have been. Her sisters came over a lot.

"Okay." He nodded. "Some other time, maybe."

"Yeah. Sure. Some other time. For sure." She was babbling. She needed to just shut up and drive away.

But somehow, the *shut up and drive away* plan was derailed when she unlocked her car, turned to him to say a friendly and casual goodbye, and found him standing so close to her that she could smell him.

Oh, holy God, his smell, all warm man and sandalwood soap, and maybe a hint of some heady cologne.

She forgot what she'd been doing, and her mind blanked.

He put his hands on her shoulders, gently, and her body said, *Yes.*

"Lacy? I'd really like to kiss you." His voice was a low rumble that she felt all the way down in some of her favorite body parts. "Would that be okay?"

She didn't answer, but instead found herself tilting her face toward his, her eyes closing, her lips parting.

He put his hand on the side of her face, his thumb slowly caressing the line of her jaw.

The kiss, when it came, was gentle at first, tentative. A feather-like touch of his lips to hers. And then, in response to her sigh, he moved in closer, fitting his mouth to hers as though they'd been made for that purpose. Just a moment of his tongue caressing hers, and then he pulled back with a gentle tug of her lower lip.

It was like time had stopped. She stood there, unmoving, her eyes still closed, her lips still slightly parted in memory of his touch.

When she roused herself, when her senses came back to her, she opened her eyes and found him so close, looking at her so intently that it was tempting to simply melt into him, to simply disappear into his eyes.

"I ... uh ... I should go," she said.

He nodded and took a step back. "Okay." He rubbed the back of his neck again. The fact that he was nervous was cute. So goddamned cute.

"Well ... okay," she said.

Before she could change her mind, she opened her car door

and got in. He stood watching her as she put the car in reverse, turned around, and started down the dirt road that led back to Highway 1.

With him standing there looking at her like that, it was a wonder she didn't plow into a tree.

The thing about it was, it wasn't a real date. Or maybe it was. They hadn't said the word *date*, and no food had been eaten—the usual standard for date vs. non-date. But there had been the kiss. For some reason, it was very important to Lacy to know how to classify this encounter in her mind. Because if it wasn't a date, then what the hell was it? And if it was, then what the hell was she thinking?

"I'd have said no, not a date," Rose weighed in later that night as they discussed it on the phone. "But then, when you factor in the kiss, it does sound datelike."

Lacy was lying on the bed in her trailer, her cell phone to her ear, miserable with longing for a guy she shouldn't even have been seeing, if she was, in fact, seeing him.

"Right? It's the kiss that throws the whole thing off. Until then, it was two friends getting together. But after, it took on all of these datelike overtones! What the hell is going on? Are we friends, or are we dating? And if we're dating …"

"Would that be so bad?" Rose asked.

"Yes. Yes, it would. Because … he's Chunky Monkey."

She could almost hear Rose's quizzical expression over the phone. "Excuse me?"

"I don't buy Chunky Monkey ice cream anymore," Lacy patiently explained. "Because when I do, I don't just get out a bowl and scoop out a reasonable portion, and enjoy that portion, and then get on with my life."

"Ah. You eat the whole carton," Rose said, catching on.

"Yes. I do. I eat the whole carton, and then I feel all sick and full, and I vow over and over again that I'll never make that same mistake again. But then, the next time ..."

"You eat the whole damn thing."

"There you go," Lacy said with satisfaction. "I can't help myself! I don't have any self-control!"

"Huh," Rose said. "So, what flavor do you usually get?"

"I get something bland, like vanilla or ... or Neapolitan. Something that tastes okay, but that I know I can stop eating."

Following Lacy's train of thought, Rose observed, "Brandon was Neapolitan."

Lacy's brow furrowed. "What? No, no. I'm just talking about Daniel here."

"But it's not just about Daniel," Rose said. "It's about more than that. It's about how you want to feel like you're in control of things, so you chose a Neapolitan man to marry instead of a Chunky Monkey one. And you were miserable, and you ended up not even eating the Neapolitan. And now you're tasting the Chunky Monkey and realizing what you were missing."

"That's not—"

"Honey," Rose said, more gently now. "Falling for a guy so hard that you feel like you can't control your emotions is scary. Believe me, I get that. When I fell in love with Will I was so freaked out that I tried to push him away about a million times."

"I remember."

"But choosing Neapolitan is not the answer. Nobody likes Neapolitan. It's boring, and the orgasms suck. If there even are orgasms."

The sudden clash of the metaphor with orgasms was too jarring, and Lacy rubbed at her eyes. "You're missing the point. I don't want the Chunky Monkey hangover, with all of that bloating and regret."

"Okay, let's switch gears for a minute," Rose said. "Back to your original question, I'd say it definitely was a date. Because when I hang out with my friends, we usually don't kiss."

"This is true," Lacy said.

"And speaking of the kiss ... how was it?"

"Oh, God," Lacy said.

"Really," Rose said with interest. "Go on."

"I wanted to eat the whole carton, Rose. I really, really did."

"Well," Rose said, "I have double fudge brownie every night, and I've got to tell you, it's pretty goddamned delicious."

"Will is double fudge brownie?"

"My version of Chunky Monkey."

"Ah."

It was all so confusing. If Lacy was dating Daniel—and it seemed like that was a real possibility—then she was in way over her head with all of the lust and the longing and the ... the *feelings*. And all of this so soon after her unsatisfying bowl of Neapolitan. But after today, and the kiss, it increasingly seemed as though it might be out of her hands. She might not be able to put down the damned spoon.

Chapter Sixteen

"Why the hell did I do that, Z?" Daniel asked. He was sitting on his sofa with the dog beside him. Zzyzx, worn out from a busy day of doing dog things, was resting his head on Daniel's blue-jean-clad thigh.

"I mean, she's on the rebound, right? Plus, she's way out of my league. That's just ... well. That's just asking for trouble."

Z gazed at him adoringly.

Daniel looked at the dog and grunted. "Why am I asking you? You're crazy about her, too."

Z's little pink tongue emerged, and he licked his own nose.

Daniel figured he had two choices: He could stick the kiss into his mental scrapbook of the high points in his life, close the book, and move on. Or, he could pursue Lacy with reckless abandon, and to hell with the consequences.

He remembered the way she'd looked, her face tipped up to him, her eyes closed, her lips gently parted.

Oh, Christ.

"You know I'm already screwed," he said to the dog. "Why don't you just say so instead of pretending I've even got a damned choice?"

Z raised his doggy eyebrows at Daniel and made a slight whimpering noise.

"You know, if you're going to live here, you're really going to have to get better at giving advice."

Z thumped his tail against the couch cushions.

Daniel wasn't sure where to take things from here. But he did have some idea who to talk to about it. Someone who could talk back to him, for one thing.

❖

Vince had some preliminary sketches of the renovation ready for Daniel's approval. Daniel had suggested that they meet at the Old Stone Station for lunch. Daniel was buying.

When they both had fish and chips and mugs of beer in front of them, Daniel broached the subject he'd really come to talk about.

"Hey, Vince?"

"Mmm?" the man said around a mouthful of fish.

"I was wondering … What would you think of me kind of … well … going out with Lacy?"

Vince's eyes widened, then he swallowed his food and wiped his mouth with his napkin. "Well, son, it's not that I don't love an good, old-fashioned gesture, but I don't really think that's up to me."

"Sure, of course," Daniel said. "I know. But … Do you think … It's just, she just broke up with that Brandon guy, and I—"

"You want to test the waters before jumping in," Vince provided.

"Well, yeah."

Vince put down his napkin, folded his arms on the table, and looked at Daniel. "I stay out of these things, generally."

"Right." Daniel nodded. "Right. I just—"

"I stay out of them," Vince continued, "because I find that's what serves me best in a domestic bliss kind of way. But that doesn't mean I don't see what's going on around me."

"Okay," Daniel said.

"Just because I keep my mouth shut, like any man with half a brain would, doesn't mean I don't have my opinions." He raised his eyebrows at Daniel meaningfully.

Daniel waited, trying to look both encouraging and upstanding.

"That Brandon guy." Vince shook his head sadly. "My wife was very big on him. Still is. But I could see that train wreck coming a mile away. Wasn't my business to say anything, but there it was. And then …" He used his hands to pantomime two trains colliding, and the ensuing wreckage.

"Right. And I don't want to—"

Vince interrupted him as though he hadn't spoken. "You live with a woman enough years, you start to understand her in ways you would have never thought possible. And I understand my daughter. Maybe better than my wife does."

They were leading up to a verdict, Daniel could feel it. He waited to see which way it would go for him.

Vince clapped Daniel on the shoulder. "You do what you've gotta do, son. Ask her out. Make your move. You've got my blessing, if you feel like you need it." With his hand still lying heavily on Daniel's shoulder, he said, "But if you hurt her, I'll tell you what … nobody's ever going to find the body."

Daniel gulped.

Vince laughed. "Son, you going to eat the rest of your fries?"

Lacy still couldn't seem to find the damned earrings.

It wouldn't have mattered if they'd been just any earrings, but they were her grandmother's. She ransacked the trailer looking for them, but they just weren't there. She had to search the main house surreptitiously, because she didn't want to admit to her mother that she couldn't find them.

She'd last worn them to the engagement party. The blue topaz had matched the color of her dress. She hadn't left them at the veterans' hall, had she? No, because she hadn't taken them off until late that night.

She was searching the meager spaces of her little trailer one more time when her cell phone buzzed with a text message.

Zzyzx misses you.

Daniel.

Suddenly, Lacy felt warm all over, and she was aware that she had a goofy smile on her face. She was silently berating herself for the warmth and the goofy smile—*Get a grip on yourself, Lacy*—when a second text came in.

I miss you, too.

Oh, God.

She didn't know how to respond. Should she admit that she missed him? That she thought about him nearly every moment? That she kept replaying the kiss in her mind, over and over, mentally taking it much further, to its logical and decidedly NC-17 conclusion?

She couldn't tell him any of that—not without losing whatever semblance of self-control she had—so instead, she typed:

How's my sweatshirt?

It was neither sexy nor clever, true. But it was friendly and chatty, and it wasn't likely to result in her being naked sooner than she was really prepared to be. The phone buzzed, and she read his response:

Warm, smashed flat, and covered in dog hair.

There was that goofy grin again. She couldn't seem to help it. Oh, she was in so much trouble.

She thought, calculated, and then composed her own text:

You said you'd buy me another one. Maybe you could just buy me dinner instead.

She looked at her screen, at what she'd written. If she pressed SEND, she'd be setting something in motion that she might not be able to control, sort of like Ebola or global warming. On the other hand, being out of control with Daniel would be so much more fun than either of those things.

Shit.

She erased the text and put down the phone. Then she paced the length of the trailer a few times, picked up her phone, and put it down again. Then she snatched up the phone, typed the text again exactly as it had been the first time, and pushed SEND before she could stop herself.

Shit. Shit. Shit.

She waited, pacing, the phone on her little dinette table. When it buzzed, she jumped slightly and lunged for the phone.

How about I buy you both? Are you free tonight?

Her heart was pounding. And how stupid was that? It was like she'd never been on a damned date before. In fact, she'd been on hundreds. Maybe thousands. And none of the invitations for those dates had made her feel like this—at least, not since Mark Brockton in the ninth grade. God, he'd been cute. She'd written *Lacy Brockton* in flowery script on her science notebook for a week afterward.

She took a deep breath and composed her answer:

Live music at Jitters tonight. I have the late shift.

She sent it, considered, and then sent another message:

Maybe you could stop by.

His answer came in less than a minute:

I'll see you then.

Okay. It wasn't anything as drastic and dangerous as a date, but she'd be seeing him again, and soon.

Oh, God.

What the hell was she doing? She sent a group text to Kate, Rose, and Gen. It contained only two words:

Emergency meeting.

It wasn't easy to pull together an emergency meeting at the

last minute early on a Friday afternoon. Everybody had work—
Lacy needed to be at Jitters at four, Kate and Gen both closed
their shops late on Fridays, and of course, Rose couldn't get
away from the wine shop, because Friday and Saturday nights
were their busiest time.

But they were all motivated, so they found a way to make it
work. Lacy's shift hadn't started yet, and both Kate and Gen had
assistants they could leave in charge for a half hour. Rose, who
was the manager of the wine shop and not the owner, was the
only one who simply couldn't leave work. So, the natural solu-
tion was for all of them to meet at De-Vine, where they gathered
at the bar during a lull in Rose's customer traffic.

Lacy was there first, sipping a glass of water Rose had
served her. Kate came in next. She took a barstool next to Lacy's
and ordered a glass of pinot grigio. She was wearing a T-shirt
that said BOOK LOVERS DO IT BETWEEN THE COVERS, and
her short, dark hair was artfully messy.

"So, what's the emergency meeting all about?" she asked.

"Let's wait for Gen," Lacy said.

"She wouldn't tell me, either, but I suspect it's got something to do with the delicious Daniel Reed," Rose observed, a
smirk on her face. Her chin-length hair was a vibrant purple, and
her belly, which had really popped out just in the last month,
stretched the front of her knit skull-and-crossbones dress.

On cue, Gen rushed into the shop, click-clicking along on
perilously high heels. She was wearing one of her sleek black
gallery dresses, and her hair, a mass of unruly red curls, had been
forced into submission with a complex arrangement of pins and
clips.

"Okay, okay," Gen said. "I'm here. What's going on? Why
the emergency meeting?" She plopped down onto a barstool and
focused on Lacy with interest.

"Daniel asked me out," Lacy said. "And also, he kissed me. But … not at the same time. Those are two separate events. But related, obviously."

"I knew about the kiss," Gen said. Kate nodded in agreement.

Lacy had only told Rose, who now shrugged her shoulders.

"What was I supposed to do, just sit on information like that?" Rose asked.

"No, no." Lacy shook her head. "It's fine. Just … what now? He asked me out to dinner, but I stalled him, because I have to work. But he's going to come by Jitters tonight, and I—"

"Wait, wait." Kate put up her hands in a *stop* gesture. "Just back up a little. We haven't deconstructed the kiss yet."

"Can we focus?" Lacy demanded. "We're on a timeline, here."

"There's always time to deconstruct a kiss," Gen said, taking Kate's side. "So … how was it?"

Lacy shot Gen a look. "He's Daniel Goddamned Reed. How do you think it was?"

Kate looked thoughtful. "If I'm guessing, I'd say about an eleven on the one to ten scale. Daniel always looked to me like he had that seething sexuality thing going on. And if Jackson asks, I never said that."

"So? Is she right? An eleven?" Gen said.

Lacy moaned. "I don't even think my scale goes that high."

"Ooh," Kate said, rubbing her hands together in glee.

"But that's the problem!" Lacy exclaimed.

"Wait. Why is that a problem?" Gen said.

"Because he's Chunky Monkey." Rose filled them in on Lacy's ice cream metaphor for relationship sustainability. Just as she was getting to the part about Brandon and the Neapolitan, a pair of middle-aged women came in, decked out in Cambria sweatshirts and carrying shopping bags from the boutiques on Main Street. They settled in at the far end of the bar, and Rose greeted them and placed tasting lists in front of them.

"But that's just crazy," Kate said when Rose had concluded her explanation. "Of course you want the Chunky Monkey. Who the hell would choose Neapolitan?"

"Oh. You serve ice cream here?" one of the tourists asked.

"No, just wine and relationship advice," Rose told her.

"But Chunky Monkey makes people fat!" Lacy exclaimed, throwing her hands into the air. "And it's expensive! And it leaves you all … all gassy and full! And you swear you will never eat it again, but then you do! You do! Because you can't help yourself!"

"Oh, honey," Gen said, putting a hand on Lacy's arm. "I think Daniel's worth the risk."

Rose poured tasting portions of two wines for the tourists, who were beginning to catch on to the gist of the conversation.

"I dated a Chunky Monkey man once," one of the women said. Her helmet-like blond hair appeared to have been recently coiffed, and her red lipstick was feathering slightly at the edges of her mouth. "He broke my heart. I cried for months."

"See?" Lacy said, gesturing toward the woman as Exhibit A.

"But it was so worth it," the woman said, a dreamy look on her face.

"I married my Neapolitan." The other woman looked at Lacy pointedly. "Do not make that mistake. Unless you think you'll enjoy twenty years of him watching football in his boxer shorts."

"Brandon—her ex-fiancé—wasn't a boxer shorts and football kind of guy," Rose told the woman. "More polo shirts and NPR."

"I suppose that could get tiresome, too," the woman said.

"Back to the question." Lacy attempted to get the conversation back to its original purpose. "I'm in trouble here. Real trouble. If I go out with Daniel, you're going to find my bloated corpse submerged in a bathtub of Chunky Monkey."

"But what a way to go," the first tourist observed.

"Look, Lacy," Kate said. "Daniel's a good guy. He's not going to hurt you. At least, not on purpose. And you deserve the Ben & Jerry's. Not the … the bargain store-brand stuff."

"But it's so soon after Brandon," Lacy said, slumping a little on her barstool.

"You can't put your love life on a schedule," Gen said. "Things happen when they happen. You've got to seize your opportunities. You've got to … grab that ice cream spoon."

The blond tourist leaned toward Lacy conspiratorially. "You should at least try one little lick."

Chapter Seventeen

Jitters usually closed around six p.m. on a weeknight. But on the weekends, when Cambria's tourism was at its peak, the coffeehouse stayed open as late as ten, serving hot drinks and snacks to people who weren't quite ready to retire to their hotel rooms.

Live music wasn't a regular evening offering at the coffeehouse, but they did it on occasion; it was usually one guy with an acoustic guitar, a tip jar, and some CDs to sell.

Tonight, Lacy had put a chalkboard sign out on the sidewalk announcing LIVE MUSIC, 8-10 P.M. She'd added a chalk drawing of a guitar and a steaming cup of coffee just to amuse herself. They weren't expecting much of a crowd, but it didn't matter; the singer worked for free, so if they got ten people drinking lattes and enjoying the music—along with some additional takeout traffic—they would consider it worth the effort.

Lacy's shift had started at four, and now, at 7:45, she and Connor were moving tables and chairs around and bringing out a platform they kept in the back room to create a stage for the guitarist, who'd just arrived with his guitar in a case slung across his back.

In a venue of this size—barely a thousand square feet—they shouldn't have needed a microphone, but they wanted the guitarist to be heard over the milk steamer and the whir of the blenders they used to make their frothy iced drinks. Plus, the owner thought that if the music was loud enough to waft out onto Main Street, it might attract more of a crowd. So Connor brought the sound system out of the back room and set up a speaker and a single microphone on a stand atop the platform.

By eight, the guitarist, a guy in his mid-forties with a blue chambray shirt and prematurely gray hair that was long enough to curl slightly at the collar, was settled into a chair on the platform, singing a cover of Jason Mraz's "I'm Yours."

They'd turned down the lights a little for the sake of atmosphere, and within twenty minutes they had a medium-sized crowd of people sitting at the café tables, sipping cappuccinos, and listening appreciatively—or at least passively—to the music.

Lacy was going through the motions of doing her job—making lattes, ringing up sales, making sure the tables were wiped and the trash cans were emptied—but she was having a hard time focusing, because she couldn't seem to stop watching the door for Daniel.

She'd already had to remake two drinks because she'd gotten them wrong—a mocha that was missing the chocolate and a latte sans the drizzle of caramel sauce the customer had requested—and she mentally berated herself for her silly, teenage behavior.

When she dropped a drink behind the counter and had to retrieve the mop from the back room to clean up her mess, Connor gave her a pointed look.

"What's going on with you, Lacy?" he asked, not unkindly. "Is everything okay?"

"Yeah, yeah. Of course. Yes," Lacy answered as she mopped up coffee and milk.

"Because if this is about a guy, I can kick his ass for you."

Lacy had been working with Connor for a couple of years now, and the boy—she thought of him as a boy, since he was nearly ten years younger than she was—had been flirting with her for that entire time. She didn't mind, though. It was the kind of benign, companionable flirting a guy did when both he and the object of his flirtation knew that he was hopelessly out of his depth.

"It's not about a guy," Lacy lied. Just then, the front door of the shop opened, and the unmistakable form of Daniel Reed filled the doorway. Lacy froze in the middle of her cleanup efforts, having completely forgotten what she was supposed to be doing.

"Oh, really?" Connor said, glancing at Daniel and then at Lacy, a smirk on his face.

"What?" Lacy asked him. "I'm sorry, did you say something?"

When Daniel walked in the door, his eyes went to Lacy immediately. It just seemed to work that way. His attention had a way of going right to her, wherever she was, whatever she was doing. It didn't matter that she was crouched halfway down behind the counter. He didn't have to look for her; he could feel her.

The guy on the makeshift stage was singing "More Than Words" to maybe a dozen people scattered among the café tables. Daniel didn't know the singer, and he thought that he knew just about everybody in Cambria. Must have been a guy from Morro Bay, or maybe Paso Robles.

Daniel didn't want to disturb Lacy when she was trying to do her job, so he found himself a table and sat down to relax and take in the atmosphere.

It had been a long day. Daniel had been commissioned to do a large piece for a hotel in Los Angeles: a five-foot-tall sculpture that would sit on a table in the center of the lobby. He'd toured the place—all cool, modern minimalism—and he knew how he wanted the sculpture to look. The trouble was, he couldn't do a piece of that size and weight alone. And the assistant he'd used on the Eden job had just moved up to the Bay

Area. Daniel needed someone new.

He didn't have time to train someone from the ground up. He'd talked to the guys down in Harmony—they did a lot of glass work down there—in the hopes of borrowing somebody for a short period, but that hadn't panned out. Now, he was going to have to use a student from the Art and Design program at Fresno State. You never knew what you were going to get with a student. He'd interviewed one today, and after an hour of conversation, Daniel doubted the guy would be able to find his ass with a mirror and a GPS program. That left him back at square one.

He'd have to deal with that tomorrow, though. Now, the presence of Lacy Jordan—she didn't have to be with him, she just had to be in the room—was washing over him like a cool, gentle breeze.

He caught her eye, and he grinned at her with what he knew had to be a pathetic, lovestruck expression.

The kiss.

He kept remembering the kiss.

Lacy gave him a little wave, but she was busy doing her job, so he just sat and watched her. Faded blue jeans, torn at the knees. A fitted white tee with a low neckline that showed a creamy expanse of tanned skin. A white apron tied around her waist. Golden hair piled atop her head in a messy bun. Her usual, effortless grace was nowhere in evidence at the moment; as he watched, she nearly dropped a tray of drinks on a customer's head before righting herself at the last moment.

She seemed rattled by something.

It occurred to him that he might be that something, and the thought wasn't an unwelcome one.

He liked the idea that he might have gotten under her skin—though he would have preferred to be on it instead.

Once all of the customers had been served and she got a brief break, she came to his table and hovered nervously over him. "Hey," she said. She was holding a round tray, and she partially released her death grip on it to wave at him with the fingers of one hand.

"Hey," he said back. "Can you sit for a minute?"

Lacy looked around to make sure the other customers were all well tended, then slid into the seat across from Daniel. "Glad you could make it," she said, giving him a shy smile that just slayed him. Then her eyes widened. "Oh. Can I get you a coffee?"

"Nah, I'm good," he told her. And he was. Better than good, in fact, now that she was sitting with him.

The guitarist segued into "And I Love Her," a classic from the Beatles, and Daniel thought he sounded pretty good, which wasn't a given; these coffeehouse deals could go either way. The other customers seemed to be enjoying themselves, either talking quietly among themselves or swaying gently to the music.

The nervous tension between Daniel and Lacy was thick; it was the tension of having had a first kiss, and not knowing where things would go from there. Would they date? Would they kiss again? Would they perhaps, God willing, sleep together? Would it be more than that? And did both of them want the same things?

Daniel thought about making small talk, things about his day or hers, observations about the weather, or about the annual Scarecrow Festival that had just ended the weekend before.

Instead, he opted to directly address the elephant in the room.

"About the kiss," he said, leaning toward her.

Lacy looked a little bit startled. "What about it?" she said.

"I'd like to do it again." He felt the flutter of butterflies in his stomach, but plowed ahead anyway. "Not right here, obviously. But sometime. Sometime soon. Just so you understand my thought processes here. I really enjoyed the kiss. A lot. And, yeah. I'd like to … explore that further."

He wasn't sure that this was wise, but he also wasn't sure it was still a decision he could make, a thing he could think about and say yes or no to. If she was agreeable, then he could no more stop himself from kissing her again—as soon as possible—than he could stop himself from breathing or blinking.

"Daniel—"

"Just think about it," he said, interrupting her. He'd interrupted her because, if she was going to say she didn't want that, too, then he hoped to delay hearing it as long as he could.

A couple of people strolled in the front door from Main Street and headed up to the counter.

"I'd better get back," she said. She gathered up her tray and went behind the counter to make lattes or hot teas or whatever the hell the new arrivals had come for.

The fact that she hadn't answered him—that she'd hurried off without any indication of where she stood on the matter—rattled him.

Of course she had to work. Of course she did. But had she hurried away just a little more quickly than she otherwise would have? And if so, what did that mean?

Well, hell. He'd stated his intentions—the information was out there. And now she had her job to do, so he figured he should get the hell out of there just in case her answer was no.

The ball was in her court, and if she chose not to lob it back over the net, then continuing to sit here would be awkward.

Not that it wasn't already.

He was still pondering what to do when the lights went out and he heard a crash.

Chapter Eighteen

Blackouts at Jitters weren't an unusual occurrence. It was an old building that hadn't been updated in a while, and sometimes the circuit breakers tripped when somebody in the building—maybe the hair salon on one side of Jitters, or the bar on the other—used too many appliances at the same time.

The blackout itself wasn't that big of an issue. The bigger issue was that Daniel had rattled her, and that, combined with the sudden extinguishing of the lights, had caused her to trip while she was carrying a tray full of used water glasses to the dishwasher.

The crash had been deafening.

She wasn't hurt, but now she was in pitch darkness, sprawled on the floor, surrounded by broken glass.

Shit.

She heard the swinging door that led to the front of the shop open, and heard someone step into the back room.

"Connor?"

"He went to check the breaker." The voice was Daniel's. "Are you all right?"

"Oh, yeah, fine," she quipped in a light and airy voice. "Just, you know, face-planted on the floor with about ten broken glasses all around me. The usual."

"Are you hurt? Are you cut?" His voice was sharp with concern.

"No, no. But be careful if you're coming in here. There's glass everywhere."

"Okay. Don't move."

She heard him rustling about, coming toward her in the darkness. Then she felt a hand on her back as he felt around to figure out where she was.

"I've got you," he said. He found her hand, took it, and helped her up.

"Let's just … over here." His hand in hers, he guided her away from the broken shards and toward the door leading back to the front of the shop.

They went back through the swinging door and into the area behind the counter, where the espresso machines and the cash register stood silently in the darkness.

"Is everybody all right?" Lacy called out into the blackness. She received answers in the affirmative.

The guitarist, apparently realizing that he didn't need electricity, resumed playing without the benefit of the sound system. Keeping with the Beatles theme he'd started earlier, he began a slow, lilting rendition of "My Love."

Maybe it was the darkness. Maybe it was the music, and the guitar player's sensuous voice. Or the fact that Daniel had come to rescue her. Maybe it was because he was still holding her hand, warm and safe in his. Or, maybe it was because she'd spent the last couple of days wanting him so badly it felt like a high fever.

Whatever it was, she couldn't seem to help herself. She pressed her body to his, reached up to put her hands in his hair, and drew him to her. She touched her lips to his, gently at first, and then devoured him with a hunger that surprised even her.

At the first touch, she felt his surprised hesitation. And then, she felt him let go of all resistance and give everything back to her: the desire, the need.

Lacy had kissed a lot of people. A lot of boys, and then men. But never had her body responded like this, with this kind of intensity, this kind of fire. She seemed to mold herself to him, every inch of her, as everything else ceased to matter. The taste of his lips, of his tongue, were like a sweet promise; the feeling was like lightning in her blood.

Neither of them noticed when the lights came back on.

By the time they did, by the time Lacy roused herself to conscious thought and opened her eyes to see the glow of the overhead lights, Daniel was still adhered to her as though they had somehow fused into one person. And everyone in the coffeehouse was staring directly at them.

Connor, who had switched the breaker back on, came into the room through the back, having picked his way through the broken glass. "What the hell happened back th—" He froze in midword as he emerged to see Lacy and Daniel looking as though they might consummate their lust next to the coffee filters and the grinding machine.

Lacy, finally conscious enough to fully get the situation, gasped slightly and shoved Daniel away with both hands. He was a little slower than she was to rouse himself, but when he did, he cleared his throat and ran his hands through his hair in an effort to regain his composure.

"Oh. Okay. Ah … wow," he said, to no one in particular.

After a few more moments of silence, the guitarist resumed playing, and the customers went back to talking among themselves, a few tittering and side-eyeing Daniel and Lacy, who were still behind the counter looking embarrassed as hell.

"I … ah … I should probably go," Daniel said.

"Yeah. You probably should," Connor said bitterly.

"And so I went into the back room to clean up the broken glass. I could barely look at Connor. It was mortifying," Lacy concluded. She was in her workout clothes, breathing hard, hiking briskly at Fiscalini Ranch in the morning fog. Cassie had called her on her cell phone, and Lacy figured they would talk for as long as the spotty cell service held out.

The thing about this historic small town was that the actual infrastructure—like the cell phone service and the electrical grid—was sluggish, while the gossip network functioned like a Swiss watch. By the time Lacy had awakened at seven a.m., her family had heard all about the incident at Jitters, and they were calling her, one by one, to get the full scoop.

"Sounds like the guitarist wasn't the only entertainment," Cassie observed wryly.

"Yeah, well." Lacy powered past an older couple walking a poodle on a leash, and headed up into the trees of the Forest Loop Trail. The fog laid a gentle layer of gauze over the woodsy landscape, and the cool, crisp air felt good on Lacy's skin. She could hear the crashing waves off the bluffs to her left. Above, a bird cawed in the branch of a tree.

"So, how was the kiss? Dish!" Cassie insisted.

How could she describe the kiss? How could a person describe feeling as though their body had quite pleasurably been turned inside out and then set right again? And did she even want to tell that to Cassie? It was one thing to tell the truth to her friends about her raging, rampaging lust and the confusion that raised in her. But it was quite another to say such things to her little sister. Also, Lacy knew that whatever she told Cassie would soon get to her mother. And nobody wanted their mother to know about their raging lust.

So, she downplayed it.

"It was … fine," she said.

"That's not what I heard," Cassie said.

"What do you mean?"

"I didn't hear 'fine.' I heard, 'just inches from dropping to the floor and going for it right there in Jitters.' That's what I heard."

The image that raised—of Lacy and Daniel on the floor, going for it—made Lacy temporarily lose her train of thought. But then, with considerable effort, she rallied.

"Well, that's just … You know how things get twisted. People exaggerate."

"So, it wasn't so hot you were about to burst into flames?" Cassie pressed her.

Just then, Cassie's voice started to break up, and the call got dropped. Lacy sighed in relief. Saved by the poor cell coverage. She tucked the phone into the pocket of her warm-up jacket and focused on physical fitness.

And the image of herself and Daniel on the floor, naked.

Jesus, Lacy. Stop it.

When she passed again into an area where the cell service worked, her phone chirped with an incoming call. She checked it: Jess. Lacy put the phone back into her pocket and ignored the call.

While Lacy was walking off her sexual tension, Daniel was coping another way. He was throwing his energy into the glass.

All morning he'd been working on a piece for the Porter Gallery, a tall sculpture with streaks of red and orange, with a shape that mimicked flames licking toward the sky. It was the biggest thing Daniel could comfortably handle without an assistant, since he was still searching for one.

The Eden piece had invoked water; this one was fire. And both of them had made him think of Lacy.

God, Lacy. He had to get her out of his head, and yet a part of him wanted her to just live there forever. He turned the glass inside the furnace and thought of heat, of passion.

The problem with him and Lacy was that she threw off his equilibrium. He'd more or less had his life settled. He had his house, his work, his friends. He'd date somebody every now and then, and that was fun. But he had the distinct feeling that if he went with this Lacy thing—if he got involved with her and then just let it go wherever it was going to go—then his life would be altered in ways that were both frightening and unpredictable. They wouldn't just go out a few times, maybe sleep together a few times, and then part on good terms.

Good or bad, positive or negative, it was going to be more than that. Daniel wasn't sure how he felt about that prospect.

Increasingly, though, he was starting to feel as though he didn't have much choice in the matter. Walking away from this thing with Lacy after last night's kiss would require superhuman levels of self-control that he knew he just couldn't muster.

The whole thing was like jumping out of an airplane with your eyes closed, without knowing for sure whether you were even wearing a parachute.

But, hell, he guessed he was going to have to jump, because life inside the airplane no longer seemed sustainable.

Daniel turned the rod, shaped the glass, added color, fired it again, shaped it again.

And then blew the transfer and sent the whole thing crashing to the concrete floor.

"Fuck," he said, looking down at the shattered and misshapen remains of his work. "Fuck, fuck, fuck."

One thing about infatuation: It was playing hell with his career.

Chapter Nineteen

"So, I heard you made out with Daniel last night, but it wasn't that great," Kate said. She was standing across the counter from Lacy at Jitters, waiting for her coffee order.

"Wait, what? Where did you hear that?" Lacy froze in the middle of steaming a pitcher of low-fat milk.

"Which part? The making out part, or the part about how it wasn't that great?"

"The part about how it wasn't that great." Lacy didn't have to ask how Kate had heard about the making out, since she'd done it in front of about twenty people, many of whom were locals who were regular contributors to the gossip mill. That part just went without saying.

"Oh. Whitney told me. She came into the shop this morning for the new John Sandford release, and we got to chatting."

Lacy set down the pitcher and planted one fist on her cocked hip. "*Whitney* told you? How does Whitney even know?"

"Apparently Cassie called her."

"Ah." Lacy sighed, then shook her head slightly to refocus on her work. She went back to making Kate's drink.

"So, was she right? It wasn't very good? Because that would surprise me. Partly because Daniel seems like he'd be a great kisser, and partly because the eyewitnesses are fairly unanimous that there was enough heat between you two to melt the ceiling tiles." Kate grinned gleefully at Lacy.

"The eyewitnesses," Lacy repeated.

"Well, yeah. The bookstore was all abuzz."

Lacy didn't know how to feel about being the object of the

Swept Away buzz, but it wasn't as though she had any say in the matter. The thing to do, she supposed, was to keep her head down and wait for someone else to do something more buzz-worthy.

"Well … it was," Lacy said. She slid the coffee in its paper cup across the counter to Kate.

"Wait, wait, wait." Kate waved a hand in front of her face. "What was? Cassie was right? It was awful? It was good, or …?"

"It was freaking *amazing*." Lacy lowered her voice so only Kate could hear. She couldn't help grinning as the memory of the kiss flooded her with fresh, new lust.

"Oh! Oh, good!" Kate clapped her hands happily and bounced a few times on her toes. "So, what now? I mean, what's next for you two?"

"I don't know." Lacy sighed. "I mean, yeah, I want to go out with him. But we don't have a date set or anything. I keep waiting for him to text. Because, you know, I'm basically twelve." Lacy scowled at herself.

"Oh!" Kate held up a finger as she suddenly remembered something. "Speaking of setting dates, Rose wants to have her baby shower on the tenth of December. Will that work?"

Lacy thought for a moment. It was early November now, with Thanksgiving looming. It might be hard to pull together a shower with all of the various holiday preparations that had to be considered. On the other hand, Rose's baby wasn't going to wait just because it was the holiday season. And if they put the shower off any longer, they were either going to conflict with Christmas, or they would end up waiting too long, and the baby would be attending as a guest.

"Sure," Lacy said, mulling it over. "December tenth it is."

"Great." Kate picked up her coffee, slipped a cardboard sleeve onto the cup, and got ready to head back to the bookstore. "We'll get together to talk about themes, food, stupid party games, all that."

"Does Rose even want stupid party games?" Lacy wondered.

"Rose actually insisted on stupid party games. She said, and I quote, 'As God is my witness, somebody at that party is going to wear a diaper.' End quote."

"Ah. Well. Maybe it'll be her mother."

Kate snickered. "Now, there's an image." She tapped her knuckles once on the counter. "I gotta go. Text me when you hear from Daniel!"

"I will."

But, in fact, she probably wouldn't have to. Kate could just hear it from Whitney, who heard it from Cassie.

Families.

"Hey, there, Lacy. Can I get a large coffee?"

Lacy turned to see Hank Lawson, an elderly gentleman, standing at the counter.

"Oh. Sure, Hank. Coming right up."

"I heard about you and that Daniel Reed," Hank said, leering a little from under his John Deere cap as she rang up his purchase. "Be still my heart."

"Just drink your damned coffee, Hank," Lacy barked at him, shoving a full cup across the counter.

It occurred to her that she and Daniel might as well have just gone for it on the floor.

That was the way people were going to retell it, anyway.

Daniel and Lacy had their first date a couple of days later. They danced around it a little—where they would go, and what they would do, and when—and then settled on dinner at Neptune.

Dinner at a nice restaurant—it was a classic for a reason.

Lacy didn't have anything to wear, other than the one standard black dress her sisters had rejected for the engagement party, and the engagement party dress itself. Obviously, both of those were out. So, Whitney came over with an armload of clothes from her own closet for Lacy to try. Not only was Whitney the most fashionable of Lacy's sisters, she was also the one closest to Lacy in height and build.

When Whitney got there and plunked the clothes she'd brought onto the bed in Lacy's trailer, she looked around her and scowled.

"I don't know why we can't do this in the house. This place isn't big enough to spread out. And do you even have a full-length mirror?"

"I've got one in the bathroom," Lacy told her. "And you know why I can't do it in the house. Mom would grill me about why I was going out with someone new so soon after Brandon, and why I broke up with Brandon in the first place, and how she could call him and smooth things over …"

"That's true," Whitney admitted thoughtfully. "But she does have a point."

Lacy stopped browsing through the clothes and looked at Whitney. "About which part?"

"Both. I mean, just a month ago you were at your engagement party, all happy and looking forward to being married. And then this Daniel Reed comes along …"

"First of all, I wasn't happy," Lacy said, sitting on the edge of the bed beside the pile of dresses, skirts, and blouses. "I only thought I was. And second, the breakup didn't have anything to do with Daniel."

"Well … okay." Whitney tossed her hands up in confusion. "Fine. But he did step into the void pretty quickly, didn't he?

And Cassie said the kiss at Jitters wasn't even that good!"

Lacy could have corrected Whitney and told her how the kiss had practically melted her nether regions, but she didn't see the point. Instead, she said, "You don't really like Daniel, do you?"

"I don't know him that well," Whitney said, deflecting the question.

"Uh-huh. But?" Lacy prompted her.

"But, one of my friends from high school dated him a couple of years ago, and he broke her heart."

"Well … how? How did he break her heart? I mean, was it one of those things where she fell for him and it just didn't work out? Or did he do something mean, or …?" Lacy felt the strong need to defend him, even without knowing any of the details.

Whitney shrugged. "I don't know. She didn't give me a blow by blow. It's just …"

"It's just what, Whitney?"

Whitney gathered herself, faced Lacy, and spoke with new conviction. "It's just that a guy who looks like he does probably thinks he can use women however he wants. And you should be careful."

"He's not like that," Lacy said, stung a little on Daniel's behalf.

"Okay, whatever you say." Whitney's face was set in her *nobody ever listens to me* pout. "Just, be careful."

Lacy settled on an emerald green halter dress with a flowing, midlength skirt. She didn't have any shoes to go with it, but Whitney had thought of that and had brought a selection. The only problem was that Whitney's feet were half a size smaller than Lacy's. As a result, Lacy hobbled to the trailer door when Daniel came to pick her up.

"You look gorgeous," Daniel said when Lacy opened the door. He blinked a few times as though acclimating himself to a too-bright light.

"It's Whitney's. The dress, I mean," Lacy said. "And the shoes. I didn't have any nice shoes, except the ones I wore to the engagement party, and I figured, the less to remind us of that, the better, so …"

She was babbling. She knew it, but couldn't seem to stop herself. And she also had reminded them both of her engagement, even while commenting that she didn't want to remind them of it. *Shut up, Lacy,* she told herself.

"Do you want to come in for a minute?" she asked, figuring that, at least, was safe territory, conversation-wise. Though it might not be safe in other ways.

He climbed up the steps and into the trailer, peering around with interest.

"You live here full-time?" he asked. "This place is great." He poked around with no self-consciousness about the fact that he was in someone else's home, looking at all of their stuff. He peeked into the bathroom, into the tiny closet. He opened a kitchen cabinet or two, marveling at the ingenious use of space. "Do you leave it parked here all the time, or do you ever take it camping? There are some good RV parks near Yosemite."

Lacy was, for a moment, speechless. Nobody had ever loved her Airstream the way she did. Her mother was eager to get her married off so she could have a "real" home. Brandon had refused to even come inside. And Whitney fretted over the lack of closet space, bemoaning the sorry state of Lacy's wardrobe, considering how few belongings she could fit into the trailer. Nobody really saw it the way she did: the simplicity. The efficiency. The feeling of being inside a safe and warm burrow, a cozy cocoon.

Now, here was Daniel marveling at the place in pure glee.

"I … uh … yeah. We've taken it to Yosemite," Lacy said, recovering herself. "I bought this place from my mom and dad. They got it when I was about fourteen, for family road trips. We went to Sequoia, Kings Canyon. The Grand Canyon. Yellowstone, one time."

"Wow." Daniel peered into the storage area under the bed, which was where Lacy kept her shoes all lined up in a neat row. "Do you still travel with it?"

"Not for a while." Lacy sat down on the bed and watched him, amused and charmed by his boyish enthusiasm. What was it with men and vehicles—or things that you pulled behind vehicles? "The road trips were more of a family thing—Mom and Dad, my brother and my sisters. Now that we're all grown and my parents can't force us to go on vacation together, we don't really do it anymore. Kind of a shame," she said as an afterthought.

"Wait. There are, what? Five kids in your family? How did you fit everybody in here?"

"We didn't. The trailer was kind of a headquarters, for showering and cooking. Everybody slept in tents and sleeping bags. Except for Whitney—she got the bed. I think she came out of the womb too prissy for camping." Lacy smiled fondly at the memory.

"Man. I wish we'd had one of these when we were doing our quest to visit all fifty states," Daniel said. He shoved his hands into the pockets of his dress pants, his face aglow with enthusiasm. "I think I've stayed in every Motel 6 in the continental United States."

They both fell quiet, and something in the air between them changed, subtly but noticeably, as they both realized they were alone in a place with a bed. The way he was looking at her made her feel hot suddenly. She stood up on the too-tight heels, intending to tell him that they should get going, thinking that she should get him out of the trailer and into public before she was tempted to strip naked and offer herself to him like an early Christmas present.

She knew what she was supposed to say: *Well, should we get going?* But instead of saying that, she stepped a little closer to him. She could see his Adam's apple working as he swallowed. Then, he reached out one hand and ran it gently down her arm.

The effect was immediate and profound. His touch sent a wave of tingling warmth through her body, and she let out an involuntary sigh.

He moved in as if to kiss her, and she breathed in his smell—shaving cream and some kind of minty mouthwash, and a warm and musky scent that was just him.

Sleeping with him on the first date would show an appalling lack of self-control. How much worse would it be if she slept with him before the date even happened?

He was just inches from her now, just a breath away.

"Dinner?" she said, and her voice cracked.

"Huh?" He looked as though he were entirely unfamiliar with the word.

"We … uh … shall we go? To dinner?"

She could almost see him turning his brain back on, coming fully back into consciousness.

"Oh. Right." He held out his hand to her, and she took it in hers. "Shall we?"

They had thought to go to Neptune, where Jackson was the head chef, because the atmosphere was nice and the food was even better. But they were halfway between Lacy's place and the restaurant—a distance of less than a mile—when Daniel's cell phone rang, and he answered it through the Bluetooth in his SUV.

"Daniel?" the voice said. "This is Earlene Drummond."

Earlene Drummond was the closest thing Daniel had to a neighbor; her place was down the road from his in the hills south of Cambria.

"Oh. Hey, Earlene. How are you?" he said.

"Well, I have your little dog. He is yours, right? I didn't think you had a dog, but I see your number on his collar."

What the hell? Zzyzx had been in the house when Daniel had left to get Lacy. How had he gotten out?

"Uh … yeah, I've only had him a little while. Where'd you find him?"

"He was wandering down the road in front of my place. He looked lost." As an afterthought, she added, "He certainly is … interesting looking."

"Ah, shit. Oh. Sorry, Earlene. Excuse the language." Earlene was in her seventies, and it occurred to him that his mother wouldn't approve of him swearing to her.

"I've got him here in my kitchen, and I don't have a fenced yard …"

Earlene sounded somewhat distressed about the situation. He glanced over at Lacy, looking lovely in her green dress. She gave him a wry smile.

"Okay, Earlene. I'll be right out. Just sit tight."

He disconnected the call and pulled the SUV over to the curb on Main Street a couple of blocks from the restaurant.

"Lacy, I—"

"It's okay. We can go get him," she said.

"Really?"

"Sure. He's kind of my dog, too, when you think about it. We can't just leave him there."

"All right. Thanks. I'm going to wring his furry little neck when I get him. I don't even know how he got out of the house. Probably stood on a chair and turned the knob."

Zzyzx was proving to be surprisingly smart for a dog. If he wanted out, and there was a way, Daniel wasn't surprised that he'd found it. Z didn't like it when Daniel left the house; his whines, accompanied by the sound of his little claws scratching at the door, struck guilt into Daniel's heart whenever he tried to go anywhere these days.

He pulled the SUV back out onto Main Street and headed toward Highway 1, then drove south in the direction of Harmony. It didn't seem quite fair that he'd saved Z's life, and this was how the dog was repaying him.

If Z ruined his chances with Lacy, the mutt was never going to lay eyes on another Milk-Bone as long as he lived.

Chapter Twenty

They picked up Z from Earlene's, and when the dog saw Lacy, he went into a hysterical display of pleasure, jumping and spinning and whining as though she were his long lost mother. She scooped him up and held him to her chest, and he squirmed in delight, licking her face with his little pink tongue.

"Oh, you're both so dressed up," Earlene remarked. "I hope I didn't ruin your evening."

As a matter of fact, Daniel thought. But instead of saying that, he just thanked her, and they bundled the errant dog into the car for the drive home.

In the SUV, Z continued to whine with pleasure, gazing at Lacy in pure, worshipful love.

"I'm the one who feeds him," Daniel grumbled as they drove toward his place. "I'm the one who cleans up his pee when he goes in the house. It's like I don't even exist."

"Aww. You're jealous," Lacy said as Z looked up at her with adoring eyes.

"A little." He grinned in the glow of the dashboard lights. "I get it, though. If I had the chance to curl up in your lap, I'd sure as hell take it."

"Maybe later," Lacy remarked. "We'll have to see how the evening goes."

It turned out that Z had climbed onto a table and squeezed through a window that Daniel had left partially open. The dog hair on the tabletop was a dead giveaway.

They let him run around the yard to pee, then put him

inside the house, closed the window, checked his food and water bowls to make sure he was adequately provisioned, and then left the house to give their date another try. But with Lacy's presence, his drama over being left was even more heartrending than usual. He whined, howled, yelped, scratched at the door, and did everything short of hiring a skywriter to ask them not to go.

They didn't even make it all the way to the SUV before Lacy cracked.

"We can't just leave him." She looked at Daniel apologetically. "He's sad."

"He's always sad when I leave," Daniel remarked. "Am I supposed to just stay in my house for the rest of his life, having groceries delivered and chatting with women on the Internet?"

"It kind of seems like he'd like that," she said. The sound of Z's moaning and sobbing—or the canine equivalent, anyway—came through the door to where they stood beside the car.

They both waited there indecisively for a minute, listening to the pitiful racket on the other side of the door.

"Let's just go," Daniel said finally, moving in the direction of Lacy's door, intending to open it for her. "He'll settle down."

Lacy looked at the house, then at Daniel, then at the house.

"Now, listen," Daniel said, his face stern. "He's gonna have to learn. He'll live. He's not gonna die of loneliness." But even as he said it, he already knew he'd lost.

Z continued to whine in abject misery.

"Maybe we could just stay with him for a little while?" Lacy suggested. "He sounds so sad."

"Oh, for—" Daniel took his keys out of his pocket and headed back toward the house. "Come on," he said to Lacy. "I think I have some pizza in the freezer."

He did have a pizza, and also the makings for a salad. As he was moving around the kitchen with Zzyzx at his feet, getting the food ready, he noticed that Lacy was having a little trouble with her shoes, so he suggested that she take them off.

Her sigh of ecstasy when her feet were freed made him think of other ways he might make her sigh, under other, infinitely nicer, circumstances.

And *that* was how he almost set the kitchen on fire.

He was so distracted by the sigh, and by the associations it created in his mind, that he accidentally hit the dial for the front right burner on the stove, rather than the dial for the oven. It just so happened that there was a dishcloth sitting right there, and before either of them knew what was happening, flames were licking at the corner of the cloth, and the smoke alarm overhead started screaming in distress.

"Oh, God," Lacy exclaimed, jumping back from where she'd been leaning against the kitchen counter.

Fortunately, Daniel dealt with fire every day, so a minor dishcloth incident was no cause for panic. Cursing to himself, he grabbed the end of the cloth that wasn't on fire, dropped the cloth in the sink, and turned on the tap, putting out the flames.

That still left the problem of the smoke alarm—and the problem of Z, who was so frightened by the noise that he was howling a high-pitched, musical wail to accompany the blaring scream.

"Here. Just let me …" Daniel opened the window over the kitchen sink, grabbed a dishcloth that wasn't on fire, and fanned at the smoke alarm until it finally quieted down. Lacy picked up Z to comfort him, and he quieted down, too.

Now there was only the shocked silence, the thick fog of Daniel's embarrassment, and the lingering scent of charred cotton/poly blend.

"Jesus," Daniel said when the immediate crisis was over.

"I'm sorry about that. I guess I hit the wrong dial."

"I guess you did." Lacy stroked Z's head. "I'm a little worried now about letting you make the pizza. We could be putting our lives at risk."

"I was … a little nervous," he admitted. He leaned against the kitchen counter, his hands tucked into the safety of his armpits.

"Nervous? About me?"

He shrugged. "I just … I wanted our date to go well, but there was the thing with Z, and then you made that noise …"

Lacy frowned, bemused. "What noise?"

"When you took off your shoes." He gestured vaguely toward her discarded shoes with one finger. "You made this … this sighing sound."

"I sighed," she said, as if trying to make sense of whatever the hell he was saying.

"Yeah. But it wasn't just a sigh, it was … Look. Let's just forget it, okay? Maybe I should just take you home." He rubbed at his eyes miserably.

Lacy put Z down on the kitchen floor and stood. "Is that what you want? You want me to go home?"

"No." Daniel shook his head. "Hell, no. I don't *ever* want you to go home. But I don't want to ruin your evening any more than I have already, so—"

"Daniel." She interrupted him.

"What?" There was that misery in his voice again, that weary defeat.

"Just come over here and kiss me."

At first, he wasn't sure he'd heard her right. Then, he just hoped to God that he had. He went to her, feeling tentative and unsure. A lock of her golden hair lay on her shoulder, and he picked it up between his fingertips.

"Daniel. Kiss me," she said again.

His body thrummed with anticipation before he even touched her, before he even tasted her. He reached out and touched the side of her face with his hand. Then he drew closer, until their lips were barely a breath apart. He hesitated just a moment, and then took her mouth with his.

She was all softness, all comfort and promise. He sank more deeply into the kiss, exploring her with his lips, his tongue, the gentle tug of his teeth.

And there was that sound again, that sigh that was also a moan. The idea that he was making that sound come out of her caused his pulse to race. His arms went around her and he pulled her closer. His hands tangled themselves in the glorious bounty of her hair.

He forgot everything else except this. The date, the dog, the fire—everything else faded into the gauzy haze of distant memory. This was the only thing that was real, the only thing that mattered.

He felt as though his body recognized her. As though it were saying, *This is the one.* He folded her against him and bent his head to taste the soft skin beneath her jaw.

"Daniel?" she murmured. He roused himself just enough to pull away from her, to search her eyes.

"Show me your bedroom," she whispered. She found his hand with hers, and held it, pulling him gently toward the back of the house.

And just like that, he was gone. He knew it, and there was no sense fighting it. She owned him, his body, his spirit. Nothing to do but just give in and follow her.

Lacy wondered, as she led him toward a door that she assumed was the bedroom, what exactly she thought she was doing. This wasn't going to be a fun dalliance that could be forgotten tomorrow. This wasn't casual. This was her getting in over her head, into something that would make her terrifyingly vulnerable.

She was quickly moving toward a point of no return, a place where her heart would be his to protect or to destroy. If she slept with him, if it was everything she thought it was going to be, she'd be lost.

And yet, she felt helpless to do anything else. She wanted him more than she wanted to go on breathing, to go on living. And so she walked with him into his bedroom, her fear warring with her desire.

"Lacy?" he murmured when they were standing beside the bed. The room was dark, except for the light filtering in from the kitchen. "Are you sure?"

She didn't answer him. Instead, her trembling fingers went to the buttons of his shirt. She undid them one by one, revealing his bare skin inch by inch.

He watched her raptly as she moved down, down, until at last she pulled his shirt free from where it had been tucked into his pants and unbuttoned it the rest of the way. She slid the fabric off of his broad shoulders and down, until it fell to the floor at his feet.

She ran her hands over his chest, his shoulders, the muscular planes of his arms. And now he was the one letting out a guttural sound of pleasure.

He reached for the tie at the back of her dress, but she gently moved his hands away. "It's still my turn," she said, with a hint of mischief in her eyes.

He kicked off his shoes, and her hands went to his belt buckle. He held still as she unbuckled the belt and slid it out of its loops, but she could see his breath quickening in the rise and fall of his chest.

She unsnapped, unzipped, and then slid his remaining clothes down and off until he stood there, naked in the faint glow from the kitchen light.

And oh, God, he was gorgeous. Every bit of his body told the story of his work and the strength it required. His arms, his chest, his legs were hard and muscled, and pure man.

For a moment, she just looked.

"I've wanted to see you like this for a long time," she said, her voice a little hoarse with desire.

And it was true. Even when he was just a friend, even when she'd been with Brandon, the curiosity about him, the little flame of want, had been there, burning in her. She'd ignored it then. But she couldn't ignore it now.

She ran her hands over his skin, and he drew in a breath. He reached around to untie her dress, and then gathered the silky fabric in his hands and drew it up, over her head, and off of her. She'd worn tiny, silk underthings for him—in anticipation of this moment—and something in his face changed when he saw her. What had been rapt attention was now raw hunger.

She began to reach back to unclasp her bra, but he took her hand to stop her.

"Wait a little," he said, his voice a low rumble. "I like this." He traced the line of her bra with his finger.

He lowered his head to take her lace-covered breast into his mouth, his hot tongue pressing against the peak through the fabric. Lacy felt it like a jolt of fire through her body. She threw her head back, grabbed his hair in her fists, and let out a low humming sound from the depths of her throat.

Then, when the anticipation was almost too much, he scooped her up into his arms and carried her to the bed.

She was just so goddamned perfect. Golden hair, sun-kissed skin, and that body. That body that she was giving to him, as though he had any hope in hell of deserving such a gift.

He lowered her onto the bed and tasted the hollow plane between her breasts.

"Lacy." Her name came out on a sigh.

He wanted to take it slowly, to make this last forever. But he couldn't help himself. He ran his hand down her body, pushed the tiny, tantalizing panties aside, and thrust his fingers into the warm, hot core of her.

She gasped, and her eyes opened wide.

"Tell me how you want me to touch you," he murmured into her ear. "Is this what you want?" He caressed her engorged nub with his thumb while his fingers stroked inside her.

"Oh, God, yes. Yes. Like that," she said, and her eyes, which had moments ago opened in surprise, now slid shut in bliss.

Watching her like this, seeing on her face the way he made her feel, was almost more than he could bear. But he didn't stop, couldn't stop. His fingers moved inside her as she writhed and arched her back on the bed.

The orgasm ripped through her like an earthquake, like a hurricane. Like some epic event that left devastation in its path. She cried out, and then fought to catch her breath.

When she opened her eyes to look at him, his face was pure, intense need.

He knelt at her feet, slid the silky panties off of her, and then eased her thighs apart and slid into her.

Her body hadn't recovered from the things he'd already done to her, so the feeling of him inside her, his insistence, his intensity, could have been too much. But she kept up with him, giving back everything beat for beat. She wrapped her body around him, her arms, her legs, savoring every sensation.

She couldn't get enough of him, of this.

She clung to him, reveling in the pleasure, until he grew still and shuddered against her.

When it was over, neither one of them moved for a while. He was sprawled half on top of her, his arm wrapped around her. His body was heavy on hers, but it felt delicious, as though it belonged there.

Finally, he let out a groan and scrubbed at his face with his hand.

"Jesus," he said. "That was … are you …?" Apparently, eloquence escaped him. Lacy didn't blame him. She doubted she could have done much better.

She turned her body toward him and kissed him so she wouldn't have to try.

"Oh, shit," he muttered. "I didn't think about …"

"I'm on the pill," she told him. "If that's what you were worried about."

"It was, yeah." He rolled onto his side and pulled her into his arms.

"You're still wearing your bra," he observed.

"I am. You said you liked it."

"I do." He looked down at the garment in question with a lecherous grin. "Still, kind of a shame …"

She raised her eyebrows. "We could try it again without, just to see which works better."

"A kind of experiment," he said.

"For science," she added.

He unhooked the bra and slid it off of her shoulders.

"Who am I to argue with scientific discovery?" he said.

Chapter Twenty-One

"So the dog ruined the date, and then Daniel set the kitchen on fire, and then you had smoking hot, earth-shattering sex." Rose recapped Lacy's rundown of her date as she, Lacy, Kate, and Gen gathered at Rose's house over dinner to plan the baby shower.

At least, they had intended to plan the baby shower. Instead, they seemed to have abandoned all discussion of girl-themed cupcakes and decorations in favor of sex talk.

Because who didn't like a good sex talk?

"That's pretty much how it happened," Lacy agreed. "Except he didn't really set the whole kitchen on fire. It was just the dish towel."

"And your pants," Gen added, smirking.

"God. I don't mean to trash-talk Brandon," Lacy said, a glass of chardonnay in her hand. "But I didn't realize how mediocre the sex with him was, until …"

"Until Mr. Hottie Artist Guy rocked your world?" Kate suggested.

"Well … yes."

Rose's house, a rustic cabin on the outskirts of Cambria, was scattered with shower invitations, decorations still in their packaging, the components to make party favors, and ideas printed from Pinterest. The women were gathered around Rose's kitchen table, which was laden with wine bottles and glasses, Mexican takeout packages, and plates bearing the remnants of their dinner.

Will, with the keen sense of self-preservation common in most men faced with baby shower planning, had fled the house to go play with his friends.

"Sweetie, I'm so happy for you," Kate said, laying a hand on Lacy's forearm.

"I'm happy for me, too," Lacy said. "I think. It's just …"

"Uh-oh. It's just what?" Gen prompted her.

"It's … I just got out of a relationship that was smothering. That made me feel like I wasn't myself. And now here I am, jumping right into this thing with Daniel." Lacy poked at the remains of an enchilada with her fork. "But the thing is, I don't feel smothered. I feel … like me. Only better."

"That's how it's supposed to feel," Kate said. "Like you, only better. And happier."

"And with more orgasms," Rose put in.

"Orgasms are good," Lacy agreed. "Better than good. But … I think I might be in trouble here." She looked up from her plate at her friends. "This isn't going to be something I can just get over if it goes wrong."

"Who says it's going to go wrong?" Gen asked, her voice full of sympathy.

"Because it always goes wrong!" Lacy tossed her hands up for emphasis. "When has one of my relationships ever not gone wrong?"

"That's how it works," Rose said, giving Lacy an indulgent look, like a parent with a child who still has much to learn. "You get into relationships, and they all go wrong until you get to the one that doesn't."

Kate and Gen nodded in agreement.

"Besides," Rose went on. "You're not the first person to get freaked out by good sex. And feelings." She wiggled her fingers in the air to illustrate the word *feelings*. "I ran away from Will so fast you'd have thought he was chasing me with an ax. Good thing he caught me." She rubbed her pregnant belly with amused affection.

"Right. Shit. You're right," Lacy said. "I feel like one of those stupid cartoon characters. You know, the ones where you know they're in love because they float a foot above the ground and they've got little cartoon hearts and birds over their heads."

"Okay, that really *was* good sex," Kate observed.

"As someone who's going to be very sex-deprived, very soon," Rose said, "I say you should just enjoy it. Wear him out. Emerge only for occasional hydration."

To Lacy, that did sound like an attractive option.

"In the meantime," Rose said, "let's talk cake. Should we go with the pink chevrons or the baby bootie design?"

The guys had gathered at Ted's, since the women were all tied up with party planning and they had nothing else to do. Jackson and Will were absorbed in a game of pool; Jackson was winning, of course, since Will was crap at pool. Daniel wasn't talking about his date with Lacy, because he didn't want to be ungentlemanly. But he was brooding about it, all the same, as he sat on a barstool next to Ryan, drinking a beer and watching Will get the snot beat out of him.

"You didn't show up at Neptune last night," Jackson observed as he lined up a shot toward a corner pocket. "You had a reservation."

"Yeah. I was supposed to be bringing Lacy, but the dog had other plans." He told them about Zzyzx getting out through an open window, about retrieving him from the neighbor's house, and about the way he'd thrown a holy tantrum when they'd tried to leave.

"Well, that's a shame," Will said, as he stood with his pool cue waiting for Jackson to finish his turn. "So, what did you end up doing?"

Daniel wasn't much of a blusher, but he must have. Either that, or he got some kind of telltale look on his face, because the other three stared at him, and then began giving him these smug, know-it-all grins.

"What?" Daniel demanded.

"Seems like maybe it wasn't such a bad thing that the Neptune deal didn't work out," Ryan observed.

"That's not … I never said …"

"You didn't have to," Jackson said. He took his shot, and sank the nine ball into the corner pocket.

"Well, you didn't hear anything from me," Daniel grumbled irritably. "I'm not gonna talk about her like that."

"If you did, I'd have to kick your ass," Jackson said as he moved around the table, looking for his next shot. "Since she's practically my sister-in-law."

"The question is," Ryan said, "since it seems like the date might not have been a total bust after all, why do you look so pissed off?"

"What? I'm not." And it was true; he wasn't. Pissed off wasn't an accurate description of what he was feeling. He was more … troubled. Because everything was changing—he could feel it—and he wasn't sure what he thought about that.

He scowled, picked up his beer mug, and then put it back down again on the little round table where he and Ryan sat.

"I like my life," he said finally, in a non sequitur that had the others peering at him quizzically.

"Okay," Will said. "Well … that's a good thing."

"Yeah," Daniel said, mostly to himself. "Yeah."

Jackson straightened up from where he'd been bent over the pool table, leaned against his cue, and said, "Let me try to translate. You had a good time with Lacy. A very good time. And now you're thinking maybe it was *more* than just a good time. Maybe it was *so* much more that it's going to throw your whole universe out of whack, with things like marriage and kids to go with that dog of yours."

Will's eyebrows rose behind his glasses. "Daniel? Is he right?"

Daniel shrugged. "I don't know. Shit. I guess he's right, yeah." With the door to the conversation opened, he figured he might as well walk through it. Who the hell else was he going to talk to about all of this?

"The thing is … if we do this—and it looks like we're doing it—it's not going to be just fun. It's not going to be friends with benefits. She's not like that, and, hell, neither am I."

"Okay. So why is that a problem?" Ryan asked.

"It's not." Daniel scrubbed at his face with his hands. "Jesus, I don't know what my issue is."

"Sure you do," Jackson said.

"You seem to know everything about what I'm thinking," Daniel said irritably. "Why don't you just tell me, then?"

"All right." Jackson leaned his cue against the wall and stood with his arms crossed over his chest. "You're thinking about how Lacy wants kids and a house and the whole bit, and you're not sure what you want, but you know that you're already in this pretty deep, and it's going to be hard, if not impossible, for you to walk away. So you're trying to adjust to your new reality. But you're a guy, so instead of just dealing with all of that, you're sitting around looking like someone pissed in your corn chips, when you should be on top of the world after enjoying the sweet, sweet attentions of the spectacular Lacy Jordan—something we've all fantasized about at one time or another."

Daniel looked at Jackson sharply. "You've fantasized about Lacy?"

Jackson put up his hands in helpless surrender. "Not lately.

Not since Kate. But, I'm only human."

Daniel looked to the others for any indication that they might have been lusting after Lacy, so he'd know whether he needed to punch any of them in the face.

Ryan just shrugged. "You're living the dream, man. Seems like kind of a shame not to enjoy it."

Once Daniel and Lacy started seeing each other regularly, and once that became general knowledge around town, Daniel noticed an unsettling phenomenon.

The men he came in contact with were all treating him differently.

It seemed like these days he got treated one of two ways: either as some kind of folk hero, or as the asshole who had what everyone else wanted, thus ensuring that they, themselves, never would.

One morning as he walked into Jitters, he experienced both within the space of five minutes.

The bell on top of the front door was still jingling from his arrival when Bert Wexler, the guy who ran the hardware store down the street, walked past on his way out and clapped Daniel on the shoulder.

"Lacy Jordan, huh?" he said with a leer. "Nice job." And then Bert went out the door with his coffee cup in his hand, making a kind of wolf-whistle sound.

Then, when Daniel got to the counter, Connor glared at him as though Daniel had bad-mouthed the guy's sister. As far as he knew, Connor didn't even have a sister.

"What do you want?" Connor said flatly, no friendly greeting, no chitchat about anybody's day.

"Uh … large coffee."

Connor grunted and rang him up.

"Dude. Everything okay?" Daniel asked him.

"It is for you, apparently." Connor took Daniel's money, slapped it into the register, slammed the drawer shut, and then threw Daniel's receipt at him.

Daniel supposed he should be grateful it was just the receipt that had been thrown, and not the coffee.

Chapter Twenty-Two

An interesting thing happened when you started seeing someone right before the holidays, Daniel thought. Actually, it was a series of interesting things.

One, it was taken for granted that you would spend the holidays together. That was reasonable enough. Why wouldn't you?

Two, since you were spending the holidays together, that necessarily meant that you'd be mingling with the other person's family in a fairly intense way that involved food, distant relatives, and long-established rituals and traditions.

And three, the fact that you were mingling with the other person's family and participating in their rituals and traditions led everyone to assume that you were just moments away from pulling a ring out of your pocket and having a flash mob propose to the tune of an Ed Sheeran song.

Daniel figured that was inevitable. People always wanted to know what would happen next. And if there were no answers—at least, not yet—then they'd invent their own.

Still, the whole thing made him feel a little bit twitchy when he showed up for Thanksgiving dinner with Lacy's family.

He'd brought a bottle of wine and a pie. Because who didn't like pie? But he hadn't been in the door for two minutes before it became apparent that his pie—and his wine, for that matter—was irrelevant.

The Jordan house looked like it had been invaded by a crew of Thanksgiving elves who had not only loaded the place down with every type of pie, side dish, appetizer, and fall-themed cookie imaginable, but who also had buried the place in fall-leaf wreaths, crepe paper turkeys, and cardboard Pilgrims.

Having come from a small family, he stood inside the doorway and gaped at the sheer magnitude of it.

"Oh, pie!" Lacy said enthusiastically as she took his arm and
pulled him toward the kitchen. "And chardonnay. We'll need
that. Cassie's already hit the wine pretty hard. But don't tell her I
said that."

As he entered the kitchen, it was readily apparent why the
Jordans needed so much food, and so much wine. The kitchen
was crammed with people. Parents. Sisters. Sisters' boyfriends.
Children. The brother was probably here somewhere, too,
though Daniel couldn't spot him among the various men who
were here as the women's other halves.

He looked for a place to set his pie and wine, but every possible counter surface was occupied with food, ingredients to
make food, or crockery that would be used to serve food.

"Daniel!" Cassie greeted him enthusiastically, and took the
items from his hands. He could see from the pink of her cheeks
that Lacy had been right about the wine. "It's good to see you!"
she said. She leaned in conspiratorially and said, out of the corner of her mouth, "I was dreading spending the holidays with *you
know who*." She theatrically mouthed the word *Brandon*. "Thank
God that's over!"

From there, he greeted, was introduced to, shook hands
with, or otherwise interacted with both of Lacy's parents, three
sisters, one brother, one brother-in-law, one sister's boyfriend,
three neighbors, and three kids.

Mostly, the greetings were warm and friendly, with one not-
able exception.

"Happy Thanksgiving," Nancy Jordan said, her hands on
her hips, which were swathed in a turkey-themed apron. The
words were amiable enough, but the tone said, *Go screw yourself.*
Lacy had told him this might happen. Nancy had been thrilled

by the idea of having a chiropractor as a son-in-law, and all that had been shot to hell. There would be no free spinal adjustments in her future, and it didn't take much to see that she blamed Daniel.

"Everything smells great, Nancy," he told her, in a lame bid to get into her good graces.

"Well, it should," she snapped. "I would think I know how to put together a turkey dinner by now."

With that, she turned her back to him and went to baste the bird.

Vince, with two bottles of cold beer in his hands, appeared at Daniel's side and thrust one of the bottles into his hand. "I figure you're gonna need this," Vince said. "You want to come on into my study and take a look at something?"

Vince's study was upstairs and down the hall, sandwiched between a large, messy bathroom and a bedroom that had been repurposed as a sewing room. The study had dark wood paneling, a large window that let in the afternoon light, and a big oak desk that was scattered with papers. In the corner was a drafting table with a tilted top.

Vince gestured for Daniel to follow him behind the desk. Then he unrolled a large sheet of paper and spread it out on the desk.

"These are just sketches," Vince told him as Daniel looked over Vince's shoulder. "Once you settle on a design, I'll do up the plans on the computer. See here?" He pointed with a meaty finger at one part of the drawing. "This is what we talked about. Here's the new room you wanted, and the loft. Plus, it wouldn't take much to expand the size of the kitchen. Bring it out here and here"—he pointed—"and you get five more feet of usable space." It was the same design they'd talked about at the Old

Stone Station, but more detailed, and with a few refinements.

"Wow." Daniel looked at the sketches with interest. "That's great. Really great. It's just what I had in mind."

"Now, before you get attached to that," Vince said, reaching for another rolled sheet of paper, "I want you to have a look at this."

He opened up another sketch, this one of a much more extensive renovation. Not only did this drawing add square footage to the house's basic footprint, it also added an entire second floor.

"See? With this plan, you get a study downstairs, plus the bigger kitchen, and you get bedrooms and a full bath upstairs. The budget for this one's a lot bigger, obviously, but it's something to think about."

"But …" Daniel said.

Vince clapped him on the shoulder. "The way things are going, I figure you might need a couple-three more bedrooms."

Daniel started to say something, then closed his mouth. He looked at the beer in his hand and wondered if there was any Scotch in the house.

By the time Daniel left that evening with a couple of Tupperware containers full of leftovers, he found himself feeling irritable and, more than that, misunderstood.

Didn't Vince realize that he and Lacy had only been seeing each other for a few weeks? Didn't Nancy realize that he wasn't to blame for Lacy and Brandon's breakup? And didn't Lacy's sisters realize that just because he showed up for Thanksgiving, it didn't mean he was ready to sweep Lacy off her feet and join the family?

"So, how did your talk with my dad go?" Lacy asked in the car on the way to Daniel's place, after the cleanup was done and the football was watched and they were finally able to get free and get out of there.

At first, Daniel thought she was asking about the part where Vince had obliquely suggested that he should impregnate Lacy and move her in with him. Of course that's what Daniel thought; he seemed to keep rerunning the conversation over and over in his mind.

But Lacy couldn't be referring to that, could she?

"Huh?" he said.

"Didn't he talk to you about your renovations?" Lacy asked. She was holding the leftovers on her lap as they drove down Highway 1. "He said he had some sketches to show you."

"Ah. Yeah, yeah. He had … a couple of different versions." He didn't tell her that one of the versions was designed to accommodate their multiple children. Though, he supposed it was possible that she already knew. And *that* idea made him feel ganged up on, as though there was some kind of conspiracy to direct his life in ways that were beyond his control.

"So? Are you going to do it?" She asked the question guilelessly, her face open and innocent and so beautiful it made his soul ache.

"I don't know." He focused his gaze on the road, so he wouldn't have to look at her. Because if he did, if he looked, then he would say yes to everything: to the house, and the couple-three bedrooms, and the flash mob, and the Ed Sheeran song. "I think I'm maybe gonna hold off for a little bit."

"But why? I thought it was what you wanted."

Daniel turned off of the highway and headed onto the road that led to his house. What was he supposed to say? It *was* what he wanted. In so many ways, it was exactly what he wanted, but it was all happening so fast. There was no time to think. He just needed to think.

"I just don't see why I have to rush into something," he said irritably as he pulled up in front of his house. "Does everything have to happen so fast? Does everything have to change right this second? Why can't I have some time to breathe? Why can't I just ... think?"

He turned off the ignition, put on the parking break, and looked over at Lacy, who was staring at him with more than a small level of concern. That was when he realized that they'd each been talking about entirely different things, and that Lacy had no idea what the hell he was going on about.

"Are you okay?" she asked.

He forced his shoulders down from where they'd been hunched around his ears. "Ah ... yeah. Yeah, I'm fine. It's just that today was a little ... intense." He reached over, put a hand on Lacy's shoulder, leaned in, and kissed her. The kiss made the tension drain out of him like bathwater from a tub.

"I know my family can be a lot to handle," she said sympathetically. "But we have pie." She held up one of the Tupperware containers hopefully.

"I like pie," he said.

"And after the pie," she said, leaning in closer to purr into his ear, "I have some ideas for what we can do with the extra whipped cream."

Oh, Jesus.

He swallowed audibly.

Had he thought that he needed time to breathe? Breathing was probably overrated anyway.

Chapter Twenty-Three

They had decided that Rose's baby shower wouldn't be a female-only event. Instead, it would be a big, mixed-gender party with all of the trappings of a traditional shower—including the stupid games Rose was so looking forward to—but also with the music, beer, and barbecue more common to a regular get-together.

The deciding factor was that Will didn't want to be left out, which all of the women thought was completely adorable.

They had worried that the weather might not work out for barbecue, given the date in December. But Mother Nature was cooperative, and the temperatures hovered in the low seventies with clear blue skies.

The party was held at Ryan and Gen's house on the Delaney Ranch, because the rest of them had places that were too small for the number of guests Rose had in mind.

By the time Daniel rolled up in his SUV at two p.m. on that Saturday, the Porter-Delaney house was filled with Rose and Will's friends, Rose's mother, Gen and Ryan's family, Will's parents, various customers from De-Vine who had wheedled invitations, neighbors of the ranch, and just about everyone else in town who'd heard about the party and wanted to be included.

People were milling about on the big front porch, music was wafting out of doors and windows that had been left open, and Jackson was manning a big barbecue in the front yard, supervising a selection of steaks, chicken pieces, burgers, and brats.

Daniel was a little late. That was partly because he'd finally hired a new assistant, and the two of them had spent the morning working on the piece for the hotel in Los Angeles. But it was also because Lacy had called him when he was on his way and asked him to stop by the winery in Harmony to pick up a case of wine that the owner—who knew Rose well through her work at De-Vine—was contributing to the party as a gift.

He got the carton of wine bottles out of the back of the SUV and had hefted it into his arms when Lacy came out to greet him.

"Hey, you made it," she said with pleasure as she leaned past the bulk of the box to kiss him.

She looked lovely, her cheeks flushed with happiness. She was wearing her usual jeans, T-shirt, and sneakers, with no makeup, or at least none that Daniel could see. That meant that this impossible abundance of beauty was pure Lacy. Something in him relaxed when he saw her; some element of stress or annoyance, some unsettled thing in his chest, released and tamed itself with a sigh at her touch.

"I've got the wine," he said, unnecessarily.

"Great! Come on, let's take it inside."

He followed her up the porch steps and into the big house, nodding his greetings to people as he went. He hadn't put the box down yet when Rose came to meet him, grinning with infectious joy.

"Thanks for doing that," she said, gesturing toward the box of wine. "Just put it in the kitchen. Look how many people showed up! This is going to be so much fun. God, it's a nice day, right? I wasn't sure how the weather would turn out, but it's great. Jackson's making brats. I love brats!"

Daniel had to grin at Rose's bubbly enthusiasm. In honor of her baby's gender, she had dyed her hair a cotton-candy pink. Somewhere, she'd managed to find a Ramones maternity T-shirt, and she was wearing it with black leggings and motorcycle boots. The piercings in her eyebrow and her nose glinted in the overhead lights.

Once he'd had a chance to put down the box, Daniel enveloped Rose in a hug. "You look great," he told her when he'd let her go. "Not long now, huh?"

"Just a few more weeks," she said. "God, I can't wait. I know I'm going to be cranky and sleep-deprived and all covered in poop and baby vomit, but I can't wait to meet her." She rubbed her round belly with love.

Daniel, who'd heard about the Baby Name Derby from Will, asked whether anyone had won yet.

"Will won." For some reason, Rose was beaming as she told him.

"So, the name's Harper, then?" Daniel asked.

"Nope." Rose bounced on her toes. "That was his shower gift to me. He won the derby, but he gave me the naming rights anyway. She's going to be Poppy Wren Bachman." Rose was grinning so hard that Daniel couldn't help but laugh.

"A flower for you, a bird for him," he remarked. Will was an evolutionary biologist who had done his doctoral research on a species of bird common to the Cambria area.

"Isn't it perfect?" she said.

"It's great. I'm happy for you," Daniel said, meaning it.

Lacy had to rush off to get some of the games ready, so Daniel mingled among the crowd, greeting his friends, introducing himself to people he didn't already know.

He grabbed a beer from the kitchen, popped the top, and went out to where the barbecue was set up to say hello to Jackson.

Jackson was manning the grill with typical Jackson-like intensity, turning meat and applying sauce with a basting brush, and Will's father—a guy in his sixties with a balding head, a paunch, and studious-looking glasses that looked just like

Will's—was ferrying platters of raw meat from the kitchen to Jackson for grilling.

"Hey," Jackson said, greeting him with a glance up from the grill. "You finally made it."

"Yeah, yeah," Daniel said. "I'd have been here earlier, but I had to go back for the wine."

A group of kids that included Ryan's nephews and Lacy's nieces ran around on the lawn, playing some kind of game with rules that were incomprehensible to Daniel. Something involving a stick, an invisible line, a particular method of jumping on one foot, and a cape fashioned out of a dinner napkin.

Even without understanding the rules, Daniel would have put his money on the girls' team, hands down.

"Nice grill," Daniel remarked, gesturing toward the gleaming stainless steel behemoth that looked big enough to hold the parts of not just one chicken, but flocks of them. "This Ryan's?"

"Nah. I brought it from the restaurant in my truck."

Daniel's eyebrows rose. "You do outdoor grilling at Neptune?"

"Sometimes," Jackson answered. "We had that Fourth of July deal."

The smell of the meat, marinated with some concoction only Jackson knew the mystical secrets to, made Daniel's stomach growl, but he figured he should make an attempt to be social for a while before he dug into the food.

"Rose looks happy," he commented, making conversation.

"She's over the moon. She's probably going to deck the baby out in punk rock T-shirts and temporary tattoos."

"I'd like to see that," Daniel said.

A big outdoor table had been set up with a white tablecloth, place settings, and a centerpiece of red roses, presumably inspired by the guest of honor. Some of the women, and Will's dad, were bringing platters of food out to the table. Lacy came out of the house with a big bowl of some kind of salad in her hands, and Daniel followed her with his eyes.

Jackson said something that Daniel didn't hear. "Huh?" Daniel asked, distracted.

"I said, it seems like you're a goner," Jackson said, looking pointedly at Daniel and then at Lacy.

"That's not what you said."

"No, but it's still true."

Daniel's first impulse was to be annoyed and to deny that he was seriously hung up on Lacy, or anyone else for that matter. But what would the point of that be? He wasn't in damned third grade, after all. Denying feeling for girls was no longer a matter of manly honor.

He sighed. "Yeah. I guess it is."

"Well, you could do one hell of a lot worse," Jackson said jovially, flipping a row of chicken parts.

"That's what worries me." Daniel watched Lacy as she put the salad on the table, exchanged a few words with one of Ryan's relatives, and then went back up the porch stairs and into the house.

"What's that supposed to mean?" Jackson looked up from the grill to squint at Daniel.

Daniel shrugged. "It means, I kind of feel like I'm playing A-ball and Lacy's the Major Leagues. Like I'm out of my depth."

"Ah, that's bullshit," Jackson said, gesturing at Daniel with his barbecue tongs. "It's shallow as hell, and it's unfair to Lacy, and it's not what's really bothering you."

Daniel scowled, surprised. "What are you—"

"It's shallow and unfair because it assumes that an especially beautiful woman only wants some European underwear model named Javier." He pointed at Daniel with the tongs. "And that because you're no Javier, she's going to get bored and run off with some other guy."

"Well." Daniel had to admit that it sounded pretty stupid when Jackson put it that way.

"And it's bullshit," Jackson continued, "because what you're really worried about is that this is the big one."

"The big one?" Daniel said.

"The big one. The big L. And that doesn't stand for Lacy."

"Ah … you're an asshole," Daniel said, lacking a more trenchant response.

"I'm just saying." Jackson turned his attention back to the meat on the grill. "You think it was easy for me when I fell for Kate? It took me a while to start thinking like part of a couple. It's worth it, though. I'm just saying."

Daniel scowled. "Ah … just cook your damned meat."

After everyone had eaten and the plates had been stacked in the kitchen for some later cleanup, Rose opened her gifts, gasping and clapping with glee over each onesie, each diapering accessory, each piece of gear intended to make the baby sleep better, or stay safer, or look cuter. Daniel didn't know what he and Lacy had given her, but it rankled him slightly that they'd given a joint gift. Like he was already losing his identity, becoming less *Daniel* and more *Lacy and Daniel*. Not that it was fair for him to be rankled. It wasn't like he'd even mentioned the issue to Lacy. So why was he feeling pissy about it now?

After the gifts, the girls did their party games while the guys hovered around the edges uncomfortably, drinking beer and muttering about the incomprehensibility of women.

One game involved using streamers of toilet paper to estimate Rose's girth. Another required the participants to wear necklaces made of diaper pins while trying to avoid saying the word "baby." And yet another involved the timed diapering of a roughly baby-sized teddy bear.

As Daniel sipped from a longneck bottle and watched, Lacy got on her knees in front of the teddy bear and raced to diaper the thing's butt while the other women cheered her on.

She won by a good five seconds, and received a prize of some bath salts and a scented candle.

"This is so much fun!" Lacy beamed, holding up her treasures so someone could take a photo. "I can't wait to have kids of my own. I want at least six."

Daniel felt like he'd been hit in the head with a hammer.

"You look a little green there, son," Ryan observed.

Daniel looked at the beer in his hand and decided that wasn't going to cut it. He wandered off into the kitchen to see if Ryan had anything stronger.

A little morphine would be soothing.

Chapter Twenty-Four

Daniel did what he often did when a situation in his life was troubling him. He called his mother.

A day or two after the shower, he finished work for the day, cleaned up his studio, took a shower, put on clean jeans and a T-shirt, towel dried his hair, and then settled in on his sofa with a cold beer and his cell phone.

"Hey, Mom. It's me."

"Hi, honey." His mother sounded so happy to hear from him, and he was so comforted by the sound of her voice, that it transported him back to a childhood of road trips, Little League, and grilled cheese sandwiches served with a side of Campbell's tomato soup.

"How are you guys? How's Dad?"

"Oh, you know your father," Irene Reed said, as though that explained everything, as though no other words needed to be said.

They chatted for a little while about his work, and her health—her most recent physical had gone without a hitch—about the house where he'd grown up and where his parents still lived, about Zzyzx, and about Winston the beagle, whom they both were still mourning.

"Now that we've gotten the small talk out of the way," Irene said, "what's wrong?"

Daniel's eyebrows shot up in surprise. "What do you mean, what's wrong?"

"Just what I said, Daniel. I can read you, even over the phone, even from a thousand miles away. I've had more than thirty years of practice. So, get on with it. What's wrong?"

He chuckled and shook his head in wonder. Damned if she couldn't read him. It was comforting to be understood so deeply, but it was also a little unsettling.

"It's nothing. It's just … I've started seeing someone...."

Irene said nothing, which was something of a surprise. He'd have thought news of a romantic involvement would provoke enthusiasm, curiosity—anything other than silence.

He rubbed at the stubble on his chin. "You're not saying anything."

"Well, honey, you need to give me a minute to get over the shock."

He fidgeted in his seat, irritated. "Shock that I'm seeing someone? What's that supposed to mean? I see people."

"Not shock that you're seeing someone. Shock that you're telling me about it. You never tell me about your girlfriends."

He thought about whether that was true. Surely it couldn't be. "I tell you things. I told you about Sharon Murphy."

"No, you didn't. I heard about Sharon Murphy from Sharon's mother."

"You did not."

"Yes, I did. I was in the housewares section at Walmart, and she came up all friendly, asking what I thought of this budding romance between my boy and her daughter. I didn't know a thing about it."

Daniel stared at his beer bottle. "Well … there was Katrina Ames. Now, I know I told you about her, because—"

"You told your father, you didn't tell me," Irene said. "You have never told me about a girl or woman you were dating, Daniel. Not one girl, not one time."

He tried to think of some response, but couldn't. He sank back against his sofa and sighed.

"I figure that has to mean this one's different," Irene continued. "So tell me, honey. What's going on?"

He told her about Lacy, and about his insecurities. He told her about how Lacy's family seemed to assume they were headed toward marriage, except for her mother, who didn't like him much. He told her about his unsettled feelings. He told her about everything except the stupendous sex; he and his mother, like sons and mothers everywhere, had an unspoken pact to pretend that he was celibate, and would be until the day he took his wedding vows.

"It's just all going really fast," he finally admitted. "And I'm not sure I'm ready for that."

Irene took a moment to absorb all that Daniel had told her. Then she said, "Let me tell you about how your father and I met."

"Mom." He rubbed at his forehead. "I know all that. You were in a play together in college. *Death of a Salesman.* He was Willy Loman and you were—jeez, I forget. You were some kind of bar girl or hooker, right?"

"I was Miss Forsythe. In any event, there were some things about our early relationship that I didn't tell you."

He sat up straighter, intrigued and more than a little worried about what childhood illusions his mother was about to shatter. "Like what?"

"Like how long we dated before we got married."

Daniel scratched at the back of his neck, unsettled. "Okay, then. How long?"

"Three months."

"Three ... *What?*"

"That's right. Three months." Irene's voice sounded just a touch smug.

"Well, that's ... jeez. Are you going to tell me you were pregnant? Because I don't really think I wanna—"

"No, Daniel. I wasn't pregnant. I was just in love."

Daniel would never have thought of his mother as an impulsive romantic, someone who would plunge headlong into a lifetime commitment without considering the consequences. Now, he was clearly going to have to reevaluate.

"Why didn't you ever tell me that?" he asked.

She chuckled. "Because I didn't want you to follow my example. I figured that if you ever got involved in a bad relationship, and I wanted to encourage you to slow down and be careful, I wouldn't have a leg to stand on."

He could see her point. "But you're telling me now," he said.

"Well, right now, it seems to me, you need to consider the idea that fast isn't always bad. Sometimes things move fast because they're right. Look at me and your father. Thirty-five years of marriage and I haven't strangled him yet. Though I have my moments."

Daniel grinned. Talking to his mom just made him feel better. It always had.

"What if I'm just not sure where I want things to go?" he said.

"Well." The tone of her *well* suggested that she'd been waiting for him to ask that very question. "That would mean one of three things. One, you really do need more time to figure things out. Two, she's not the right one for you. Or three, she is the right one for you, and you're having trouble opening yourself up to her for your own reasons."

"You think I'm, what, emotionally stunted? Is that what you're saying? Because I—"

"I didn't say that, Daniel."

She hadn't. But still, he wondered if that was what she was getting at. And he wondered whether it was true. After all, how many relationships had he been in since reaching adulthood? Dozens. And how many had progressed beyond casually dating and sleeping together, with each party returning to their own home at the end of the night, or, at the very most, the next morning?

None.

"Honey. You're being awfully quiet. Did I hurt your feelings?" Irene said.

"No, no. I'm just … thinking."

"Daniel. Do you *want* a committed relationship?"

He thought about the question. About his parents, still married after thirty-five years. He thought about the way they finished each other's sentences, the way they just fit together emotionally, like Russian nesting dolls. God, yes, he wanted that.

"Yeah. I do." His throat felt unaccountably thick.

"Well, it's not going to happen if you don't take a risk."

He thought that she likely was right. But on the other hand, the trouble with risk was that it made you think of everything you had to lose.

Like Daniel, Lacy had been talking to her own mother about her relationship issues. The problem was, her relationship with Daniel wasn't the one Nancy was interested in.

Lacy's mother simply would not stop talking about Brandon.

Of course, Nancy was still seeing Brandon for her back problems. Every week after her adjustments, she'd get on the phone to Lacy or cross the yard to the trailer and tell her everything Brandon had said, how he looked, what he was wearing.

Lacy dreaded the conversations, but she didn't see much point in having it out with her mother. What would that accomplish? Nancy would still mourn the loss of Lacy and Brandon's relationship, and Lacy would still not want to marry Brandon. So, in the interest of making her own life easier and avoiding conflict, Lacy just listened to her mother's reports, made appropriate mouth sounds feigning interest, and then got off the phone or out of the room as soon as possible.

This time, though, the conversation took a troubling turn. Instead of simply telling Lacy about what Brandon was doing, Nancy had started talking about the possibility of the two of them getting back together.

"So I told him that there wasn't anything going on between you and Daniel Reed, and that you'd just said that because you were angry," Nancy told Lacy one morning over coffee at the Jordan kitchen table. "He seemed to really be interested in that piece of news. I think he'd take you back. I really do."

Exasperated, Lacy pushed her coffee mug aside. "Mom, there *is* something going on between me and Daniel. You know that."

Nancy waved it off. "Oh, but there wasn't when you were still engaged to Brandon. You didn't *cheat* on him. That's the point. I think now that he understands that you were faithful, there's room to work things out."

"But—"

"I told him you were just hurt and upset about that fight you'd had. That you just said what you did to lash out. I told him you were sorry, and Lacy, you should have seen the look on his face. You're going to get back together, I know you are. I told Josie Smith at the Cookie Crock, and she said—"

"Wait." Lacy held up a hand to stop her mother. "You're telling people at the Cookie Crock that Brandon and I are getting back together?"

"Well," Nancy said, looking defensive, "you will. Just wait."

Lacy got up from her seat at the table, picked up her coffee mug, and carried it to the sink. She poured out the rest of the coffee, rinsed the mug, and placed it on the top rack of the dishwasher. Then, having calmed herself through the rote task, she turned to her mother.

"Mom. Why don't you like Daniel?"

Nancy looked surprised, as though Daniel Reed were entirely beside the point.

"I don't dislike him," she said, which Lacy noted was very different from saying that she did like him. "He's nice enough, I suppose. And it's perfectly understandable that you'd want to seek … I don't know … *comfort* after a breakup. But, honey, it's not too late to fix things with Brandon. I just know—"

"Mom." Lacy tried to interrupt her.

"If you'd only seen how he looked when I told him, you'd know that he misses you, honey. He wants—"

"Mom."

"Why, it's probably not too late to plan a spring wedding, if only—"

"*Mom!*"

Nancy stopped in midsentence, looking surprised to discover that Lacy was yelling at her.

"Well, what is it, Lacy?"

"It's over," Lacy said, exasperated. "Me and Brandon. It's over. We're not getting married. We're not getting back together. I'm with Daniel now."

Nancy pressed her lips together in a stern and unforgiving line. "This is pre-wedding jitters, is what it is. You proved your point bringing Daniel to Thanksgiving, I guess. But now, Lacy, it's time to—"

"I was not proving a point! I'm not playing some kind of *game* with Daniel."

"Well, you can't possibly *love* him," Nancy said.

"Yes, Mom! I do! I love him! I'm in love with Daniel!"

Lacy stood gaping at her mother, shocked by her own words. She hadn't articulated it before now, even to herself.

It was true: She loved Daniel.

"I guess you and Josie Smith are just going to be disappointed," Lacy said, and walked out the back door and across the yard to her trailer.

Chapter Twenty-Five

Lacy needed to get away from her mother. But more than that, she needed to see Daniel. Now that she knew she loved him, she was ready to get down to the business of loving him. And the sooner the better.

She didn't call him, she didn't text to let him know she was on her way. She just left her parents' place, left the trailer, and drove south toward Daniel's house. As she drove down Highway 1, she felt a growing urgency building in her center. She needed to tell him what she felt, what she now knew to be true. She needed to show him.

His SUV was parked in front of his house. She parked beside it, got out of the car, and rushed up onto his front porch, because this couldn't wait. This mattered.

Lacy's heart pounded as she knocked on the front door of Daniel's house. The house was at the end of a winding road, and she had the sensation of herself, the house, and Daniel—wherever he was—being completely alone in the world. At her knock, she heard the sound of Zzyzx whining and scratching at the other side of the door, but she didn't hear Daniel. No footsteps from inside the house, no call in answer to her knock.

Besides the dog, the only sound she heard was the wind whispering through the tall grass that carpeted the rolling hills.

If he wasn't in the house, he had to be in the studio. The outbuilding, about the same size as the house, stood at the end of a twenty-yard path that led from the back door of the little cottage.

She descended the porch steps into the yard, got on the dirt path that led to the studio, and marched forward, her hands in fists at her sides, her heart pounding. She got to the studio, threw open the door, and stepped inside.

Daniel was just finishing the second version of a bowl he'd screwed up the first time because he was too busy thinking about Lacy. The shape was right, the color was right, and he'd stayed pretty much focused long enough to get to the last steps without major incident. He'd detached the piece from the punty, had used a torch to smooth out the bottom of the bowl, and was just putting the thing into the annealer to gradually cool when he became aware that he wasn't alone in the room.

He closed the door of the annealer, took off his safety glasses, turned—and felt his heart stutter when he saw Lacy, gloriously silhouetted in the sunlight pouring through the door.

He said, "Lacy. What—"

That was all he got out before she strode purposefully across the room, threw herself into his arms, and kissed him as though her life, her future, her very soul depended on it.

It was as though the switch that governed his rational thought was turned off with a resounding *click*. The thoughts that had been tormenting him—the ones about the house, and kids, and where this relationship was going—vanished like a forgotten dream. He had no more power to stop her or himself than he had to change the orbit of the earth.

He did have enough presence of mind to shove her away from the hot furnaces and toward a corner of the room where nothing was likely to produce third-degree burns, so he hadn't gone completely stupid. Once the danger of severe injury was averted, though, he gave himself to the moment and they simply consumed each other.

Before he even knew what he was doing, he had wrapped his hands in her hair and was caressing her tongue with his. Was there anything else in the world besides this? Did it even matter if there was? The heat of the studio combined with the heat of Lacy's body to make him feel as though he were melting into a steaming mass of pure pleasure.

She smelled like white jasmine and she tasted like his own hopes and dreams. He wrapped his arms around her and felt her clinging to him.

She didn't say anything—didn't tell him what she felt. Instead, she showed him with her body, her touch, the pure, blazing intensity of her desire.

He didn't question it. He just responded to her in kind, his own passion, his own fire, rising to meet hers.

Her mouth savored his, and her hands were on him everywhere at once. He shoved her backward and onto a big wooden worktable until she was sprawled across it with his body covering hers. A glass bowl that had been sitting on the table fell to the concrete floor with a crash.

She wasn't thinking, couldn't think anything except *Yes* and *More*. She tore at his shirt, pulling it off over his head, then ran her hands over the delicious lines of his torso.

Lacy's button-down shirt was too much of an obstacle, so he tore it off of her, sending buttons flying. He pulled down the cups of her bra to free her breasts, taking one and then the other into his mouth. The feel of his hot tongue on her made her gasp.

Instinctively, she wrapped her legs around him, gripping him to her. He pulled away just long enough to unbutton her jeans and drag them down her body. Her sandals clattered to the floor as he yanked the jeans off of her and threw them aside.

There was no time for him to get fully undressed. No time. He unzipped, freed himself, and plunged into her.

She wrapped herself around him and clung to him as he

thrust into her, his body shimmering with sweat from the heat of the room and from the heat of his desire.

"Oh." She heard the one syllable coming out of her own mouth over and over: "Oh, oh, oh." Because this was something she hadn't known about. This level of pleasure, this height of maddening, impossible arousal. It was discovery and revelation, rising on a crashing wave of urgent need.

He stiffened and shuddered against her with a gasp. And then, while he was still inside her, he brought his fingers down between her thighs to caress her until she spasmed in release.

Afterward, she lay on the table with Daniel bent over her, both of them limp, their breathing ragged.

"Jesus," he rasped out. "I didn't … expect … to see you today." He was still trying to catch his breath.

"Didn't you hear?" She could barely speak, breathless, her body under the weight of his. "It's take … your girlfriend … to work day."

He laughed, and she felt it as a low rumble that traveled from his body to hers.

When he finally got up off of her, he zipped up and raked his hands through his hair. "It was time for a break anyway, but I was just looking forward to a cup of coffee. This was better."

She started to get down off of the table, but he stopped her. "Oh, wait. Whoa. Hang on a minute."

He gestured, and she saw the issue: She was barefoot, and the broken shards of the bowl they'd knocked over littered the floor. He got a broom and swept it up, then handed over her clothes and shoes.

"I'm never gonna look at that table the same way again," he remarked as she began to get dressed. She put on her jeans and her shoes and rearranged her bra, then realized that she couldn't finish dressing because her shirt was in shreds.

"Well, this is a problem." She held up the shirt with its missing buttons and its long tear across the front.

"Ah. Jeez. I'm sorry about that," he said, looking embarrassed.

"Don't be. I can always get another shirt. Believe me, it was worth the twenty dollars." She could feel the wide, silly smile on her face, but couldn't seem to do anything about it.

He picked up his own T-shirt off of the floor and handed it to her, and she put it on. When they were both as reassembled as they could reasonably be—he was still naked from the waist up, a situation she wasn't in any hurry to remedy—he came to her and pulled her into his arms.

"Not that I'm complaining, but what's going on? Is everything okay?" She felt his voice as a low vibration through his chest.

"Yeah. Yeah, I'm fine. Better than fine, especially now. It's just …"

He pulled back a little so he could look into her eyes.

"Just what?"

"I … I was talking to my mother, and I said something to her, and it made me realize … and I had to come out here to tell you. It couldn't wait." Her heart was thumping with the gravity of what she was about to say to him.

"Lacy? You had to tell me what?" His voice was soft, gentle. And sexy as hell.

"I had to tell you … that I love you, Daniel. I do. And it's real, and it's not going to go away. I needed you to know that. I love you."

Daniel froze with the words still in the air between them. He knew what he was supposed to say, but when he opened his mouth to say it, no words came out.

This thing he was feeling, was it love? The sense that he was only half a person when he wasn't with her, was that love? The relief that flooded him when he saw her after they'd been apart, was that what love felt like? And if it was, was he ready to accept that?

"Lacy …" He caressed her shoulders with his hands.

Something happened in her eyes as he watched her, as she realized he wasn't going to say it back. Her look of hope and pleasure turned to hurt. The thought that he'd put that pain in her eyes gut-punched him, but goddamn it, was he supposed to say something he wasn't ready to say?

"Lacy …"

"No, that's fine." She gave him a small, forced smile and pulled out of his arms. "You don't have to say it back. You don't have to say anything."

He could see it, though, could see that it wasn't fine. Disappointment played on her face as she avoided his gaze.

"Well, look," she said. "I should go. I mean, you were working.…" She turned and walked out of the studio and headed toward her car, her arms clutched across her chest, her footsteps determined.

He scrubbed at the back of his neck with his hand. How had something so perfect turned to shit so quickly?

Chapter Twenty-Six

"So he didn't say it back. So what? It's not important. It's stupid to let it bother me." Lacy quickly wiped a tear from her cheek as Gen looked on sympathetically. Lacy had needed someone to talk to, and she couldn't pull together an emergency meeting of her friends on such short notice. So she'd gone to the Porter Gallery, and had, mercifully, found Gen there alone. She'd laid out the sequence of events, starting with her revelation about being in love with Daniel and ending with his panicked look when she'd declared that love.

"Honey, it's not stupid. If it bothers you, it bothers you." Gen rubbed Lacy's shoulder as the two of them sat in big leather office chairs behind Gen's desk.

"I mean, it's reasonable if he doesn't know. We've only been seeing each other for two months." She blew her nose with a tissue from the box on Gen's desk. "Why the hell did I have to say it first? Why did I do that?"

Gen looked wistful. "Ah, the *who says it first* dilemma. I know it well."

"Who said it first between you and Ryan?" Lacy asked.

"I did. I almost said it about five different times before I finally came out with it. He said it back, thank God, or I'd have had to beat him to death with my shoe."

They both looked down at Gen's shoes, which had three-inch heels sharp enough to impale somebody.

"God," Lacy said miserably. "I said it first, and he didn't say it back, even after crazy hot studio sex. Gen, he *threw* me onto the table and he *tore my shirt off.* Can you imagine Brandon doing something like that?"

"He probably would have stopped everything to whip out a little mending kit," Gen mused. "With one of those tomato-shaped pin cushions." Amused by her own observation, Gen chuckled.

"Can we focus?" Lacy said. "I'm having a crisis here."

"All right." Gen looked at Lacy with sympathy. "Look, Lacy. I think it took some serious guts for you to say it first. Telling someone about your feelings for them is never a bad thing. You know how you feel, and now he does, too."

"But what now?" Lacy said. "Now that I've humiliated my-self with my declaration of apparently unrequited love?"

"Let's just put aside the whole idea of humiliation," Gen said. "What do you want to have happen?"

What did she want? She wanted him to love her, and for that to be so obvious to both of them that there would be no question of whether to say it. But if she couldn't have that, then, God help her, she still wanted Daniel. No matter what.

"Honestly?" she said. "I want to turn back the clock and take back what I said. But since I can't do that ... I guess I just have to pretend I didn't say it. Be patient. And hope like hell that he's not too freaked out and we can just ... keep doing what we're doing."

"Including hot studio sex," Gen put in.

"From your lips to God's ears."

"You know," Gen began tentatively, "if he doesn't know how he feels yet, that's okay. It's still pretty early in the rela-tionship."

"I know," Lacy replied, her voice glum.

"But it's possible that he does feel the same as you do, and that he's just too big of a wussy to admit it yet."

Lacy looked at Gen. "You think?"

"Well, he is a man, after all," Gen said. "Wussiness, where

love is concerned, would not be completely out of the question."

That was true. But what kind of wussiness were they talking about, exactly? The kind that made a person cautious? Or the kind that made someone run like hell?

"Ah, Jesus. I'm an idiot. And I'm a total wimp," Daniel moaned to Will as the two of them jogged on the bluff trail at Fiscalini Ranch. It was late afternoon, and the sun, partially hidden behind a layer of fog, was beginning its descent toward the western horizon. A chill nipped the air, but Daniel didn't feel it because he was warm from the run. He was sweating a little, enjoying the exertion. The sound of waves crashing into the bluffs blended with the noise of barking sea lions.

"There she was, all gorgeous and perfect and ... and so *Lacy,*" he went on as they crested a hill. "And this *goddess* tells me she loves me. And what did I do? I froze. I couldn't say it, man. What the hell's wrong with me?"

"Maybe you don't love her," Will suggested, keeping pace beside Daniel, his blond hair damp with perspiration.

"Ah, bullshit," Daniel said.

"So, then you do love her," Will said, not unreasonably.

"Why wouldn't I? I'd have to be an idiot not to love her," Daniel said.

"I notice you dodged the question," Will said.

Yeah, he had. But why?

He stopped on the trail and bent forward, hands on his knees, breathing hard. Then he straightened and ran his hands through hair damp with sweat.

"I have the feelings," he said. "All right? Jesus. Yeah. I have the feelings. So why can't I just say that?"

"Because you're just like Rose," Will said. "Not in every way, obviously. But in terms of behavior in love relationships ...

yes."

"I'm like Rose," he repeated, mulling it over.

"She couldn't admit to having feelings for me because of her previous problems with men." Will squinted, probably because he wasn't wearing his glasses.

"I don't have any previous problems with men," Daniel said.

"Ha. Funny." Will lifted up his left foot to stretch his quadriceps.

"I don't have any previous problems with women, either," Daniel insisted.

"Well ..."

"Well, what?" He turned to face Will, hands on his hips.

"Nothing," Will said. "It's just ... you haven't had a lot of serious relationships, have you?"

Daniel scratched at the back of his neck. "What the hell are you getting at?"

Will shrugged. "Just saying."

Daniel started running again, thinking that would put an end to Will's speculations about him and his love life. Daniel had been the one to bring it up, yeah. But he'd expected the kind of sympathy guys usually gave each other in situations like this. He hadn't expected actual *insight*.

But now that Will had said what he had, now that it was out there, Daniel couldn't help but think about it. *Was* he like Rose? Was he pretending that he didn't feel something he did, just to avoid the uncomfortable implications of loving someone?

And if so, how did he get to be such a coward?

And, most importantly, what should he do now?

"Try flowers," Will suggested, as though reading his mind. "Girls love flowers. And the best part is that you can apologize without saying that you apologize."

"I don't have anything to apologize for," Daniel protested.

"Exactly why you apologize without *saying* you apologize." Will said it as though it were completely obvious, which Daniel supposed it probably was to a guy whose significant other was expecting a baby. Will probably had abundant experience in apologizing for things that he didn't even understand, let alone had actually done.

Daniel grunted in response.

"Cambria Nursery's always good for flowers," Will remarked.

The flowers were delivered to Jitters, probably because the Airstream didn't have its own address. Lacy was prepared to be hard-hearted about it—to scoff at the cliché of sending flowers after hurting a woman's feelings—but then she laughed out loud when she read the card.

Lacy—

Will says I'm being Rose. Don't ask.

—D

"What the hell does that even mean?" Lacy wondered out loud, holding the card in her hands, the scent of a dozen long-stemmed red roses filling her senses.

Coincidentally, the actual Rose just happened to be there getting a half-caff latte when the delivery arrived. She took the card from Lacy's hand and peered at it.

"Ha!" She barked out a laugh. "It's true. He's totally being me."

"How do you figure?" Lacy said.

"He can't admit his feelings. Hell, I wouldn't even admit that Will and I were dating until I was already duplicating his DNA."

Lacy took back the card and slapped it down on the counter. "Huh. Seems like you and Daniel are a perfect match. Maybe you should be the one dating him."

"I would, if my honey bunny wasn't so damned cute," she said cheerfully. She looked down at her vast, round midsection. "And if I wasn't carrying his child."

Lacy finished up Rose's latte and passed it across the counter to her. "Flowers," she mused. "Now I can't even enjoy being mad. Well, not mad, exactly. Irked."

"Must have been Will's idea," Rose said. "I've gotten a lot of flowers since I've been knocked up."

When Rose was gone, Lacy bustled around behind the counter, washing cups and restocking filters and napkins.

The card hadn't said *I love you.* On the other hand, it appeared he wasn't going to run like hell.

That was something, anyway.

Chapter Twenty-Seven

Things between Daniel and Lacy had just gotten back on track, with the turmoil of the "I love you" declaration behind them, when Lacy's mother did something unconscionable.

And then Brandon did the thing *he* did, which made it all so much worse.

It turned out that Nancy hadn't just been talking to people at the Cookie Crock about Lacy and Brandon getting back together. She hadn't just been talking to Brandon about how Lacy had been faithful. She'd also told Brandon—contrary to all fact, and contrary to everything Lacy had said on the matter—that Lacy was willing, nay, *eager*, to reconcile.

And that was what led Brandon to bring Lacy's topaz earrings, which he'd found in his luggage and had been holding onto all along out of spite, to Jitters, presenting them to her with a story about how he'd just discovered them.

Lacy was so happy to see the earrings that she leaped into Brandon's arms during the morning rush at Jitters, when the place was packed with locals filling up on their prework caffeine fixes.

By ten a.m. on the day of the hug, no fewer than four people had told Daniel about the embrace, and about how happy Lacy had looked in her ex-fiancé's arms. Three of those reported hearing from Brandon himself, or from sources close to Brandon, that a reconciliation was imminent.

Five additional people offered Daniel condolences while he was doing errands on Main Street, consoling him by saying that at least he'd had fun while it lasted.

He didn't know what the fuck was going on, but he was pretty sure he was being played somehow, by somebody.

And he knew he didn't want any part of it.

Lacy had just gotten home from work and was putting her grandmother's earrings into her jewelry box, which she then tucked inside her underwear drawer for safekeeping, when her phone buzzed with a text message.

Brandon.

It was so good to see you this morning. Can we maybe have dinner and talk?

Lacy stared at the message. What was this? She sighed, thinking that she shouldn't have hugged him. It was a stupid, impulsive thing to do, but she'd been so happy to get the earrings back that she'd acted before she'd thought.

She tapped in a response to his message:

I don't think that's a good idea.

A moment later, her phone buzzed again:

I don't understand. Your mother said you were ready to try again.

Lacy's eyes widened as she read the message. Surely she was reading it wrong. She called Brandon, and when he answered, she snapped into the phone, "What did you mean about my mother?"

So he told her about the conversation he'd had with Nancy while the woman had been on his table getting her spine realigned. "She said you'd never cheated on me with Daniel Reed. Was she wrong?"

"Well … no, but—"

"And she said that you were sorry for everything that happened. That you regretted breaking up. She said you might even go ahead with the wedding if I were to just talk to you and smooth things over."

Lacy was so outraged that she could only sputter.

"She … I …"

"So it's not true?"

Lacy almost felt sorry for Brandon, he sounded so crest-fallen.

"No, Brandon, it's not true. I wasn't with Daniel while you and I were together, but I am now. My mother misled you. I'm sorry."

"But, Lacy. I just know that if you and I could—"

"Brandon? I have to go." She hung up on him while he was still talking.

And then she charged out of the trailer, down the stairs, across the lawn, and into her mother's kitchen.

She found Nancy sitting at the kitchen table with a cup of tea and a book.

"Mom? What did you do?" Lacy demanded.

"Why, Lacy. What in the world …?"

"I just talked to Brandon. What. Did. You. Do?"

Nancy had always gotten along well with her daughters, particularly Lacy, who had been a happy, parent-pleasing, good-natured child. So now, the pure fury in Lacy's face and in her voice caused Nancy to lean back in her chair, squinting like a newborn kitten still trying to acclimate to the world.

"Well, I … Lacy, I didn't *do* anything."

"Did you tell him I wanted to get back together? Did you tell him that I wanted to go ahead with the wedding? The wedding I canceled for many, many good reasons, not the least of which is that I'm in love with another man?"

Nancy, who normally wouldn't tolerate one of her children raising their voice to her, now just appeared flustered and defensive. "Well, I might have said it was *possible*. But only because it seems to me that it is! You've taught him a lesson by breaking up, by going out with Daniel Reed right under his nose. But now he's learned the lesson, Lacy! He's not going to take you for granted anymore! Don't you see, he's ready now!"

"But I'm not! And I never will be! Not for him! Because I love Daniel, Mom, and I don't love Brandon!"

Nancy pressed her lips into a taut line and shook her head sadly. "Oh, Lacy."

"What, Mom?" Lacy demanded. " 'Oh, Lacy' what?"

Nancy set aside the book that had been in her hand, seeming to remember for the first time that she was holding it. "Honey, you might think you're in love with this Daniel Reed. But you can't be. A person doesn't break up with their fiancé and … and just immediately fall into true love with someone else!"

"Except that I did," Lacy said, more quietly now.

"Oh, honey. I know it seems that way right now, but it's like I was telling Ellie MacKay at the Joslyn Center, I don't think you—"

"You talked about this to Ellie MacKay. And Brandon. And to Josie Smith at the Cookie Crock," Lacy said, by way of recap. "Did you tell *all* of them that Brandon and I are getting back together?"

"Well, it wasn't like I told people it was a sure thing," Nancy said, a whine in her voice. "It was more like a prediction."

"A prediction," Lacy said.

"Yes! And I still think I'm right!" Nancy insisted.

Lacy walked out of the kitchen with Nancy still calling after her.

"Did you know that Mom was telling everybody in town that Brandon and I are getting back together?" Lacy asked Whitney over the phone about twenty minutes later, after she'd had time to calm down.

"Well … yeah. I told her you were going to be mad."

"Damned right I'm mad!" Lacy bellowed. She could imagine Whitney holding the phone away from her ear to avoid auditory damage.

"Look, Lacy," Whitney said, trying to placate her. "You know Mom means well. She thinks Brandon is your key to happiness. A nice house. Kids. A retirement plan. All that."

Lacy rubbed her eyes with one hand. "Okay, yeah. I know that. But while I was enjoying the house and the kids and the retirement plan, I'd have to be married to Brandon."

Whitney let out a very un-Whitneylike guffaw. "Fair point," she said. "So, are you going to forgive Mom?"

Lacy sighed. "Of course. Eventually. But not today."

"All right, well, in the meantime, try to calm down, and tell that delicious Daniel hello from me."

Lacy didn't know how she felt about the lecherous tone in Whitney's voice.

"Get your own man," she said.

Even if Lacy had wanted to tell the delicious Daniel hello from Whitney, she wouldn't have been able to.

Daniel wasn't taking her calls.

He scowled at his phone as it rang, Lacy's name on the screen, and shoved it back into his pocket.

He just couldn't deal with this right now. Maybe ever.

Daniel had tried to work earlier in the day, but in his current state of mind, it would be hazardous to get too close to the roaring flames of his furnaces. So instead, he'd put Zzyzx in the car and had driven out to Leffingwell Landing, where he sat at a picnic table and looked out at Moonstone Beach as Z ran around in dog heaven, peeing on things and sniffing the poop of the bunnies and squirrels who had gone before.

The idea of Lacy getting back together with Brandon infected him like an illness. It wasn't the jealousy. At least, it wasn't entirely that. It was the idea that he'd been a fool. What had made him think that this thing with Lacy was anything more than a rebound fling, a way for her to show Brandon what he was missing? Had she been using Daniel for that purpose? Even if she hadn't, if what she'd felt for him was real, then it was still unlikely that things between them would ever work. After all, just months ago, she'd been ready to pledge her lifelong devotion to another man.

And anyway, what she wanted out of life—marriage, a house, multiple kids—was something Brandon was more ideally suited to give her than Daniel was. Brandon had a six-figure job, probably a goddamned investment portfolio and a pension. Daniel had the uncertainty of a career as an artist: a heady and dangerous mix of occasional financial bounty followed by long stretches in which he was spinning his metaphorical wheels, eating up his earlier profits and wondering if the last big sale, would, indeed, be his last big sale.

How the hell was he supposed to provide what Lacy wanted? While it was true that she was one of the least materialistic women he'd ever met, happy for the moment with little but an Airstream trailer and so few belongings she could fit them into one suitcase, it was also true that she eventually wanted multiple kids, and multiple kids had to live somewhere. They weren't going to fit in Daniel's small house, and they sure as hell weren't going to fit in Lacy's trailer.

Multiple kids needed clothes and food and health insurance; they needed braces and college educations. Daniel's bank account was flush now because of the Eden job, but he couldn't count on such a state of affairs continuing. His unstable income was fine for just him; he'd never had a problem with scaling back on his expenses as needed. He didn't require a hell of a lot.

But multiple kids would, collectively, be a money-burning machine, and he wasn't sure he could keep such a machine running.

But Brandon could.

Hell, if he were Lacy, he'd probably choose Brandon. If you could ignore the fact that that the guy was an insufferable shitbag, he was practically perfect.

She should have told Daniel, though. If she was dumping him and going back to the insufferable shitbag, she should have just said so.

Zzyzx caught sight of a squirrel that was munching on some kind of greenery about ten feet away from the picnic table where Daniel sat. Daniel would have expected the dog to go off in hot, barking pursuit, but instead Z sat down on his haunches and let out a quiet and tentative *woof.*

Daniel understood the feeling of having something right in front of you and not knowing what the hell to do with it.

"You're a wuss, too," Daniel told the dog. "Ah, come here."

He patted his lap, and Z obligingly jumped up onto him. Daniel held the dog and rubbed him behind his oddly shaped, fuzzy ears as they both felt the ocean breeze and watched the white surf.

It was good to have somebody who understood you, who was there to comfort you when you needed it.

Though Daniel suspected that Z would throw him over for Lacy in a hot minute, given the chance.

"*Et tu,* Z," he said, rubbing the dog's ears. "*Et tu.*"

Chapter Twenty-Eight

"He's ghosting me. I'm being ghosted."

Lacy and Kate were working out side by side on stair climbers at the gym. At seven a.m., before the beginning of the work day, the place was moderately busy with people of various sizes, ages, and descriptions plodding along on the treadmills or toiling away at the elliptical machines. Wall-mounted TVs showed a variety of offerings ranging from CNN to ESPN to the morning talk shows. In the background, the sound system played Justin Timberlake's "Can't Stop the Feeling" at a volume that was barely audible above the whirring of the fitness machines.

"He can't be ghosting you," Kate said. A fine sheen of sweat shimmered across her skin, and she wiped at her face with a small white towel.

"I've left four phone messages and sent five texts over the last two days," Lacy said. "He's definitely ghosting me. Who does that? We're adults. We're not in middle school, for God's sake."

"Huh," Kate said. Having finished her warm-up, she shifted her stair climber to a higher setting. "Well, if your mother told Brandon you wanted to get back together, she probably told other people the same thing."

"I know! She pretty much admitted it!" Lacy gestured with her hands so emphatically that she almost lost her balance on the machine.

"Plus, there was the hug."

"God, the hug." Lacy shook her head in disgust.

"I'm sure at least half the people in Jitters that day spread the word about the hug to Daniel. So now, he's got rumors of you desperate to reunite with Brandon, and he's got eyewitness accounts of you pretty much leaping into Brandon's arms."

Lacy felt almost sick with guilt, but what did she have to feel guilty about? She hadn't done anything wrong. And she could *tell* Daniel that she hadn't done anything wrong, if only he would pick up the goddamned phone.

"He's being an idiot," she grumbled. "Why can't he just ask me? Why does he have to … to ignore me like some offended teenager? Why can't we talk like human beings?"

As her indignation rose, so did her level of exertion on the stair climber. She began to breathe heavily, and sweat dripped into her eyes. She took a long drink from her water bottle without breaking stride.

"Why, indeed," Kate said.

"And this is after the hot studio sex!" Lacy said. "Who ghosts somebody after hot studio sex?"

"You could always go to his place," Kate suggested. "Talk to him face to face."

Lacy had been thinking the same thing for the past two days. But she hadn't done it, and wasn't going to do it, because she shouldn't have to. She shouldn't have to defend herself for something she didn't do.

"Screw that," Lacy said, summing up her feelings with eloquence.

"Well, okay," Kate said.

Lacy climbed stair after stair to nowhere, and the more she thought about what was going on with Daniel, the more she felt a deep despair welling up in the center of her chest. She brought the machine to a stop, and tears blurred her vision.

"Is this it? Is this really it? I thought …"

"What, honey?" Kate brought her own machine to a stop

and stepped off so she could stand next to Lacy. She put a hand on Lacy's arm and looked up into a face clouded with despair.

"I love him. And I thought maybe … I thought he loved me. Even though he wouldn't say it." Lacy dabbed at her eyes with her towel.

"Oh, sweetie." Kate rubbed Lacy's arm. "Men are assholes. Some are assholes all of the time, and some are assholes part of the time. But men who are never assholes are like unicorns or Santa Claus. They don't exist."

Lacy smirked and shrugged one shoulder. "I guess."

"But it seems like Daniel's asshole quotient is pretty low overall," Kate went on.

That was true enough. But if he didn't trust her enough to dismiss rumors for what they were—just small-town gossip— then he had just enough asshole in him that she thought it might be a deal breaker.

"She's not going back to him, you know. She hugged him because he gave her back some earrings that had a lot of sentimental value, that she thought she'd lost. And the rest of it? The talk that she wants him back? Her mother spread that around. Lacy had nothing to do with it."

Gen was standing in the front room of the Porter Gallery, her hands on her hips, confronting Daniel about his standoff with Lacy. Daniel had just come to drop off some glass pieces to be shown at the gallery. He'd neither expected nor wanted an intervention regarding his love life.

He hadn't even had a chance to put down the box he was holding before Gen started in on him. Her stern, form-fitting black dress and her wild red hair, along with the scowl on her face, made him feel like he was being reprimanded by the headmistress at a boarding school run by really hot nuns.

"I don't even know what you're talking about," he lied. "Can I just put this down? It's damned heavy."

"Fine," she said, somewhat grudgingly.

He put the box down, thinking that he should have just stayed home. But it wasn't like he could avoid Lacy and her friends forever. Cambria wasn't big enough.

His defensiveness over her tone and the way she was confronting him had blocked out the content of what she'd said. Now, without the burden of the box, and having had a moment for things to sink in, it started to hit him.

"Wait. What? Her mother did what?"

Gen sighed, her patience wearing thin.

"Lacy's mother had a hard time with the engagement being canceled. She had some idea in her head that Lacy and Brandon would work things out and get back together. So, she started spreading rumors that they *were* getting back together. Either because it was a ploy to somehow make it happen, or because she really believed it. I'm not sure which."

"Ah … okay." He rubbed the back of his neck with his hand. "But then, why's she throwing herself at him at Jitters, if it was all her mother's deal?"

Gen rolled her eyes, still standing in her confrontational, avenging Sister Mary pose.

"I told you. Lacy had lost some earrings that belonged to her grandmother. She was upset about it, because they meant a lot to her. Brandon found them and gave them back. She threw herself at him because she was happy about the earrings. That's it."

He was still having a hard time making sense of everything. But he did seem to remember something about some earrings, and Lacy being sad about them.

All of that made him start to feel like maybe he'd gotten

everything horribly wrong. That and the Sister Mary thing made him defensive.

"Well ... why the hell didn't she tell me all of that?"

"Because you wouldn't answer your phone, you idiot! And you wouldn't answer her texts! What was she supposed to do, send a message by carrier pigeon?!" She reached out and smacked him on the arm, hard.

"Hey!" He rubbed his arm, not because it hurt, but because it was easier to play the victim if she thought it did.

"She's really hurt, you know," Gen said.

Daniel tried to recalibrate his thoughts, given the new information. It made sense that Nancy would be working behind the scenes to get Lacy and Brandon back together, given her coldness toward Daniel at Thanksgiving. And the earring thing was plausible, too, he guessed.

But he'd picked up so much forward momentum in his conviction that Lacy had thrown him over that it was hard to slow down the speeding train of his indignation and bring the thing to a stop.

"But ... she could have come to the house to see me. She could have—"

"Why should she have to?" Gen had stopped yelling at him, and her tone was calmer now. More reasonable. Which made him feel even more like an idiot. "Why should she have to chase you down and beg you to give her the benefit of the doubt? I get you being upset, Daniel, but didn't she at least deserve a conversation?"

"Yeah." He couldn't quite meet Gen's gaze. "Jesus. Yeah."

The idea that he'd made a terrible mistake settled into his gut like a stomach virus. He felt relief that maybe Lacy hadn't chosen someone else over him, but beneath that was shame at how he'd treated her, and something else he couldn't quite name.

Or maybe he just didn't want to name it, because if he had, its name would have been Fear. And that would have been less than flattering to Daniel's manly self-image.

"Look … just … ease up, would you?" he said. "I'll talk to her."

"You need to do more than talk to her," Gen said, her eyes hard and accusing. "You need to decide how you feel about her. Because she loves you. She's in it. And if you're not, then it's better that she knows that now."

Gen turned to the box Daniel had brought in. "Now, what did you bring me?"

Daniel hadn't gone into Jitters for his coffee for days, because he was avoiding Lacy. Instead, he'd been making it himself at home, or going into the Redwood Café for his caffeine fix.

So when he finally bolstered his courage and walked through the doors into Jitters, it was with some trepidation that Lacy might serve him his hot coffee by pouring it down his pants.

As he walked in, the bells above the front door jingled. Lacy, who was standing behind the counter, turned to see who had entered, a professional, pleasant expression on her face. When she saw who it was, she froze, and the smile dissolved.

"Hey," he said. He gave her a tentative little wave with his fingers.

"Oh," she said, as though his arrival had somehow answered a question for her.

"Listen." He stepped up to the counter and lowered his voice. "Could we maybe talk?"

"I'm working." To demonstrate, she picked up an empty stainless steel milk pitcher and began to wash it in the sink. She looked so tense that if the pitcher had been ceramic or glass, it probably would have shattered in her hands.

"Lacy—"

"Do you want to order something? If not, then you should probably leave, because the table space is for customers only."

It hurt to be treated this way by her, especially when the memory of their last encounter, when she'd given herself to him with all of the lust and intensity of his secret fantasies, was so fresh that he could still smell her skin. But he figured he deserved it. He just had to ride it out until her anger started to wane, and then they could talk. And once they were talking, he was sure they would be able to work this thing out.

"Ah … yeah." He rubbed the stubble on his chin. "Give me a large coffee."

"That's it? That's all you're going to order?" Lacy scowled. "We've got a business to run here, and I don't know what you think we're going to do with a dollar seventy-five."

Okay, so that was how this was going to go. He let out a sigh.

"Fine. Give me a café mocha. And one of those cinnamon roll kind of deals over there." He pointed to an item in the bakery case. "And … a blueberry muffin."

"God, Daniel. You don't even eat pastries. Now you're just humoring me."

She was glaring at him as though she wanted to rip his face off and wear it as a hat.

Maybe this was going to be harder than he thought.

"Just the mocha, then."

She rang up the purchase, took his money by snatching it out of his hand, and slapped his change down on the counter before turning crisply to make his drink. He hoped she didn't have any rat poison back there that she could slip in instead of sweetener.

There was only one other person in the coffeehouse—a middle-aged guy who'd settled in at a table with his coffee and a crossword puzzle—so Daniel figured he could try talking to her here and now, if she wouldn't let him do it any other way.

She was busy making his drink, so he used the opportunity to lean across the counter and plead his case while she worked.

"Look. All I knew was that you'd been hugging that guy. And people kept coming up to me and telling me they were sorry about our breakup. That you were going to marry him after all. What the hell was I supposed to think?"

"You were supposed to take my phone calls, so I could explain it!" she hissed at him as she steamed his milk.

"Fair enough. I was hurt, so I acted like an ass. I get that. And I'm sorry."

She poured his steamed milk into the cup, finished the drink, slapped a lid on it, and plunked it on the counter.

Daniel lifted the lid and peered inside.

"Where's my whipped cream?"

"You can shove your whipped cream up your ass."

So, no whipped cream, then.

"Lacy. It was just a misunderstanding. People have misunderstandings. I said I'm sorry, and I really am. Can't we just move past this?"

She propped a hand on her hip and blew a stray lock of hair out of her face. "No, I don't think we can."

"Why not?"

"Because you didn't trust me." Her face started to redden, and he was horrified to see tears welling up in her eyes. "When people started saying things, you didn't give me the benefit of the doubt. You just believed the rumors. And then you didn't even respect me enough to talk to me about it."

A fat tear fell from her eye and down her cheek, and she

wiped it away with the heel of her hand.

"I can't have a relationship with someone who can just … just write me off that easily."

She went to the bakery case and grabbed the blueberry muffin he'd initially ordered.

"Take the muffin. On the house."

And she wound up like a Major League pitcher and threw it at him with all of the force her girly arm could muster.

The muffin hit him in the center of the chest and exploded into a mess of blueberry-scented crumbs.

The guy with the crossword puzzle looked up, raised his eyebrows questioningly, then looked back down at his puzzle.

Chapter Twenty-Nine

Daniel tried to look on the bright side and just get on with things. The bright side being that now his life, with its quiet, its routine, its order, would continue uninterrupted. He wouldn't have to worry about what his relationship with Lacy, with her desire for six children, would bring. He didn't have to feel threatened by every asshole who leered at her or flirted with her, or hugged her at Jitters. He didn't have to think about things like adding a second story onto his house.

But he also wouldn't get to laugh with her, or walk Zzyzx with her, or do any of the other little things he did with her that seemed impossibly perfect—like small glimpses of some better, shining world—now that he would never do them again.

He wouldn't get to make love to her on the table in his studio again, wouldn't touch her skin, wouldn't taste the delicious hollow of her throat.

There was no bright side here, no matter how hard he tried to find one.

So, he tried to just get on with his days.

He worked. He watched football on TV. He let Zzyzx sleep on the bed with him, so he wouldn't feel so alone.

He avoided Vince Jordan, leaving the house renovation plans up in the air. He didn't think he could face Lacy's father, and even if he could, there was always the chance that he would run into Lacy if he tried to talk to the man.

When they were in public, she'd thrown a muffin at him. What might she throw at him, or even bludgeon him with, on her own home territory?

"It's good to be single guys," he told Zzyzx one night as

they were settling in on the couch to watch some TV. Daniel had a bottle of beer on the table beside him, and Z had a chew toy between his paws. They had everything they needed.

Z looked up at him and whined.

"Yeah, I know it's bullshit. But I'm trying here," he told the dog.

He took a long pull from the bottle and flipped the channels, hoping to find something that could distract him from the growing ache in his chest.

He'd had a good thing—possibly the very best thing—and he'd blown it.

"I'm an idiot," he told Zzyzx.

The dog didn't argue.

Lacy didn't want to talk about it.

Her friends had heard about the muffin-throwing incident—apparently it was possible for gossip to spread even when the only witness was one man with a crossword puzzle—and had approached her with concern.

She brushed them off, insisting she was fine. She'd had breakups before, and she'd survived them. Of course, she would survive this.

It didn't matter, she said. Daniel was just her rebound man, anyway.

Of course, it was all a steaming pile of horseshit. Even she didn't believe what she was telling them.

Normally, she would deal with any disappointment in her life by hashing it out with her friends, but this particular disappointment was so real, so raw, so immense in its awfulness that the only thing to do was to deny its existence.

Not that this approach was helping.

She went to work every day, and then she went home.

Christmas came and went, without the joy it usually brought her. She buried herself in her romance novels, because the books had the happy endings, the fulfillment of true love, that she apparently wasn't going to get for herself.

At least, not this time.

The trouble was, she had the nagging suspicion that this time was going to be the only time that mattered.

Because of the Titanic-like disaster that was her love life, Lacy was no longer speaking to her mother—at least, not in any substantial way. They still exchanged pleasantries, still said good night and good morning, hello and goodbye. But Lacy said the minimum she could without being blatantly rude, and then retreated into her trailer or into a room where Nancy wasn't.

If Nancy had just refrained from meddling, if she had just kept her opinions and her comments out of Lacy's business, none of this would have happened. Of course, Nancy's interference hadn't caused the issue of Daniel not trusting her, of him shutting her out as soon as her true feelings for him had come into question. Nancy had only exposed those issues. And if she hadn't done it, someone else—or something else—would have.

Still, it hadn't been someone or something else. It had been Nancy.

And Lacy could barely look at her.

It had been a week of Lacy holing up in her Airstream, avoiding the family home, when Jess came over one day and knocked on the Airstream door, tentatively poking her head in when she found it unlocked.

"Lacy?" Jess seemed reluctant to come in, as though Lacy might bite her head off if she attempted to enter. Which she might have done, had it been Nancy.

Lacy was lying on her bed reading a novel about a medieval

knight and a hot maiden he'd accidentally married through a case of mistaken identity. She'd been reading so long that when she looked up at Jess, it took a moment for her to readjust her reality.

"Oh. Hey," Lacy said in listless greeting.

"Are you okay?" Jess asked. "Mom says you haven't been to the house in a while."

"Yeah, well." Lacy marked her place and put down the book. "That's because I don't really want to talk to her."

Jess scowled at her. "Well, you have to forgive her. She's our mom."

Lacy sat up on her bed, glowering at Jess. "I know she's our mom. And I love her, and I will forgive her. I'm just not ready yet."

Jess sighed and sat down on the bed next to Lacy. "That's fair enough, I guess."

Jess patted Lacy's knee in a very motherly, Jess-like fashion. "You know, while you're thinking about forgiving people, you could forgive Daniel."

Lacy looked at Jess curiously. "I thought everybody wanted me to marry Brandon."

Jess made a scoffing sound. "Not everybody. I've always thought he was kind of an ass."

"Why didn't you say anything?"

"What was I supposed to say?" Jess got up from the bed and started to pace the tiny trailer. "I thought you were in love. You don't tell somebody that the person they're in love with is an ass. What if he'd become my brother-in-law? Then that's always there between us, that you love him and I think he's an ass."

"Well, okay," Lacy said.

"I don't think Daniel's an ass," Jess added. "I think he's a

guy who acted like an ass once. But I think he can get over that."
She grinned slightly. "I don't think it's a curable condition for
Brandon."

Of course, the idea of simply forgiving Daniel wasn't entirely new to Lacy. She was tempted every minute of every day to
just go over to his place and tell him she was over it, and she had
to constantly remind herself to be strong. Because forgiving him
wouldn't change the fact that the first moment something had
gone wrong between them, he'd shut her out.

It wouldn't change his awkward silence when she'd said she
loved him.

"Tell Mom I'm okay," Lacy said.

"You could tell her yourself."

"Not yet."

When Jess left, Lacy went back to her book. Fictional love
was better than no love at all.

Chapter Thirty

I t was one thing when Lacy told her friends she didn't want to talk about Daniel. But when she stopped spending time with them, opting instead to hide inside her trailer like a woodland animal barricading itself in a burrow whenever she wasn't at Jitters, they decided they had to do something.

More specifically, Rose decided *she* had to do something.

If she'd called Lacy and said, *I want you to come to my house so I can force you to talk to Daniel,* Lacy would have balked. So instead, she told Lacy that she needed help painting the baby's room.

Lacy resisted, claiming first that she was too busy, then that she had to work. Finally, she admitted that she was just too damned sad to leave the trailer. Rose, who was committed to her plan, put as much stress into her voice as she could muster, complaining that Will was sick, and the baby was going to come any day, and she had nothing ready. What was she supposed to do? Did Lacy want her to do it all herself? Was she expected to get on a ladder in her compromised state, possibly falling off and risking the lives of both the baby and herself? Was that what Lacy wanted?

At last, Lacy had agreed to drag herself out of the Airstream and come to Rose's house.

What she didn't know was that the nursery was already painted, and had been for more than a week. She also didn't know that Will had called Daniel with pretty much the same story, minus the bit about falling off a ladder.

And that was how it came to pass that Lacy walked in the front door of Rose's house at ten a.m. on a Tuesday to find Rose with a smug look on her face, and Daniel just looking confused.

❖

"What's going on?" Lacy looked at Rose accusingly, and then at Daniel. He was standing there looking awkward as hell, his hands stuffed into the pockets of his jeans, carefully avoiding eye contact.

"What's going on is I lied to you to get you here so you could work things out. Deal with it," Rose said.

"Ah, jeez," Daniel groaned.

Lacy turned and started to walk toward the door, but Rose, moving faster than one would expect given her girth, blocked the door with her body.

"You're not going anywhere, so you might as well sit down," she said.

"I don't want to sit down." Lacy sounded, even to herself, like a petulant child refusing to clean her room. She turned to Daniel. "Was this your idea?"

He raised his hands in helpless surrender. "I had nothing to do with it. I thought I was here to help paint." He rubbed the back of his neck. "Though, now that we're here, I wouldn't mind talking."

"There you go," Rose said encouragingly.

"This is pointless," Lacy said, crossing her arms over her chest and glaring at Rose.

"Well, that might be. But you're at least going to try to sort things out." Rose sounded surprisingly cheerful, though she looked tired, as though she hadn't slept well. "I've got pizza, wine, and premium ice cream. You're welcome to any and all of it, as long as you talk to each other."

"It's ten in the morning," Daniel pointed out.

"So what? That's never stopped me," Rose said.

Daniel, apparently clinging to the fiction under which he'd been brought there, said, "Where the hell is Will?"

"He's teaching a class," Rose said.

"That son of a bitch lied to me," Daniel grumbled.

"Yeah, but it was for a good cause," Rose replied.

Rose told them she was going to her room so they could have some privacy to talk about whatever needed to be talked about. She acknowledged that there would be nothing to keep them from leaving, but she let it be known that anyone who was too pigheaded to at least try to work things out would be permanently stained by shame and disgrace.

"Well, I don't want to be stained by shame and disgrace," Daniel said when Rose was gone. "You want the pizza or the ice cream?"

Lacy glared at him. "What kind of ice cream?"

Daniel went into the kitchen and peeked into the freezer. "Chunky Monkey."

Lacy rolled her eyes. Rose was playing dirty.

"Hand it over," Lacy said.

Daniel brought her the carton and a spoon.

Lacy took the lid off the carton and took a spoonful of ice cream, partly because she couldn't resist Chunky Monkey—as Rose well knew—and partly because it allowed her to avoid looking at Daniel.

Daniel took a slice of pizza from a box on the kitchen counter, wondering aloud where she'd managed to get pizza at this time of the morning. He put the slice on a plate that Rose had left beside the box.

"Look," he said. "Rose went to a lot of trouble here. We might as well … you know." He gestured toward the kitchen table, and Lacy reluctantly sat down.

Lacy was aware that she might be overreacting, given the relative magnitude of Daniel's offense. He hadn't cheated on her. He hadn't emotionally abused her. He wasn't hiding a secret drug addiction, nor had he turned out to be into deal-breaking kinky sex practices.

He just hadn't trusted her, and he hadn't said he loved her.

It was possible that her stubborn refusal to forgive him was more about her being hurt than it was about any flaw in Daniel so big that it would make any ongoing relationship impossible.

Still, he'd hurt her feelings, and she wasn't quite ready to stop being mad about it.

"I miss you," he said, as a way of kicking things off. "Zzyzx misses you. He keeps whining and standing at the front door, like he's waiting for you. He carries your sweatshirt around. It's kinda pathetic, actually."

"You don't get to do that," Lacy said, pointing her ice cream spoon at him accusingly.

"Do what?"

"You don't get to use the dog to make me feel bad. It's … it's underhanded."

"Fine." He shoved his plate aside and leaned his elbows on the table. "I miss you. Lacy, if we could just—"

"You didn't trust me."

"Well, but—"

"The first time someone spread a rumor around town that I was seeing somebody else, you just … you just *believed* it. That hurt, Daniel." She stabbed her spoon into the ice cream and took another angry bite, as though she were somehow trying to kill the ice cream rather than eat it.

"I know, but I—"

"And then, you refused to even *talk* to me. You wouldn't even take my *calls*. Do you know how that felt? To think that I could just be dismissed like I didn't even matter?" She felt the hot pressure of tears building in her eyes, and she squeezed them shut to clear it away.

"You matter," he said under his breath, looking at the table-top rather than at her.

"What?"

"I said, you matter." His voice was louder, clearer this time. He raised his gaze to meet hers. "You matter a lot. It's just …"

"It's just what? What, Daniel?"

He took a deep breath and straightened in his chair. "I don't think I ever really believed that you could go for a guy like me. And then when people started talking about you and Brandon … Well. It seemed like I'd been right."

Lacy gaped at him in disbelief.

"What do you mean, a guy like you? What does that even mean?"

He shrugged. "Just ask your mom. I don't have a steady job. My income is inconsistent. I don't have a pension, I don't have paid vacation. I don't have a damned 401K …"

"Those are my mother's priorities! They aren't mine!"

"And," he continued, "I'm not some hot *GQ* model, some guy who looks like a movie star.…"

Neither was Brandon, so she wasn't sure what the hell he was even talking about.

And then, suddenly, she *did* know what he was talking about, and it made her so angry she wanted to stab him with the handle of her spoon.

"This is about *looks*?" She stared at him in disbelief.

"Wait, Lacy, I—"

"You believe that because I look the way I look, it must mean that I'm so shallow, so vapid, that I couldn't possibly have feelings for you unless you look like *Brad fucking Pitt*?"

"Now, wait, Lacy, I never said—"

"You know what?" Lacy stood up, the ice cream carton in one hand and the spoon in the other, holding them at the ready, as though she were going to repeat the muffin incident and hurl one or both of them at his goddamned face. "I have fucking *had* it with people who judge me by how I look. I have a pretty face and a body that's maybe above average, so I've got to be stupid, I've got to be shallow, I've got to be an *object,* right, Daniel? If that's what you think, then you're no better than that guy in the bar at Eden who tried to haul me off with him like I wasn't even a *person*!"

She slammed the ice cream carton and the spoon onto the table and turned toward the door.

"Where are you going?" he said.

"I'm done here."

"No, you're not. We're not done. Lacy, just let me—"

"Guys?"

Rose was standing in the bedroom door, looking pale.

"You tried, Rose, but I'm done," Lacy said. "I'm leaving."

"Uh, okay," Rose said, her voice weak and tremulous. "But … if you're going, could you maybe take me to the hospital?"

They both turned to look at Rose, who was holding her massive belly, her face lined with pain.

Chapter Thirty-One

At first, Daniel thought it had to be a joke. This was Rose, after all. And everybody knew that it was only in sitcoms and soap operas that women went into labor at exactly the most awkward time. In real life, things were much more uneventful.

At least, he assumed they were. Not that he'd had much experience with laboring women.

"Oh, my God," Lacy said, crossing over to where Rose stood. "Are you okay? What's happening? Is it the baby?"

"Either that or my uterus is trying to come out through my nose," Rose said. "Given the choice, I'm rooting for the baby."

At that moment, Rose doubled over and groaned. "Ahh, jeez," she moaned, nearly sinking to the floor as Lacy held on to her to give her support. " 'Have a baby,' people said. 'It'll be fun,' they said." Rose's voice was weak and trembly.

The nearest hospital was half an hour away, in Templeton. That was if there wasn't any traffic, or anything obstructing the road.

"But there's time, right?" Daniel said hopefully. "I mean, usually people are in labor for a really long time before …"

"Well, I kind of think maybe I've been in labor since last night," Rose said.

"What?!" Lacy demanded. "And Will went to work anyway?!"

"Well, he didn't know. I didn't tell him. I didn't—" Rose's words broke off as she doubled over again, grasping her giant midsection and letting out a low, animal moan.

"Oh, God. Oh, God," Lacy said. "All right. Come on. We'll

take my car."

Daniel, being the man in the group, felt like he had to do something concretely helpful, so he said to Lacy, "No, I'll drive. She's going to need you to ride in the back seat with her, so you can … I don't know. Hold her hand, or give her something to bite down on, or whatever people do when somebody's in a lot of pain."

"Aaaaaahhhhhh!" Rose yelled.

"Okay, fine, you drive." Lacy looked panicked. "Let's just go!"

They rushed around, grabbing Rose's purse, and Lacy's purse, and everybody's cell phones.

"I need to call Will!" Rose said.

"We'll call him from the car," Daniel said. "Let's go, let's go!"

They all piled into Daniel's SUV, with Rose and Lacy in the back. Lacy called Will on her cell phone, and Daniel screeched out onto the road, headed toward the hospital in Templeton.

Will said he would leave work immediately. He was actually closer to the hospital than they were, so it was likely he would already be there when they arrived.

With that taken care of, Lacy called the hospital and Rose's OB-GYN to let them know the situation. Contractions less than a minute apart, the patient thirty minutes out.

By the time Lacy got off the phone, it seemed to Daniel that the contractions were MUCH less than a minute apart, based on the truly alarming noises Rose was making.

"How the hell did you not know you were in labor?" Daniel demanded.

"I … oh, God. My back hurt … and I … I didn't think … It wasn't until this morning that I … OH JESUS GOD THAT HURTS. AAAAHHHHHH!!!!!"

"Jeez, Daniel, could you go a little faster? Maybe not drive like my grandmother?" Lacy said.

Daniel had his foot on the gas, and the speedometer was inching up toward eighty.

"I could, but if we crash, we're gonna have a bigger problem than Rose being in labor," he said.

They hit Highway 46 and headed east, Daniel praying to God that there wouldn't be any traffic, a deer in the road, an overturned big rig, or fallen trees to hinder their progress.

"So. Did you … oh, God. Did … you two … work things out?" Rose grunted out.

"Daniel thinks I'm a shallow, vapid, narcissistic pretty girl, he doesn't trust me, and he's too big a coward to admit his true feelings for me, so no," Lacy remarked.

"That's not what I said," Daniel insisted, keeping his eyes on the road.

"You might as well have," Lacy said.

"You're twisting my words," Daniel shot back. "And if that's what you think of me, then I don't know why you'd even want—"

"OOOOHHHH GOD!" Rose yelled. "CAN YOU TWO JUST … AAAAH … JUST ADMIT YOU'RE IN LOVE AND SHUT THE HELL UP?"

"He's the one who won't admit it," Lacy said. "He's the one who's afraid of the goddamned word."

"I didn't—"

"Ohhh, Jesus," Rose said. "Uh … guys? You guys? I … aaaahhhh … I don't mean to interrupt you, but … I think I feel the baby's head."

Lacy looked at Rose in disbelief. "What? Oh, God. Its head? That can't be right. How can that be? Your water didn't even break."

"Yes, it did."

"What?"

"It did. Before … before we left the house."

"Oh, God. Oh, God. How did we not know that?"

"I changed clothes. I … aaaahhhhh … I didn't want to … mention it …"

"Pull over, Daniel! Goddamn it, pull over!" Lacy screamed.

Daniel swerved to the side of the road and parked the SUV in the scrubby grass on the side of the highway. Lacy and Rose unbuckled themselves, and Rose, looking pale and sweaty, leaned back into the seat. Rose started blowing out puffs of air rhythmically, making a sound something like *hee … hee … hee … hee.*

"Is that Lamaze breathing?" Lacy said.

"Oh, who the hell knows?" Rose blurted out. "We didn't … take the class … OH GOD OH GOD OH GOD. You have to look," she told Lacy. "You … ah, Jesus … you have to look. I think she's coming. AAAAHHHHH!"

Rose wriggled out of her maternity stretch pants and her giant over-the-belly undies, and Lacy steeled herself to take a peek. Between Rose's legs, a small patch of scalp with swirls of dark hair was peeking out.

Suddenly, the world went all dark and blurry, and things started to spin.

"Lacy!" Rose yelled.

"What's happening?" Daniel called back to them.

"She's … I think she's about to faint," Rose said.

"Ah, God," Daniel said. "Should I … Is it okay if I come back there?"

"Jesus! Yes! I need … SOMEBODY FREAKING HELP ME WHO'S CONSCIOUS!"

So Daniel got out of the driver's seat and came around to

the back.

❖

Daniel helped Lacy out of the back seat and she walked, on unsteady legs, to the front passenger seat. He handed her his cell phone.

"Okay, call 911, and just ... don't look back there. Don't pass out. I need you on the phone with the emergency guys." He peered into her eyes to see if she was with him. "Okay?"

"Yeah." She nodded, looking a little steadier now. "I'm sorry. I just ..."

"Don't worry about it. Just call."

"AAAHHHH! OH, SHIT. SHIT! SHIT! MOTHER-FUCKER!" Rose yelled.

Daniel left Lacy in the front seat and went back to where Rose was lying across the back seat. "Is it okay if I look?" Daniel said, not wanting to violate a woman's privacy.

"Goddamn it!" Rose yelled. "Yes! Yes! Get the hell back here and LOOK AT MY VAGINA!"

So he did.

He could understand why Lacy had nearly passed out; the sight in front of him was not for the fainthearted. The baby was crowning, and it was coming now whether any of them liked it or not.

"Nine-one-one, what is your emergency?" a voice on the speakerphone said.

"Is she supposed to push? Should you tell her to push?" Lacy said.

"How the hell should I know?" Daniel shot back. "I'm not a goddamned doctor!"

"I'm having a baby!" Rose yelled to the dispatcher. "Right now! In a car! And these two are idiots! Help me!"

The 911 guy proved to be a necessary voice of calm, walking them through the details of what was happening and where they were located, and then reassuring them that an ambulance was on the way. It was clear the baby wasn't going to wait for the ambulance, though, nor was it going to wait for instructions from the dispatcher.

While Daniel was crouched there, waiting to be told what to do, the baby's head emerged fully, looking alarmingly purple. Amid the fluids and the body parts and the screaming, Daniel could just make out something around the baby's neck.

"Ah … the cord. The cord's around the baby's neck," Daniel called into the speakerphone as Lacy held it up over the back of the car so everyone could hear.

"Oh, no. Oh, no," Rose moaned. "Oh, God. Please let my baby be okay. Please God."

Lacy had started to cry.

Daniel, surprising even himself, felt a kind of calm wash over him, a certainty that whatever was required, he would be able to do it. He hushed Rose and made reassuring noises, then said to the dispatcher, "Okay, the head is out, but there's something around the neck. What do I do?"

"That's the umbilical cord," the 911 guy said. "Is it pulsing?"

"Uh … yeah."

"Okay, good. Tell the mother not to push."

"Don't push," Daniel told Rose.

"I heard him! I'm not deaf! But I have to push! I have to! Oh, God …"

Daniel said some more soothing things to Rose, things like *You can do this* and *It's going to be okay* and *We're going to get you through this.*

The 911 guy said, "Is the cord loose enough that you can get a finger under it?"

Daniel gently slid one finger between the cord and the baby's neck. "Yeah. I got it. I got it."

"Okay, now gently slip the cord over the baby's head," the guy on the phone instructed him.

"Okay, okay. Wait a minute. I think …" Daniel eased the cord over the baby's head. "I've got it. I've got it," he said.

"You've got it?" Lacy said. "Oh my God. Oh my God."

Rose, who was pale and sweating, her face contorted in pain, wept with relief.

"Okay, now you want to gently support the head as it comes out," the 911 guy said. "Don't pull it. Just support it. You got that?"

"Yeah, yeah."

Rose pushed with a low, animal growl, and the baby turned slightly as first one shoulder and then the other popped into view. And then the baby, pinched and purple, came sliding out into Daniel's waiting hands.

The baby took in her first, shuddering breath and then let out a wail, and that frightening purple color began to change to something much more babylike and much less alien and alarming.

"Give her to me!" Rose reached for the baby, and Daniel put her gently into her mother's arms.

"You did it! Oh, God, you did it! Rose! Daniel, oh my God. She's beautiful," Lacy said.

"Okay, now, am I supposed to cut the cord?" Daniel asked the 911 guy.

"No, let the EMTs do that. They should be there any time now."

And Daniel did hear a siren in the distance, the sweet sound that meant this would soon be out of his hands and under the control of someone who actually knew what they were doing.

The look on Rose's face was pure love and blessed relief as she gazed into her baby's face. "Hi, baby," she cooed into the small, pinched features. "I'm your mom. Hi, sweetie."

Lacy was leaning over the back of the seat stroking Rose's hair. And Daniel felt simultaneously as though he might faint, and as though he were the king of the goddamned world.

He'd done it. He'd delivered Rose's baby. And now help was coming, and everything was going to be okay.

He straightened up from where he'd been crouching just outside the open car door, and the world spun and his knees went weak. He leaned against the car for support.

Lacy got out of the car to see how he was doing, just in time to see him wobble in his attempts to stand.

"Are you okay?" She put her hand on his arm.

"Yeah, I'm … I'm good, actually. Better than okay. I'm good."

"You did it," she said. "You were amazing."

"Rose was amazing," he said.

Lacy enfolded him in her arms, and he felt, for that moment, like he had all of the things in the world that mattered. He had the pride of having performed well in a crisis, he had the comfort of knowing his friend and her child were okay, and he had the soothing warmth of Lacy as he clung to her, breathing her in, savoring the feel of her body and the smell of her hair.

Right now, in this moment, he had everything.

Chapter Thirty-Two

The EMTs had Rose and the baby bundled into the ambulance and headed for the hospital in no time, and once they were gone, Daniel got on the phone to Will to tell him what happened.

Lacy listened to Daniel's side of the conversation as he determined where Will was. He didn't want to shock Will with the news if he was still on the road—that could only lead to sudden swerving and the possibility of a collision with a tree. It turned out that Will had arrived at the hospital moments before, and was just now running around trying to figure out if Rose had gotten there yet, and if so, where she was.

"Dude, you've got a daughter," Daniel said into the phone, a grin on his face, looking buoyant. "It's over. Rose gave birth on the side of Highway 46."

As Lacy watched, Daniel listened to something Will was saying and then let out a laugh. "They're both doing great. They're on their way in an ambulance. We'll be right behind them."

Pause.

"No, it's—Look, I'll tell you all about it when I get there. Congratulations, Dad."

Daniel hung up and just stood there for a minute, the phone in his hand and a big grin on his face.

"I can't believe that just happened," Lacy said.

"Me neither. But it did," he said. And then the reality of it hit him, and he paled. "That could have gone really wrong. The cord. The baby could have—"

"But she didn't," Lacy said. "Because of you, she didn't."

She knew she was supposed to be angry with him. She was angry before all of this happened, so there was no reason she shouldn't still be angry now. But somehow, all of that had evaporated from the moment Rose had begun to give birth. All of Lacy's resentments and frustrations, the hurts she'd been clinging to, had vanished into the atmosphere in the presence of the bigger picture, the very balance between life and death.

It was as though some magical game show wheel marked MIRACLE and TRAGEDY had been spun, and as the studio audience had waited with bated breath, it had come up MIRACLE. Lacy felt profoundly grateful and awed.

And beyond that, she felt love. Love for Rose, love for the new baby, love for Will. Love for the children she would have one day, for the moment of discovery when they would one day be laid, wailing and new, onto her own chest.

And she felt love, overwhelming, passionate love for Daniel. He had been magnificent.

Lacy drove to the hospital with Daniel in the passenger seat. It had seemed like a good idea for her to take the wheel, because Daniel was still a little shaken up. He didn't say much on the way there; he just sat there with a distant smile on his face, watching the passing landscape on the way to Templeton.

When they arrived at the hospital, Will was in with Rose and the baby while the doctors checked them out. Over the next hour, people started arriving, most of them bearing flowers and baby gifts: Kate and Jackson, Gen and Ryan, Rose's mother. Will's parents would be coming in from Minnesota as soon as they could arrange it.

Once Rose was settled into a room and was allowed to have visitors, Lacy and Daniel peeked in to find her sitting up in bed with the baby in her arms, looking pale and tired but glowing with happiness.

Will was sitting in a plastic hospital chair next to Rose, while Rose's mother bustled around the room, straightening blankets and rearranging the pink plastic pitcher and cup on the tray beside the bed.

"Come in, come in!" Rose said when she saw the two of them hovering in the doorway. "Come and see her! She's so beautiful."

The baby was swaddled in a cotton hospital blanket, a little knit cap on her head. She still looked a little red and pinched, to Daniel's eye, but was doubtlessly relieved to be through with her difficult journey into the world. Her eyes were closed and her little lips were pursed, as though she were in deep thought.

"Congratulations, you guys," Daniel said. He felt flushed with pleasure, and with the feeling that, at this moment, all possible things were right with the world.

Will, who looked as though he'd been crying, embraced Daniel and clapped him on the back, as men did.

"Listen," he said. "Thank you. Just … thank you. When I think of what could have happened …"

"It was my privilege, man," Daniel said. He felt a kind of high, as though he could accomplish anything, as though he'd been chosen by fate or by God—whoever He might be—to bring this new, special person into the world.

When he and Will pulled apart, Rose's mother was standing there beside them, looking at Daniel so sternly that he wondered if he were about to get scolded for having seen parts of Rose that he wasn't intended to see.

Instead, she reached out, took hold of him, and pulled him into her arms. She was a trim woman, and he could feel the delicate structure of her bones.

"Daniel," she said, crisply and in a businesslike tone as she clung to him. "Thank you for taking care of my daughter and my granddaughter. I'm so grateful. I don't know how I can ever …"

She broke off, and when she ended the embrace, she turned away and dabbed at her eyes.

"Aw, come on, Mom," Rose said. "We're happy. We're being happy right now. No crying allowed."

Pamela nodded and went back to straightening things that didn't need straightening.

"You'll need help with the baby," Pamela said to Rose as she bustled about the room. "I can pitch in, of course. I'll have meals delivered. That little house of yours is not entirely adequate, but I guess it will do." She clucked her tongue and shook her head. "Of course, this would all be better if you two were married, but—"

"Oh, we are," Rose said offhandedly.

"A baby ought to have parents who are married, but I suppose—"

"Mom. We are married," Rose tried again.

Pamela stopped in midfuss. "What?"

"We did it a couple of months ago while we were in Vegas," Will confirmed.

"But …" Pamela sputtered. "You didn't … Why didn't …"

"We didn't tell anyone because you'd have been mad that you weren't there," Rose said. "But we figured if we waited to tell you until after the baby was born, you'd be so relieved that your grandchild wasn't born out of wedlock that it would counteract the anger."

"Did it work?" Will asked tentatively, looking a little bit scared to hear the answer.

"But …" Pamela said. "There's no ring. If you two are married …"

"Oh, I have one," Rose said happily. "And it's gorgeous.

But it won't fit on my finger right now. Bloating," she explained. "It's in a drawer at home."

"Oh, honey. Congratulations. Twice," Lacy said, embracing both Rose and the baby at the same time.

Daniel laughed and reached out to give Will a hearty handshake.

Pamela's face reflected a range of emotions before she arranged her features into a neutral expression and nodded once, crisply. "Well, I suppose it did work, then," she said. "Welcome to the family, William." She pulled Will into a hug. It was more hugging than she'd done in the past five years combined.

Daniel and Lacy were about to leave the room to give the family their privacy when Rose said, "Wait. You can't go yet. You haven't heard the baby's name."

"Poppy, right?" Lacy said. "I love it."

"Poppy Danielle," Will clarified.

Daniel froze, feeling gut-punched, but in a good way. "Danielle?"

"Yup," Rose confirmed, grinning widely.

"It was the least we could do," Will said. "The very least."

Everyone else was waiting outside in the hallway in an effort not to overwhelm Rose, Will, and the baby with too many visitors at once.

Daniel exchanged a round of handshakes with Jackson and Ryan, and hugs with the women, as he and Lacy recounted the events on the side of Highway 46 for everyone's benefit.

Once everyone had been caught up and they'd all had a chance to see Rose and the baby, Daniel raked his hands through his hair and said, "Jesus, I need a beer."

"You deserve one," Kate said. "Jackson, go take the man for a beer. We can hang out here."

Jackson turned to Ryan. "You coming?"

Gen shooed him off, and the three of them went into Templeton to look for a bar. They couldn't find one right away, so they ended up in a sandwich place that also sold beer. They settled into a booth with a pitcher between them, and they had the place pretty much to themselves, as the lunch rush had already passed.

Daniel, who had missed lunch in all of the excitement, ordered a thick sub and dove into it with the enthusiasm of someone who had earned a good meal. Jackson and Ryan ordered a plate of nachos, and they scooped up chips loaded with beans, cheese, and jalapeños as they rehashed the events of the morning and early afternoon.

"So, it seems like Lacy's not mad at you anymore," Ryan observed. He looked amused as he loaded up another chip with beans and cheese.

"Man," Jackson said. "If I'd known all you had to do to make a woman forgive you is to deliver somebody's baby, I'd have tried that a long time ago. Would have saved me some trouble."

"Ah, I don't know," Daniel said. He paused, sandwich in hand. "She's not mad anymore for now, but I don't know if it's gonna stick."

Ryan looked at him thoughtfully. "So the problem is, what? Is this still about you not saying you loved her? Which you do, by the way. Obviously."

"Yeah, I do," Daniel admitted. "But it's more than that. It's also that I believed all the rumors floating around about her and her ex. And that I wouldn't talk to her about it." He shrugged.

"So why didn't you talk to her about it, dumbass?" Jackson said with his usual subtle diplomacy. "That's Woman 101. They like to 'communicate' about everything." He made air quotes with his fingers around the word *communicate.*

"Hell, I don't know," Daniel said. He was still ravenous, and he took a big bite of his sandwich.

"I do," Ryan said.

He left it at that, until Daniel raised his eyebrows and said, "You wanna let me in on it, then, genius?"

Ryan leveled his dark brown eyes at Daniel and pointed one finger for emphasis. "You didn't talk to her about it because of the baggage."

"Baggage," Daniel repeated.

"Yeah, baggage. Everybody who knows Lacy knows that her dream is to have about a thousand kids. The whole big-family domestic bit. You're scared shitless, but you can't admit that, because it would threaten your manhood. So instead, you seize on the first problem that comes along and use that as an excuse to nix the whole thing."

"Classic," Jackson said. "I pulled that maneuver at least two times myself. In my younger days," he clarified.

"Well … shit. That makes me sound like a dick," Daniel said.

"Makes you sound like a guy who's going to be single and lonely for a long damn time, with only your dog and your memories to keep you company," Ryan said.

Daniel grunted, put down his sandwich, and drank some beer. At the moment, he really needed the beer.

"What about you guys?" he said. "I mean, you're both on that path. Marriage. Family. The idea of kids has got to freak you out, right?"

"Aw, hell no," Ryan said. "I'd love to have kids. As soon as Gen's ready, I'm good to go."

"Yeah?" Daniel said skeptically.

"Oh, yeah. I'm a Delaney. We're all about family. Got to

pass on the bloodline and all that. Besides, kids are a hell of a lot of fun. I can't wait."

"And what about you?" Daniel tipped his chin toward Jackson.

"Well …" Jackson rubbed at the stubble on the side of his face. "Kate and I aren't there yet. But, yeah, I can see it. I can see us in a few years, married with a couple of kids running around. It sounds good. Really good."

Daniel thought about Rose and Will, and how they'd fairly glowed with happiness in the hospital room, a little family unit with nothing but love and possibility in their futures.

He thought of Lacy, the touch of her hand on his skin, the way she smelled, the way she made him feel every time they were together. The way he felt whole and healed, just being in her presence.

"I dunno. God." He shook his head. "It seems like not being with her isn't an option."

"Well, there you go," Ryan said, as though that settled everything.

And maybe it actually did.

Chapter Thirty-Three

While the guys were deconstructing Daniel's love life over beer and nachos, the women grabbed some coffee at the hospital cafeteria. They sat at a round table in the corner with mediocre coffee that they'd doctored up with sugar and creamer, watching as a steady flow of doctors, nurses, and visitors wandered through with trays of food.

"You should have seen him," Lacy said. "He was amazing. He was so calm, like he delivers babies on the side of the road every day." She shook her head in amazement. "God. I almost fainted when I saw the baby crowning. I literally almost fainted. But Daniel … jeez. I wish you had seen him."

Kate looked at Lacy with amusement. "It seems like we're not mad anymore."

Lacy's shoulders fell. "I kind of still want to be mad. But after that …" She shrugged.

"Okay, so we're not mad anymore," Gen said. "So, what comes next?"

"I don't know." Lacy looked into her coffee cup, avoiding their eyes. "But … he's the man I want to spend my life with. He didn't say he loved me, and he didn't trust me, and he shut me out when he should have talked to me. All of that is still true. But … he's what I want. I can't help it. And I guess … I guess he can shut me out or not love me or whatever. I love him, and I'm not going to stop loving him. And he's who I want. I don't want anyone else."

Lacy felt hot tears come to her eyes, and she swiped them away with her fingertips.

"Oh, honey." Kate put her hand on Lacy's arm. "He's not

where you are yet. But that doesn't mean he won't get there."

"He's a man," Gen said. "Sometimes men are slower with emotional stuff than women are. But that doesn't mean anything. He may feel all of the same things you do. He might just not be able to say it or understand it yet."

"You haven't been seeing each other all that long," Kate added. "You know your mind and your heart. For you, it was, *This is what I want, and I'm ready to go after it.* But Daniel might need a little time to catch up."

Suddenly, listening to her friends, Lacy felt a little bit ashamed. Had she been pushing Daniel for too much too soon? Was she expecting more than he could reasonably give so early in the relationship?

"I never said I wanted to get married and start having kids tomorrow," she said, defending herself. "I only said that I loved him."

"And then felt hurt when he wasn't ready to say it back, even though you'd only been seeing each other a couple of months," Gen added.

Shit. Kate and Gen were right. She was pushing him too hard, too fast. Even as she told herself she wasn't.

"So, what do I do now?"

"Tell him he was magnificent today," Kate suggested. "Tell him you're not mad anymore. Then ease off a little and see what he does."

"What if he doesn't do anything?" Lacy tossed her hands skyward in despair. "What if he's already decided he's done?"

"Oh, sweetie, he's not done. He's in love," Gen said.

"Are you sure?"

"Lacy." Kate looked at her with meaning. "I know Daniel is in love. Gen knows it. All of the guys know it. The only one who doesn't know it is Daniel."

"And he'll figure it out," Gen added. "You just need to sit back and let him."

Lacy reflected that it was so much easier with Zzyzx. All she'd had to do was lure him with some Funyuns. If only men were so uncomplicated.

Lacy went to Daniel's house that night intending to talk. But as it turned out, they didn't do much talking.

He opened the door and saw her, and he pulled her into his arms. They made love once in his bedroom, and then, because the night was unseasonably mild, on a blanket spread out over plush, green grass, beneath a canopy of sparkling stars.

Afterward, when she was tucked up against him under a quilt in the cool night air, feeling his heartbeat beneath her cheek, he said, "I love you, too. I did before, I just didn't know how to say it."

The sounds of the words sent a warm calm through her, a sense of everything being just as it should be.

"I'm just not sure I'm ready for … everything," he said.

"I can wait," she told him, her arms wrapped around him, his body warm against hers. "For you, I can wait. As long as it takes."

A light breeze rippled through the trees above them.

"I won't make you wait too long," he said.

The way it happened was unexpected, at least for Daniel.

He was visiting Rose, Will, and the baby about a week after the birth. He didn't want to be a burdensome guest, given all that Rose and Will had on their hands, so he'd brought a takeout dinner from Neptune that Jackson had put together for the new parents. Daniel's plan was to drop off the food, see the baby, and go.

He'd arrived at just the wrong moment—or maybe it was the right one.

The baby was screaming, and the house was in chaos. Dirty laundry, unwashed dishes, and random baby things cluttered every surface of the little cottage. Rose looked exhausted and harried. Dark circles under her eyes indicated that she hadn't been getting much sleep, and her clothes appeared to be stained with spitup and something that might have been baby poop.

Will was up to his elbows in soapy dishwater, finally addressing what looked to be several meals' worth of dishes, as Rose bounced the baby on her shoulder, trying to get Poppy to settle down.

They greeted him quickly and distractedly, and he stood there watching the scene with all of the predictable feelings: horror, shock, sympathy, and a nagging sense of stress that couldn't be more than a fraction of what Rose and Will were experiencing.

But along with that, he also had a thought that was much less predictable.

He thought, *I can do this.*

Somehow, standing there amid the noise and the mess and Rose and Will's almost tangible exhaustion, he was hit by the quiet certainty that he could handle this, and more.

He had delivered a baby on the side of the road. He had dealt with the complication of the umbilical cord, he had faced down the responsibility of having two other people's lives in his hands.

If he could do that, he could do this.

What he couldn't do was live without Lacy, now that he'd found her.

He put down the food he'd brought, went to Rose, and said, "Can I try?"

She handed the screaming baby to him with gratitude. "Good luck," she said over the baby's wails. "She's been fed, she's been changed. I don't know what her issue is."

Daniel took the baby into his hands and looked at her face, all red and distorted with a level of anger that was unfathomable to the adults in the room.

He put her on his shoulder and breathed in her scent, feeling the weight of this little person in his hands.

"It's all right, Poppy," he said to her, bouncing her a little, his voice a gentle coo. "It's going to be all right."

Chapter Thirty-Four

Daniel came up with a plan, and part of the plan involved Lacy's mother.

He called Nancy and arranged to come over for a visit. Then he arrived carrying an expandable file folder containing his tax returns for the past five years, his bank statements, a list of regular buyers of his glass, a letter from another potential client inquiring about a piece similar to the one at Eden, and spreadsheets showing his plans for savings, investments, and college funds for any possible children. He also had written out the steps he was planning to take to expand his line of vases, bowls, plates, and other tourist-friendly items, and a contingency plan for his financial security should things go south with his glass business.

He presented it all to her over coffee at the Jordans' kitchen table. When he was finished, Nancy leafed through the papers he'd brought, looking them over with interest.

"You earned *that much* for the Las Vegas job?" she said, her voice tinged with awe.

"Yes, ma'am. With that and the savings I already had, I'll be able to pay for the renovations to the house in cash, without taking on debt. And I'll still have enough in the bank for an emergency fund, should business slow down."

"Do you expect it to slow down?" Nancy asked, shooting him a look out of the corner of her eye.

"No, ma'am. In fact, the Eden job got me a good amount of press, so I'm getting more interest than ever before. I just delivered a large piece to a buyer in Los Angeles, and I expect a significant increase in my income over the next year as a result of the increased publicity."

"Well, look at that," Nancy said thoughtfully, peering at the paperwork through half glasses perched on the end of her nose.

"I don't believe I need your approval to continue seeing Lacy," he said, with more confidence in his voice than he felt. "But I'd like to have it. I know how much Lacy respects you, and I know what it would mean to her to have your support."

Nancy put down the papers, took off her reading glasses, and looked at Daniel across the table. "I spoke to Pamela Watkins the other day," she said.

Daniel's eyebrows shot up in surprise at the mention of Rose's mother. "You did?"

"She's quite a fan of yours," Nancy said.

He felt both pleased and a little embarrassed. "Well, I—"

"She told me flat-out that I'd be an idiot not to want you seeing my daughter." A hint of a smile appeared on Nancy's face. "I'm not an idiot."

"Well, no. I never—"

"I just want what's best for my daughter," she said. She shuffled the papers, avoiding his gaze. "That's all I've ever wanted."

"I know that," he said. "And Lacy knows it, too."

"Well." She put the papers back into the folder and pushed the whole thing across the table to Daniel. "Why don't we just give it a try, and see how it goes? You can start by coming over for dinner on Sunday. Let us get to know you a little."

"Yes, ma'am," he said.

The next part of the plan involved both Vince and Lacy.

Daniel asked both of them to meet him at his house on a sunny afternoon in late January. He requested that Vince bring the sketches he'd drawn up for the renovations to the house.

"What's this about?" Lacy asked when she got there and climbed out of the passenger seat of her father's car.

"You'll see," Daniel said.

He brought them both into the house and asked Vince to go over the plans for the addition, so that Lacy could see them.

"I want to go with Plan B," Daniel said, as Vince started spreading papers out on the kitchen table.

"Plan B?" Lacy said.

"The one with the second story," Daniel clarified.

Vince gave him a look and then chuckled and shook his head slowly, amused. "The one with the couple-three more bedrooms," Vince said.

"That's right."

"You sure about that, son?" Vince asked.

"Yes, sir. I'm sure."

"Well, all right, then."

So Vince went over the plans with Lacy step by step, showing her the expanded kitchen, the new, larger studio—and the additional three bedrooms and full bath upstairs, which could easily accommodate a growing family.

"Oh, and I want one more thing," Daniel added when Vince was done.

"What's that?"

"I want to put a pad out back with electric and water hookups, where I could put an Airstream trailer."

Lacy looked at him, her eyes wide. "Daniel? What is this? What is this about?"

"I figured you wouldn't want to move without your trailer," he said. "I know how much you love it. Of course, you'll be living in the house, with me—at least, I hope you will. But you might want the trailer for reading, or having some quiet time. Or we could use it for guests."

"You want me to move in with you. With my trailer," Lacy said, just to be sure. Zzyzx was in her lap, and she stroked his fur while he whined in bliss.

"I want you here. Z wants you here. I'm ready. For all of it. The work on the house will take a while, but after that ..."

Lacy looked at Daniel, and then at Vince.

"Dad," she said. She didn't ask for his approval, not in words. But they all knew that was what she meant.

"Well, honey." Vince sniffed once and looked embarrassed. "Seems to me Daniel here is a good man." He nodded once. "I guess he'll do right by you. Not like that Brandon."

And because none of them wanted to talk about Brandon, they went outside to consider where they should put the Airstream.

The work on the house really was going to take a while. In the meantime, Daniel remembered what Lacy had said in Vegas about never having traveled.

"I was thinking that if you can get some time off work, we ought to put that Airstream to use," he told Lacy one day over olallieberry pie at Linn's.

"What did you have in mind?" she asked, scraping the last of the pie onto her fork and eating the final bite with gusto.

"I thought we might hook it up to my SUV, take it out to Boulder."

"Where your mom and dad live," Lacy said, just to clarify.

"Well, yeah."

She grinned. "Daniel, are you inviting me to meet your parents?"

"Well, I ... Yes. If you'd like to. Yes."

"I'll see if I can get time off work," she said.

"See if you can get more time than that," he amended.

"More? Why?"

"Because I've been invited to teach a few courses as a guest artist at the Abate Zanetti school in Venice this summer. I thought if you weren't doing anything ..."

"Venice? The real Venice?" Lacy's eyes grew wide.

"Right. The one without the hookers and the slot machines." He felt ridiculously pleased with himself.

She threw herself into his arms. "Oh, Daniel."

"And after that," he said, "I really need to go to Delaware. It's the only one of the fifty states I haven't seen yet. I mean, if you're up for it."

She smiled, and with her arms still wrapped around him, she leaned down and put her head on his shoulder. "I'd love to go to Delaware with you."

He was aware that Delaware was a code word for marriage, family, a future, forever.

And that was just fine with him.

He couldn't wait to get to Delaware, as long as he would be going with Lacy.

Join Linda Seed's Readers' Group

Visit Linda's website at www.lindaseed.com and sign up for her e-mail newsletter to get the latest information about new releases, events, giveaways, and more. When you join, you'll receive "Jacks Are Wild," a Main Street Merchants short story, at no cost. The story, featuring Kate and Jackson from *Moonstone Beach,* is only available to newsletter subscribers.

Stay in touch with Linda at the following places:

E-mail: linda@lindaseed.com
Facebook: www.facebook.com/LindaSeedAuthor/
Twitter: www.twitter.com/LindaSeedAuthor
Pinterest: www.pinterest.com/lindahseed/

CPSIA information can be obtained
at www.ICGtesting.com
Printed in the USA
BVHW031357131020
590922BV00001B/174